HIS HUNGER, HIS NEED, FOR HER WAS BECOMING MORE URGENT.

It wasn't just the physical need for release, though that was strong enough; he wasn't accustomed to celibacy. No, his strongest need was the primitive urge to bind her to him *now*, before she found out the truth, but he found himself uncharacteristically hesitant, his usual self-assurance fading. What if this wasn't the right time? What if she rebuffed him? What if she retreated completely? He would have lost even her friendship, and to his surprise he wanted her friendship very much, as much as he wanted her physically. He wanted all of her, her mind as well as her body.

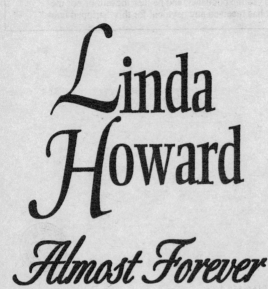

Linda Howard

Almost Forever

MIRA BOOKS

MIRA®

ISBN 1-55166-558-1

ALMOST FOREVER

Copyright © 1986 by Linda Howington.

Printed in U.S.A.

Almost Forever

Chapter One

Anson Edwards sat alone in his big plush office, his fingers steepled as he weighed the strengths of his two lieutenants, wondering which of the two would be best to send to Houston. His own strength was his ability to analyze quickly and accurately, yet in this instance he didn't want to make a snap decision. Sam Bronson was an enigma, a man who played his cards close to his chest; it wouldn't do to underestimate him. Instinct told Anson that an overt takeover attempt on Bronson's metal alloy company would fail, that Bronson was wily enough to have hidden assets. Anson had to discover what those assets were, and their value, before he could realistically expect victory in his attempt to take Bronson Alloys under Spencer-Nyle's corporate umbrella. He knew that he could take control simply by offering much more than the company could possibly be worth, but that wasn't Anson's way. He had a responsibility to the stockholders of Spencer-Nyle, and he wasn't reckless. He would do what was necessary to take Bronson, but no more.

He could set a team of investigators on the job, but that would alert Bronson, and if Bronson were given any sort of warning he might be able to take evasive action that could drag into months. Anson didn't want this; he wanted things to be over quickly. The best bet would be one man, a man whom he could trust in any situation. He trusted both Rome Matthews and Max Conroy completely, but which man would be the best one for the job?

Rome Matthews was his handpicked, personally trained successor; Rome was tough, smart, fair, and he set out to win at everything he did. But Rome had a formidable reputation. He was far too well-known in business circles, and Houston was too close to Dallas for Anson to hope that no one would know him. Rome's very presence would trigger alarm in the business community.

Max Conroy, on the other hand, wasn't that well-known. People tended not to take him as seriously as they did Rome; it was those male-model looks of his, as well as the lazy, good-humored image he projected. People just didn't expect Max to work as hard at something as Rome would. But there was steel in Max Conroy, a ruthlessness that he kept skillfully disguised. That famous affability of his was only a pose; he kept the almost fearsome intensity of his character under strict control. Those who didn't know him were always completely fooled, expecting him to be more playboy than executive.

So it would have to be Max, who would have a better chance of quietly gathering information.

Anson picked up a file again, leafing through the pages of information about key personnel with Bronson Alloys. Nothing could be learned from Bronson himself; the man was wary, and a genius. But a chain was only as strong as its weakest link, and Anson was determined to find Bronson's weak link.

He came to the photograph of Bronson's secretary and paused. Bronson appeared to trust his secretary

completely, though there was no hint of romance between them. Anson frowned as he studied the photograph; the woman was a pretty, dark-eyed blonde, but
no great beauty. There was a reserved expression in her
dark eyes. She had been married to Jeff Halsey, the heir
of a wealthy Houston family, but they had divorced five
years ago. She was thirty-one now and hadn't remar-
ried. Anson checked her name: Claire Westbrook.

Thoughtfully he leaned back in his chair. Would she
be vulnerable to Max's seductive charm? It remained to
be seen. Then he tapped the photograph in sudden decision. Claire Westbrook just might be the weak link in
Bronson's chain.

Claire slipped through the double doors onto the terrace and walked to the waist-high fieldstone wall that
separated the terrace from the flower garden. Resting
her hands on the cool stone, she stared blindly at the
garden, not seeing the masses of blooms that were
highlighted by strategically placed lights. How *could*
Virginia invite Jeff and Helene, knowing that Claire had
accepted an invitation? She'd done it deliberately, of
course; she'd been gloating at the shock that Claire
hadn't been able to hide when her ex-husband arrived
at the party with his beautiful, pregnant wife.

Tears burned at the back of Claire's eyes, and she
blinked to control them. She thought she could have
handled an accidental meeting with aplomb, but she was
stunned by Virginia's deliberate cruelty. She and Virginia had never been close friends, but still, she'd never
expected this. How ironic that Claire had accepted the
invitation only at the urging of her sister, Martine, who
thought it would do her good to get out of the apartment and socialize! So much for good intentions, Claire

thought wryly, controlling the urge to cry. The episode wasn't worth crying over, and it had taught her a lesson: never trust any of your ex-husband's old girlfriends. Evidently Virginia had never forgiven Claire for being Mrs. Jeff Halsey.

"Did the smoke and noise become too much for you, too?"

Claire whirled around, startled by the words spoken so close to her ear. She'd been certain no one else was on the terrace. Determined not to let anyone know she'd been upset, she lifted one eyebrow in casual inquiry.

The man was silhouetted by the light coming through the double glass doors behind him, making it impossible to see his features, but she was certain she didn't know him. He was tall and lean, his shoulders broad beneath the impeccable cut of his white dinner jacket, and he was so close to her that she could smell the faint clean scent of his cologne.

"I apologize; I didn't intend to startle you," he said, moving to stand beside her. "I saw you come out here and thought I'd enjoy some fresh air, too. We haven't been introduced, have we? Maxwell Benedict."

"Claire Westbrook," she murmured in return. She recognized him now; they hadn't been introduced before, true, but she'd seen him when he had arrived at the party. It was impossible not to notice him. He looked like a model, with thick blond hair and vivid eyes; Claire remembered thinking that a man with a face like his should be short, just to keep the scales balanced. Instead he was tall and moved with a casual masculine grace that drew every feminine eye to him. Despite the chiseled perfection of his face, there was nothing effeminate about him; his looks were wholly masculine, and whenever he looked at a woman, his gaze was full of male appreciation. Pretty women weren't the only ones singled out for the megaton force of his charm; every woman, young or old, plain or pretty, was treated with a mixture of courtesy and appreciation that melted them, one and all, like a snowball in hot summer sunshine.

If he expected her to melt right along with the rest, she thought wryly, he was in for a disappointment. Jeff had taught her some hard lessons about handsome charming men, and she remembered every one of them. She was safe even from this man, whose charm was so potent that it was almost a visible force. He didn't even have to flirt! His spectacular looks and flashing smile stunned, his crisp-edged British accent intrigued, and the quiet baritone of his voice soothed. Claire wondered if his feelings would be hurt when she failed to be impressed.

"I thought you seemed upset when you came out here," he said suddenly, leaning against the wall with total disregard for the condition of his crisp white evening jacket. "Is anything wrong?"

My goodness, all that and he was perceptive, too! Claire shrugged, putting lightness in her tone when she answered, "Not really. I'm just not certain how to handle an awkward situation."

"If that's the case, may I be of any assistance?"

His offer was calm, polite and coolly controlled. Claire paused, vaguely intrigued despite herself. She had expected him to be smooth and sophisticated, but that element of control she sensed in him was out of the ordinary.

"Thank you, but it isn't a major problem." All she had to do was somehow make a graceful exit without anyone noticing that she was in full retreat. It wasn't

Jeff; she was long over him. But the baby that Helene carried was a reminder of a pain that she'd never gotten over, of the baby she'd lost. She'd wanted her baby so badly....

Behind them the double doors opened again, and Claire stiffened as Virginia rushed toward her, gushing false sympathy. "Claire, darling, I'm *so* sorry! I really had no idea Jeff and Helene would be here; Lloyd invited them, and I was as horribly surprised as you. You poor dear, are you very upset? After all, we all know how crushed you were—"

Maxwell Benedict straightened beside her, and Claire sensed his acute interest. Hot color burned in her cheeks as she broke in before Virginia could say anything more. "Really, Virginia, there's no need to apologize. I'm not upset at all." The casual coolness of her voice was utterly convincing, even though it was a complete lie. She had died a little inside when she'd heard that Helene was pregnant, and the sight of Jeff's wife, so glowingly lovely and so proudly pregnant, had twisted her heart. She was still haunted by a sense of loss; that was the one pain she couldn't seem to conquer.

Virginia hesitated, disconcerted by the total lack of concern Claire was showing. "Well, if you're certain you're all right...I had visions of you crying your heart out, all alone out here."

"But she isn't all alone," Maxwell Benedict said smoothly, and Claire started as his warm arm slid around her shoulders. Automatically she began to move away, but his fingers tightened warningly on her bare shoulder, and she forced herself to stand still. "Nor is she crying, though I'd be delighted to offer her my shoulder if she felt so inclined. Well, Claire? Do you think you want to cry?"

Part of her disliked the easy way he'd used her first name, when they had only just met, but another part of her was grateful to him for giving her this opportunity to keep her pride and not let Virginia guess that her ploy had been successful, after all, though not in the way she'd planned. Tilting her head up to him the way she'd often seen her sister Martine do when intent on charming someone, Claire gave him her most brilliant smile. "I think I'd rather dance."

"Then dance you shall, my dear. Excuse us, won't you?" he said politely to Virginia, ushering Claire past their disappointed hostess and back into the house. After the relative peace of the terrace, the party seemed that much more crowded and noisy. The alcohol fumes mingled with the cigarette smoke, stifling her, but the music from the stereo rose above the clash of conversation and laughter, and they joined the group of people who were trying to dance in the middle of the room. Space was so limited that swaying in one spot was really all that could be done. Claire started to suggest that they forget about dancing, but he clasped her hand in his and drew her to him with his other arm, and she decided to dance this one dance. He wasn't holding her close despite the press of the crowd, and again she sensed the strict control that seemed to govern his actions. Perhaps she'd misjudged him, she mused. Just because his face was as precisely sculpted as that of a Greek idol, she'd automatically assumed that he was nothing but a shallow playboy, but a playboy wouldn't have that cool control. Perhaps it was his British reserve that she sensed.

"How long have you been in the States?" she asked, necessarily moving closer to him in order to be heard.

A rather whimsical smile curved his beautiful mouth. "How could you tell I'm not a native Texan?"

She chuckled. "A lucky guess."

"Actually, I have a hybrid accent. When I go home for holidays or vacations, my family constantly complains that I talk too slowly."

He hadn't answered her original question, but she let it go. It was too noisy for conversation, anyway. She let her mind drift back to her present situation, and she considered ways of handling it that would be the least awkward for all of them. She certainly didn't want to embarrass either Jeff or Helene; they had been as victimized by Virginia's petty vengeance as Claire.

Just as the dance ended, someone called his name. Claire took advantage of his distraction to say politely, "Thank you for the dance, Mr. Benedict," and walk away, while he was effectively trapped by the woman who had demanded his attention. Her mouth quirked in wry humor. It must be hell for him to have women constantly yapping at his heels; poor man, he probably suffered terribly... when he wasn't taking full advantage of it.

Out of the corner of her eye, Claire saw Virginia watching her closely, and conducting a sotto voce conversation with another woman, who was also eyeing her with intense curiosity. Gossips! She decided at that moment to defuse the situation by confronting it head-on. With her head high and a smile on her face, Claire walked up to Jeff and Helene.

Just before she reached them, she saw Jeff stiffen and an expression of alarm cross his face; he'd noticed the glitter of her eyes and probably wondered if she were going to cause a scandal with one of the passionate scenes that he remembered so well. With determined effort Claire kept the smile pasted to her lips. She had obviously made a mistake in avoiding anything except the most casual companionship with men in the five years since their divorce; her mother and sister thought she still pined for Jeff, and evidently Jeff shared that opinion, along with Virginia and the rest of their social circle. She didn't know what to do about that now, except try to be casual and polite, to show that it really meant nothing to her at all.

"Hello," she said brightly, addressing herself mostly to Helene. "I think Virginia invited the three of us to provide the entertainment for the evening, but I'm not willing to play her game. Shall we spoil her fun?"

Helene was quick; she put a smile in place. "I'd like to spoil her *face*; but by all means, let's be civilized."

As other people drifted close enough to hear what they were saying, Claire launched into a gay account of a recent shopping trip when everything had gone wrong. Helene countered with her own tale of hazardous encounters while shopping, and by that time Jeff had recovered enough to contribute by asking after Claire's parents and her sister's family. It was so civilized that she wanted to laugh aloud, but at the same time strain began to tighten her throat. How long would they have to keep this up? Pride was one thing, but standing here chatting with Helene, who was even more beautiful in her pregnancy, was almost more than she could bear.

Then a warm hand touched the small of her back, and she glanced up in surprise as Max Benedict appeared at her side. "I'm sorry I was detained," he apologized smoothly. "Are you ready to leave, Claire?"

He made it sound as if they had other plans, and Claire was desperate enough to seize the opportunity of escape. "Yes, of course. Max, I'd like you to meet Helene and Jeff Halsey."

He took over, all suave courtesy as he murmured his name, inclined his head over Helene's hand and shook Jeff's. Claire almost laughed at the dazed look in Helene's winsome blue eyes. She might be happily married and very pregnant, but that didn't make her immune to Max Benedict's charm! Then he glanced at his watch and murmured, "We really must go, dear."

"Go" was exactly what Claire wanted to do. With an effort she kept a smile on her face as she listened to Max say all the polite things; then his hand applied a steady pressure on her back as he walked with her to the bedroom, where she'd put her small evening bag. She dug it out from under a tangle of other bags, lacy shawls, a few unglamorous raincoats and several mink jackets. He stood in the doorway waiting for her; he didn't say anything, and Claire wasn't able to read anything in his expression. Why had he rescued her? It had certainly been a deliberate action on his part, but she couldn't think of any reason why he should have made the effort. After all, they were complete strangers; the brief conversation they'd had on the terrace hadn't been enough to qualify them as even casual acquaintances. She was more than a little wary of him, and all her defenses sprang into place.

But first there was an exit to make, and getting out of there took priority over everything else right then. What better way to do it than on the arm of the most breathtaking man whom she'd ever seen? Handsome, charming men had a few uses, after all; they weren't much on permanency, but they were great for making impressions.

A curiously cynical smile touched his perfectly carved lips, as if he'd read her mind. "Shall we?" he asked, holding out his hand.

She left the party on his arm, but as soon as the door was closed behind them she stepped away from his touch. The streetlights spread their silvery light over the lawn and the tangle of cars parked in the driveway and along the street, obscuring the faint stars that blinked overhead. The spring night was warm and humid as the young season celebrated its birth with an exuberant burst of heat, determined to banish the last of the winter chill. A bird chirped shyly in a tree, then fell silent as their footsteps on the sidewalk disturbed it.

"Did the bitch set that up deliberately?" he asked in such a calm, cool voice that for a moment Claire wasn't certain she'd heard the steel in his tone. She glanced up and found his face undisturbed by any hint of temper, and decided that she'd been mistaken.

"It was awkward, but not tragic," she finally said, unwilling to share with this stranger even a hint of what it had actually cost her. She'd never been able to let anyone see what went on inside her mind; the more something hurt, the more she retreated behind a meaningless smile and blank, immovable remoteness. It was a trait that, when she'd been a child, had infuriated and frustrated her mother, who had been determined that her youngest daughter would follow in the footsteps of her other daughter, who was bright and beautiful and talented and could melt stone with her sunny laughter. But the more she tried to force Claire out of her backwardness, the more Claire had retreated, until eventually Alma Westbrook had given up.

Suddenly aware from the silence that had fallen between them that her thoughts had wandered again,

Claire stopped on the sidewalk and held out her hand. "Thank you for your help, Mr. Benedict. It was nice meeting you." Her tone was polite but final, making it clear that she considered the evening at an end.

He took her hand but didn't shake it; instead his fingers clasped hers lightly, warmly, a touch that didn't demand anything. "Will you have dinner with me tomorrow night, Claire?" he asked, then added, "Please," as if he sensed the refusal that she'd been about to make.

She hesitated, vaguely disarmed by that "please," as if he didn't know that he could have the company of almost any woman he wanted, whenever he wanted. Almost. "Thank you, but no."

His eyebrow lifted slightly, and she saw the glitter of his vivid eyes. "Are you still carrying a torch for your ex-husband?"

"That's none of your business, Mr. Benedict."

"You didn't say that a moment ago. I rather thought you were relieved by my interference in something that is now none of my business," he said coolly.

Her head lifted, and she took her hand from his. "Payback time, is it? Very well. No, I'm not still in love with Jeff."

"That's good. I don't like rivals."

Claire looked at him in disbelief, then laughed. She didn't want to dignify that last statement by challenging him; what did he think she was, the biggest fool alive? She had been, once, but not again. "Goodbye, Mr. Benedict," she said in a dismissive tone and walked to her car.

When she reached out to open the car door, she found a lean, tanned hand there before hers. He opened the door for her, and Claire murmured a quiet thank-you as she got in the car and took her keys from her bag.

He rested one arm on the roof of the car and leaned down, his turquoise eyes narrowed and as dark as the sea. "I'll call you tomorrow, Claire Westbrook," he said, as cool and confident as if she hadn't already dismissed him.

"Mr. Benedict, I've tried not to be rude, but I'm not interested."

"I'm registered," he replied, amusement twitching at his mouth, and despite herself Claire found herself staring at his lips, almost spellbound by their seductive perfection. "I've had all my shots, and I'm reasonably well mannered. I'm not wanted by any law-enforcement agency, I've never been married, and I'm kind to children. Do you require references?"

A warm laugh bubbled past her control. "Is your pedigree impressive?"

He squatted in the open door of the car, smiling at her. "Impeccable. Shall we discuss it over dinner tomorrow night?"

There was a small, curious softening inside of her. Without allowing herself to dwell on it, she'd realized for some time that she was lonely. What harm could there be in having dinner with him? She certainly wasn't going to fall in love with him; they would talk and laugh, enjoy a nice meal, and perhaps she would make a friend.

She hesitated a long moment then gave in. "All right. Yes, thank you."

He laughed outright now, his white teeth gleaming. "Such enthusiasm! My dear, I promise I'll be on my best behavior. Where shall I pick you up, and at what time? Eight?"

They agreed on the time, and Claire gave him directions to her apartment. A moment later she was driving away, and by the time she stopped at the first traffic
signal, her brow was furrowed in consternation. Why
had she agreed to go out with him? She'd sworn to
avoid his type like the plague, yet he'd neatly worked
around her defenses and made her laugh, and she found
herself liking him. He didn't seem to take himself too
seriously, which would have made her run at top speed
in the opposite direction. He'd also shown kindness in
coming to her rescue....

He was far too dangerous to her peace of mind.

By the time she let herself into her apartment, she had
decided to cancel the date, but as she closed the door
and locked it, the empty silence of the rooms rushed at
her, overwhelming her. She had refused to get a cat,
feeling that would be the crowning symbol of her
aloneness, but now she wished that she had some sort
of pet, anything, to welcome her home. A cat or a dog
wouldn't care if she never quite measured up to expectations; a full belly and a warm bed, someone to scratch
it behind the ears, was all a pet would expect. Come to
think of it, she thought tiredly, that was all humans
needed. Food, shelter and affection.

Affection. She'd had the food and shelter, all the
material trappings of an upper-middle-class child-
hood. She'd even had affection, but it had been the ab-
sentminded, exasperated crumbs of the doting love that
her parents had given to Martine. Claire couldn't even
blame them; Martine was perfect. Some sisters might
have lorded it over a shy, gawky younger sister, but
Martine had always been kind and patient with Claire
and even now worried about her. No matter how busy
Martine was with her thriving law practice, her popu-

lar, outgoing children and her equally busy husband, she always made time to call Claire at least twice a week.

Still, something inside Claire had always shriveled at her parents' obvious preference for Martine. She could remember staring at herself in a mirror as a child and wondering what was wrong with her. If she had been ugly or possessed a nasty disposition, at least then she would have been able to find some reason for not being quite good enough to please her parents. But even though she hadn't been as beautiful as Martine, she'd still been a pretty child, and she'd tried so hard to please everyone, until she'd realized that her best wasn't going to be good enough and began to withdraw. That was what was wrong with her: she simply wasn't up to par. Martine was beautiful; Claire was merely pretty. Martine was a sunny, outgoing child; Claire was prone to unexplained bouts of tears and shrank from people. Martine was talented, a marvelous pianist and an outstanding art student; Claire refused to study any sort of music and often hid herself away with a book. Martine was brilliant and ambitious; Claire was bright but didn't apply herself. Martine married a handsome, equally ambitious young lawyer, went into practice with him and had two gorgeous, happy children; Claire had married Jeff—the one time in her life she'd ever pleased her mother—but the marriage had fallen apart.

Now, from a distance of five years, Claire had a very clear view of her marriage and the reasons it had failed. Most of it had honestly been her fault. She had been so terrified of failing to live up to what she thought everyone expected of her as Mrs. Jefferson Halsey that she had dashed around trying to be the perfect social hostess, the perfect homemaker, the perfect sport and had spread herself so thin that there had been almost nothing left over for Jeff. At first he'd tolerated it; then the gulf between them had widened and his eye had begun wandering...and settled on Helene, who was beautiful, older than Claire and marvelously self-assured. Only Claire's unexpected pregnancy had prevented a divorce right then. To his credit, Jeff had been tender and kind to Claire, even though her pregnancy had been the end of his relationship with Helene. He loved Helene, but Claire was his wife and carried his child, and he refused to devastate her by asking for a divorce.

Then she had miscarried. He waited until she had recovered physically then told her that he wanted out. Their divorce had probably disappointed half of Houston in its lack of acrimony. Claire had known that it was over before she'd ever lost the baby. They divorced quietly, Jeff married Helene as soon as it was legally possible, and within a year Helene had presented him with a son. Now she was pregnant again.

Claire washed her face and brushed her teeth, then got into bed and picked up her book from the night table, trying not to think of the baby she'd lost. That was the past, as was her marriage, and really, the divorce had been the best thing that had ever happened to her. It had forced her to wake up and take a good look at herself. She had been wasting her life trying to please everyone else, rather than herself. She was going to *be* herself, and for the past five years, she had been. On the whole, she was content with the life she'd made for herself. She had a good job; she read when she liked and as much as she liked. She listened to the music she preferred. She was really closer now to Martine than she'd ever been before, because Claire no longer felt threatened by her older sister. She was even on better terms with her parents...if only her mother would stop pushing her to "find a nice young man and settle down."

Claire didn't go out a lot; she couldn't see any point in it. She wasn't inclined to settle for a lukewarm marriage based on common interests, and she wasn't the type to inspire red-hot passion. She had learned control and how to protect herself with that control. If that made her cool and unresponsive, that was fine. Better that than to leave herself open to the devastating pain rejection brought.

That was the life she'd chosen and deliberately built for herself; why, then, had she accepted a dinner date with Max Benedict? Despite his sense of humor, he was still a playboy, and he had no place at all in her life. She should politely but firmly break their date. Claire closed her book, unable to read it, after all; Maxwell Benedict's handsome face kept swimming before the print. Her brown eyes were troubled as she turned out the lamp and pulled the sheet up to cover her. Despite all the warnings of her instincts, she knew that she wasn't going to break the date.

Max sat in his hotel room, his feet propped on the coffee table and a pot of coffee at his elbow. His brow was furrowed with an intense frown as he read one of the thick reports he'd received in the mail. One lean forefinger stroked his left eyebrow as he read; his reading speed was phenomenal, and he had almost finished. Absently he reached for the coffeepot, and the frown turned impatient as he realized that the pot was nearly empty. He replaced the pot on the tray and pushed it aside. Coffee! He'd become addicted to the stuff, another American habit that he'd acquired.

Swiftly he finished the report then tossed it aside. His eyes narrowed to slits. Anson had picked up hints that another company was after Bronson Alloys. That was a disturbing development in itself, but even more alarming were the rumors that this company had ties to Eastern Europe. If the rumors were true, then word had somehow gotten out that Bronson had developed an alloy that was lightweight and almost indestructible, superior to the alloy used for the SR-71 spy planes. So far, the alloy itself was only a rumor; nothing had been announced, and if anything had been developed, Sam Bronson was keeping it to himself. Still, the rumors were persistent.

He didn't like it. Any move by another company would force him to make his own move, perhaps before he was ready, which would increase the chance for failure. Max didn't intend to fail. He despised failure; his personality was too intense and fiercely controlled to accept anything less than total victory in whatever he attempted.

He picked up the report again and thumbed through it, but he allowed his thoughts to drift. The woman, Claire Westbrook...she wasn't quite what he'd expected. Anson had thought that she might be the weak link, and Max had coolly expected that he could charm her as effortlessly as he did every woman. It hadn't worked out that way. She was cool and calm, almost too controlled, and unresponsive; even though she had eventually accepted his dinner invitation, Max had the impression that she'd done so for her own reasons.

His eyes narrowed. From the time he'd reached puberty, the female sex had practically been at his feet. He appreciated women, enjoyed them, desired them, but women had come easily for him. This was the first time a woman had looked at him with a cool, blank expression then turned away in total disinterest, and he didn't like it. He was both irritated and challenged, and he shouldn't feel either of those responses. This was business. He would use his charm to get the needed information without a qualm; corporate war was just that: war, despite the outward civility of three-piece suits and board meetings. But seduction had never been a part of his plan, so his unwilling attraction to her was doubly unwelcome. He couldn't afford the distraction. He had to concentrate on the job at hand, get the information in a hurry and make his move.

He knew his nature was intensely sensual, but always before, his physical needs and responses had been controlled by the power of his icy intellect. He was master of his body, not the other way around. That was part of his character; nature had given him both a towering intelligence and a sexual appetite that would have taken control of a man of lesser intellect, but he was brilliant, and his mental capacities were so intense and focused that he controlled his physical needs and never unleashed the driving power of that portion of his nature. His unwilling attraction to Claire Westbrook both angered and disconcerted him; it was totally out of place in this situation.

She was pretty, but he'd had women who were far more beautiful. She hadn't responded to him or flirted or in any way indicated that she was attracted to him. The only unusual thing about her were her eyes, huge and velvety brown. There was no reason for him to be thinking about her, but he couldn't get her out of his mind.

Chapter Two

The shrilling of the telephone startled Claire out of sleep the next morning, and her soft mouth curved in a wry smile as she rolled over to lift the receiver and stop the intrusive noise. "Hello, Martine," she said, her voice husky with sleep.

There was a short pause, then Martine laughed. "I wish you wouldn't do that! How did you know?"

"I thought you might call this morning to check up on me. Yes, I went to Virginia's party, and no, I wasn't the belle of the ball."

"You're answering my questions before I ask them," Martine said in fond exasperation. "Did you enjoy yourself anyway?"

"I'm not the social type," Claire hedged, sitting up in bed and stuffing a pillow behind her back. She didn't mention meeting Max Benedict or that she was having dinner with him. Martine would ask a thousand questions and become all excited over something that was basically unimportant. Claire didn't expect the dinner date to be the beginning of a fabulous romance; Max could have any woman he chose, so he wasn't likely to settle for anything but the best. This was just a dinner date, nothing more or less, an evening out with a man who was new in town and didn't know many people. It was probably a respite for him to meet a woman who didn't chase him.

Martine sighed; experience had taught her that if Claire didn't want to talk about something then no amount of prying or badgering could change her mind. For someone so retiring and unassuming, Claire was stubborn. Because Martine loved her sister and recognized how vulnerable and sensitive Claire was, she refrained from badgering her and instead gracefully changed the subject, laughing as she recounted a horrendous piece of mischief that her eight-year-old son had gotten into that morning.

They chatted for a few moments then said goodbye. Claire hung up the receiver and lay back on the pillows, her dark eyes reflective as she stared at the ceiling. Her thoughts kept going back to Max Benedict, and his features formed in her mind; she saw his eyes, vivid turquoise, but the shade of turquoise kept changing. Sometimes they were more green than blue, sometimes more blue than green, and twice she had seen a flash of something in his eyes that had startled her, but she hadn't recognized it. It was as though she'd seen a shadow in the sea that was gone in an instant and left behind only the swirling, breathtaking turquoise waters, yet reminding the observer of the dangers of the sea. Perhaps he had dangers hidden in his depths, hidden behind the beauty that nature had given him. All human beings had hidden depths, of course, but some people were deeper than others, and some very shallow, but all had their private defenses. Did he use his appearance as a barrier, deflecting interest with his looks the way a mirror turns back the sun?

He was surprisingly controlled; perhaps some people wouldn't see that, but Claire was more sensitive than most. She recognized control because she had had to learn it. As a child, she had seethed with pent-up emotion, a wild flood of love and devotion just waiting to be given to someone who would love her for herself. She had thought Jeff was that person, and she had released the torrent of passion, driving herself to be the perfect wife for him, only to fail again. Now she no longer waited for that one person; she had been hurt, and she refused to let anyone hurt her ever again. She had locked her emotions and passions away and was more content without them.

But how would those turquoise eyes look if that cool control were banished and passion heated their depths? How would he look while making love?

Claire sat up, pushing away the disturbing mental image. It was Saturday; she had chores to do. She pulled off her nightgown and let the wisp of silk fall across the bed, and for a moment her eyes enjoyed the contrast of the pink silk lying on the white eyelet lace of the comforter. She loved pretty things. That part of her personality was carefully hidden away and protected, but it was expressed in her preference for exquisite lingerie, in the harmonious colors that she gathered around her. Her bed was white, the carpet a softly blushing peach color, and around the room were touches of rose and jade. The bath towels that she bought were thick and lush, and she enjoyed the feel of them on her skin. So many things delighted her: fresh rain on her face, or the warm sunshine; a ray of light through a jar of plum jelly; the translucent beauty of a green leaf in spring; the plush texture of carpet beneath her bare feet. Because she hung back, she saw more than the people who hurried through life.

She had slept late, so she had to hurry through the housekeeping and laundry that she did every Saturday in order to allow herself enough time to do her hair and nails. She was restless and on edge, all because of a man with vivid sea-colored eyes and sunshine in his hair, and that response was unusual enough to bring all her instinctive defenses springing into place. She would have to be on guard every moment, against herself more than Max. The weakness was hers, the same weakness that had let her believe that Jeff loved her as much as she loved him, because that was what she had wanted to believe. Jeff hadn't misled her; she'd misled herself. *Never again.*

Even so, pride wouldn't allow her to look anything but her best when she went out with Max, and she took a long time over her makeup. Her features were delicate, with high cheekbones and a wide, soft mouth; blusher brought color to those cheekbones, and lipstick made her mouth look even softer. Smudged eyeliner and smoky shadow turned her dark eyes into pools of mystery. After putting up her honey-blond hair, leaving a few tendrils curling loosely at her temples, she slipped pearl-drop earrings in her ears and stared at her reflection in the mirror. The old-fashioned hairstyle suited her, revealing the clean lines of her cheek and jaw, the slenderness of her throat, but she looked disturbingly solemn, as if secrets were hiding behind her eyes.

She was ready when the doorbell rang at exactly eight o'clock and had been ready long enough to become nervous; the peal of the doorbell made her jump. Quickly, before her nerve failed her, she opened the door. "Hello. Come in, please. Would you like a drink before we go?" Her voice was calm and polite, the voice of a hostess doing her duty without any real enthusiasm. Instinctively Claire moved a little away from him; she'd forgotten how tall he was, and she felt dwarfed.

His pleasant expression didn't waver as he held his hand out to her, palm up. "Thank you, but we haven't time. On such short notice, I had to take reservations that were somewhat earlier than I'd planned. Shall we go?" His outstretched hand was steady and unthreatening, but the gesture was a command. Claire had the distinct impression that he had noticed her withdrawal and was demanding her return. He wanted her to step within reach of his hand, his touch, perhaps even place her hand in his in a gesture of both trust and obedience.

She couldn't do it. The small confrontation took only a moment, and she ended it when she stepped away to get her bag and the waist-length silk jacket that went with her oyster-colored silk chemise. It wasn't until she turned around and found herself staring at his chest that she realized he hadn't let the moment end. She froze.

He plucked the jacket from her hands and held it up for her to slip her arms into the sleeves. "Allow me," he said in his cool, precise voice, so devoid of any real emotion that Claire wondered if her reaction had been an overreaction, that his out-held hand had been a mannerly gesture rather than a subtle command. Perhaps if she had gone out more, she wouldn't be so wary and skittish now; Martine had probably been right in urging her to become more socially active.

She let him help her with the jacket, and he smoothed the small collar, his touch brief and light. "You look lovely, Claire, like a Victorian cameo."

"Thank you," she murmured, disarmed by the gentle, graceful compliment. Suddenly she realized that he had sensed her agitation and was trying to put her at her ease, using his almost courtly manners to reassure her, and the odd thing was that it worked. He was controlled, unemotional, and she liked that. People who acted on the urges of their emotions and glands were unreliable.

His hand was on the small of her back, resting there with a slight warm pressure, but now it didn't disturb her. She relaxed and found that she was looking forward to the evening, after all.

His choice of car further reassured her. She would have been suspicious of a flamboyant sports car, but the sedate, solidly conservative black Mercedes-Benz wasn't the car of someone who was attracted to flash and glitter. He was dressed as conservatively as a banker, too, she noticed, glancing at his gray pin-striped suit. It was wonderfully cut, and his lean, elegant frame gave the suit a look of dash and fashion that it wouldn't have possessed on any other man, but it still wasn't the peacock attire of a playboy.

Everything he did put her more at ease. He carried on a light, casual conversation that put no pressure on her; he didn't use innuendos or sly double meanings or ask any personal questions. The restaurant he'd chosen was quiet, giving the impression of privacy but not intimacy. Nothing he did was in any way meant to impress her; he was simply dining out with a woman, with no strings attached, and that was immensely reassuring.

"What sort of work do you do?" he asked casually, dipping an enormous Gulf shrimp into cocktail sauce before biting into it with frank enjoyment. Claire watched his white even teeth sink into the pink shrimp, her pulse speeding up in spite of herself. He was just so

impossibly handsome that it was difficult to refrain
from simply staring at him.

"Secretarial."

"For a large company?"

"No. Bronson Alloys is small, but growing rapidly,
and we have outstanding prospects. It's a publicly held
company, but I work for the major stockholder and
founder, Sam Bronson."

"Do you enjoy your work? Being a secretary seems
to have lost all its attraction for a lot of people; the push
is to be an executive, with a secretary of your own."

"Someone has to be the secretary," Claire said,
smiling. "I don't have either the talents or the ambition to be an executive. What company are you with?
Will you be in Houston permanently?"

"Not permanently, but I could be here for several
months. I'm investigating certain properties for investment."

"Real estate?" Claire asked. "Are you a specula-
tor?"

"Nothing so dashing. Basically what I do is make
feasibility studies."

"How did you come to be transplanted from England to Texas?"

He gave a negligent shrug. "Business opportunities
are more plentiful over here." Max studied her smooth,
delicate face, wondering how she would look if any real
warmth ever lit her dark eyes. She was more relaxed
now than she had been, but there was still that lack of
response from her that both irritated and intrigued him.
So long as he kept the subject impersonal and made no
move that could be interpreted as that of an interested
male, she was relaxed, but she withdrew like a turtle into
its shell at the least hint of masculine aggressiveness or

sexuality. It was as if she didn't want anyone to be attracted to her or even flirt with her. The less masculine he was, the better she liked it, and the realization angered him. What he wouldn't give to force her out of that frozen nunnery she'd locked herself into, to make her acknowledge him as a man, to make her feel some sort of passion!

Claire looked away, a little rattled by the cold, unreadable expression in his eyes. For a moment his face had lost its expression of suave pleasantness and taken on the hard, determined lines of a Viking warrior. Perhaps that was the ancestry that had given him his golden hair and sea-colored eyes, rather than an Anglo-Saxon heritage.

What had she said to bring that expression to his face? It had been only a polite question; she'd been so careful not to step over the bounds she'd set for herself, saying nothing that could be construed as reflecting a personal interest in him.

"Last night," he said abruptly. "That was deliberate viciousness, wasn't it? Why?"

Claire's head jerked around, the only sign she gave that she was disturbed by the change of subject. Her dark eyes went blank. "Yes, it was deliberate, but nothing came of her efforts. It isn't important."

"I don't agree." His crisp accent bit off the words. "You were upset, though you carried it off well. Why was that little scene staged?"

She stared at him, that blank look still in her eyes, as if a wall had been erected in her mind. After a moment he realized that she wasn't going to answer him, and a powerful surge of anger shook him, made him want to grind his teeth in frustration. Why was she so damned aloof? At this rate he'd never get close enough to her to get any of the answers he needed! He wanted this damned thing over with; with business out of the way, he could concentrate on Claire and his irritating attraction to her. He had no doubt that if he were able to devote himself fully to her, he would be able to get behind those barriers to the woman. He had never yet failed to get a woman he wanted; there was no reason why Claire should be his first failure. She might be the most challenging woman of his experience, though, and the thought quickened his interest.

How could he gain her trust if she retreated every time he advanced? A small frown furrowed his brow as he studied her openly, trying to read her mind. If she retreated, then she must feel threatened by him, yet he hadn't done anything to warrant that reaction. Most women were attracted to him on sight, gravitating to him like a compass needle to the magnetic north pole, but Claire made an obvious effort to keep a certain distance from him. In a flash of insight Max realized that it was his looks that made her so wary, and his frown deepened. She had seen the playboy persona and felt threatened by it; she was probably determined not to become another one of his women. Bloody hell! She would run like a frightened rabbit if she realized that her reaction was attracting him far more surely than a blatant play for him. Max was accustomed to being pursued by women; a woman who retreated from him brought out the primitive male urge to chase fleeing prey.

She was soft, tender prey, he thought as he watched a delicate tinge of color sweep over her cheeks. She was disconcerted by the way he was staring at her, but he liked looking at her. She had a gentle, intelligent face, and he kept getting caught by those enormous dark eyes, as velvety as melted chocolate. Her coloring was exquisite, like delicate china; did she have any idea how enormously appealing her dark eyes were? Probably not. Her ex-husband's wife was a real beauty, but if he'd been given the choice between the two women, Max would unhesitatingly have chosen Claire. He'd been stunned by the courage and dignity with which she'd handled the situation at the party the night before; how many other women would have kept their poise under those circumstances? Watching her coolly, deliberately, he knew that he wanted her.

He'd have her, too, but first he had to get past those damnable barriers.

"Talk to me," he said softly. "Don't treat me as everyone else does."

Startled, Claire looked at him, her eyes widening. What did he mean? How did everyone else treat him? "I don't understand," she finally murmured.

His eyes were green ice, with no hint of blue in them. "It's poetic justice, my dear. My face makes me a target, a sexual trophy to be nailed on the wall above the bed, figuratively speaking, of course. Most women have no interest in me other than as a stud; I could be brainless for all the concern they have in me personally. I enjoy the sex, yes; I'm a healthy man. But I also enjoy conversation, music and books, and I would damn well prefer being considered as a person as well as a warm body."

Claire was stunned, so stunned that she forgot the alarm that had been racing up and down her spine as he had stared at her with such cold ferocity. "But I'm not—that is, I haven't been chasing you," she stammered.

"No, with you it's the opposite. You took one look at me and decided that with this face I can't possibly be anything more than a playboy, letting myself be used as a living ornament in any woman's bed."

She was aghast; that was exactly what she'd thought at first, and now she was ashamed of herself. Claire was unusually sensitive, and because she was so easily hurt she went out of her way to keep from hurting anyone else. The idea that she had so casually labeled this man as pretty but useless appalled her. She had other reasons for wanting to keep her distance from him, but he didn't know them; to him, it must seem as if she had simply written him off as being shallow and immoral, without getting to know him at all. He was angry, and he had every right to be.

"I'm sorry," she apologized in a soft, earnest voice. "It's true that I did think you were a playboy, but it's also true that I realize I'm not in your league."

He leaned forward, his eyes narrowed. "What do you mean by that? Just what is 'my league'?"

Claire dropped her eyes, unable to meet that piercingly bright stare, and found that his hands were in her line of vision. They were lean, aristocratic hands, beautifully fashioned, but strong for all that. Was the man like his hands?

"Claire," he prompted.

At last she looked up, her face composed, as usual, but her eyes revealed some of her vulnerability. "You're far more sophisticated than I, of course, and far more beautiful. I'm sure women chase you unmercifully, but the other side of the coin is the fact that you can probably have any woman you want. I really don't want to be your next target."

He didn't like her answer at all; his facial muscles didn't move, but still his displeasure was a definite chill brushing across her skin.

"Then why did you come out with me? I realize I was being a trifle persistent, but you allowed yourself to be persuaded."

"I was lonely," she said, then looked away again.

At that moment the waiter appeared with their dinner, and the interruption gave Max time to control the explosion of fury in his mind. Damn her to hell! So she accepted his invitation only because she was lonely? Evidently he rated above television, but only just! He wondered savagely if his ego could take much more.

When they were alone again, he reached across the table and caught her hand, holding her delicate fingers firmly when she automatically tried to draw away. "You aren't a target," he said tersely. "You're someone I met and liked, someone who looked at me without any hint of speculation about how well endowed I am or how bloody versatile I am in bed. Do you think I don't get lonely, too? I wanted to be able to talk to you; I want a *friend*. Sex is something that can be had whenever I take the urge."

There was color in her face again, as if she were faintly embarrassed, but suddenly there was a twinkle in her eyes. He'd seen it briefly the night before, and its reappearance caught his attention, made him realize how really lovely she was with that light dancing in her dark eyes. "Do they *really*?" she asked in a scandalized whisper.

He felt a bit disoriented, as if he'd just had a blow to the head. A moment before he'd been angry, but now he found himself completely bemused by the teasing humor of her expression. He shifted his grip on her hand and rubbed his thumb across the back of her fingers, absently savoring the feel of her soft flesh. "Ladies have become incredibly bold. It's disconcerting to meet a woman and five minutes later find her hand inside my trousers."

She laughed, and he felt himself become warm. At last he was gaining some ground with her! That was the way; she was lonely and badly needed a friend, while all her defenses were set up to deflect any romantic or seductive move. She wanted a friend, not a lover. Max didn't agree with her choice, but he would have to go along with it for now or risk frightening her away.

"Could we be friends?" he asked gently, determined to act with restraint. Claire simply wasn't like the women he had pursued with single-minded intensity; she was softer, more sensitive, with secret dreams in her eyes.

Claire's lips still held a little smile. Friends? Was it possible to be friends with a man who was as sleek and beautiful as a cheetah? And why would he want to be friends with her? She was nothing out of the ordinary, while he was completely unordinary. Yet perhaps he really was lonely; Claire understood loneliness. She had chosen it as the safest course in life, but there were still times when she longed for someone to whom she could talk without guarding all but her shallowest layers. It wasn't that she wanted to unburden her heart; it was the simple, everyday conversation of friends that she needed so badly. She had never had that even with Martine, dearly though she loved her. Martine was so courageous and outgoing that she couldn't understand the hurts and fears of someone who lacked that courage. Nor had Claire ever been able to confide in her mother, because she had always feared and flinched from the inevitable comparison with Martine. Even when there was no comparison, fear of it had kept Claire silent.

"You could help me look for an apartment tomorrow," he suggested, drawing her back from her thoughts. "A week in a hotel is straining my tolerance."

His tone was testy, and Claire smiled at his accent, more clipped than usual. "I'd be happy to look with you. Do you have anything in mind?"

"My dear, I don't know anything about Houston; I'm totally in your hands."

"Buy a newspaper tomorrow and circle the apartments that you like best, and we'll drive around to see them. What time would you like to start?"

"As early as it's convenient for you; after all, I'm at your mercy."

She doubted that he was ever at anyone's mercy, but a light, happy feeling was swelling in her. His eyes were a warm, brilliant turquoise now, and his smile would have turned the head of a statue. She wasn't proof against his charm, and suddenly it didn't worry her.

Their food had been cooling in front of them, and they both realized it simultaneously. As they ate, Claire began to watch him with growing amazement; how could someone so lean eat so much? His manners were faultless, but nevertheless the amount he ate would have done a stevedore proud. His metabolic rate had to be high, because his movements were characterized by an indolent grace; he didn't burn off calories with nervous energy.

She said as much, and he smiled at her. "I know. My mother used to scold me for eating too much in company. She said it made it appear as if they kept me in a dungeon on starvation rations."

"Do you have a large family?"

"There seem to be hundreds of us," he said blithely. "Aunts and uncles and cousins by the score. In the immediate family, I have one brother and three sisters, and eight assorted nieces and nephews. My father is dead, but my mother still rules us all."

"Are you the eldest?" Claire asked, fascinated by his large family.

"No, my brother is the eldest. I'm second in line. Is your family a large one?"

"No, not really. Just my parents, and my sister Martine and her family. There are cousins in Michigan and an aunt who lives in Vancouver, but the relationship isn't close."

"A large family has its advantages, but there are also times when it closely resembles a zoo. Holidays are chaos."

"Do you go home for all the holidays?"

He shrugged. "Sometimes it isn't possible, but I pop over on the odd weekend."

He made it sound as if it were only a matter of getting in a car and taking a half-hour drive, instead of "popping over" on a transatlantic flight. She was still marveling at that when he turned the conversation to her job; he asked interested questions about the sort of work done at Bronson Alloys, the market for special alloys and the uses for them. It was a fairly complicated subject, and Claire had studied intensely when she'd first gotten the job as Sam Bronson's secretary, trying to understand the processes and the practical applications of Sam's metallurgical genius; she knew her ground well but had to make a special effort to keep abreast. The ease and rapidity of Max's understanding was amazing; she could talk to him as naturally as if he also worked in the field, without having to pause continually for complicated explanations.

Then they began talking about real estate, and the way Max explained it, it sounded fascinating. "You don't actually buy the real estate yourself?"

"No. I act as a consultant, investigating properties for people who are interested buyers. Not all property is suitable for investment or expansion. There are the geological considerations, first of all; some land simply isn't stable enough to support large structures. There are other variables, of course: the depth of the water table, any bedrock, things that effect the price effectiveness of locating a building on that particular plot of ground."

"You're a geologist, too?"

"I'm a gatherer of facts. It's like putting a puzzle together, with the difference that you have no idea what the finished product will look like until it *is* finished."

They lingered over coffee, still talking, and gradually Claire realized how hungry she'd been for simple conversation, for the sharing of ideas and opinions. He was extraordinarily intelligent, but he didn't parade his mental capabilities about for anyone to admire; his intelligence was simply there, a part of him. For her part, Claire had always been unusually studious, losing herself in the varied worlds offered by books, and she was both astonished and delighted to discover that one of his favorite writers was Cameron Gregor, a wild Scotsman whose books were horribly difficult to find and who was her own favorite.

They argued fiercely for almost an hour over which book was Gregor's best; Claire forgot her reserve, leaning toward him with her eyes shining, her face lit with pleasure. After a while Max realized that he was arguing for the sheer pleasure of watching her, not because of any real difference of opinion. When passion brightened her face, she was almost incandescent; jealousy began to eat at him, because all of that fire was for *books*, and none for him.

Finally he held up both hands, laughing. "Shall we stop trying to change the other's mind and dance instead? We've totally ignored the music."

Until that moment Claire hadn't even realized that a band was playing, or that the dance floor was crowded with people swaying to the slow, bluesy tunes. A saxophone was crying pure mournful notes that almost brought tears to her eyes; it was her favorite type of music. He led her to the dance floor and took her in his arms.

They danced well together; he was tall, but her heels brought her up to a comfortable height, allowing her to nestle her head just under his chin. He knew just how to hold a woman, not so tightly that she couldn't maneuver and not so loosely that she was unable to follow his lead. Claire gave a quiet sigh of pleasure; she couldn't remember enjoying any evening more. The firm, gentle clasp of his fingers around hers told her that she was in capable hands, and still there was the sense of control about him that reassured her. Unconsciously she breathed in the faint scent of his cologne, so quiet that it was just barely there, and beneath that was the warm, musky scent of his skin.

Somehow it felt right to be in his arms, so right that she failed to notice her reaction, the way the rhythm of her heartbeat had increased just a little. She felt pleasantly warm, even though the restaurant was cool and her shoulders bare. They laughed and talked and danced together, and she hated for the evening to have to end.

When it did end, he walked her to the door of her apartment and unlocked it for her, then returned the key to her. "Good night," he said in an oddly gentle tone.

She lifted her head and smiled at him. "Good night. I enjoyed the evening very much. Thank you."

That breathtaking, whimsical smile tugged at the corners of his lips. "I should be thanking you, my dear. I'm looking forward to tomorrow. Good night again, and sleep well." He bent and pressed a light kiss on her cheek, his mouth warm and firm; then the brief pressure was lifted. It was a kiss as passionless as that of a brother, asking nothing of her, not even response. Smiling at her, he turned and left.

Claire closed and locked the door, a smile still on her lips. She liked him; she really liked him! He was intelligent, humorous, widely traveled, and remarkably comfortable to be with. He had been a perfect gentleman toward her; after all, he'd as much as told her that he could have sex any time he wanted it, so perhaps she was a welcome change for him. She was a woman who *wasn't* after him. There was no pressure to perform, no sense of being pursued because of his startling physical beauty.

While they'd been dancing, Claire couldn't help noticing that other women had followed him with their eyes, sometimes unconsciously. It was true that some women stared at him openly, with curiosity and even hunger evident in their expressions, but even those who would never think of leaving their own escorts hadn't been able to keep from looking at him periodically. His golden good looks drew the eye like a natural magnet.

Even her own. Lying in her bed, pleasantly tired and relaxed on her silk sheets, she kept seeing his face in her mind's eye. Her memory was a loop of film spliced to run endlessly, and she replayed every changing expression she'd seen, from anger to humor and every nuance in between. His eyes were green when he was angry, blue when he was thoughtful, and that vivid, wicked turquoise when he was laughing or teasing.

Her cheek tingled warmly where he'd kissed it, and sleepily she pressed her fingers to the spot. Sharp curiosity and a sense of regret pierced her; what would it have been like if he'd kissed her mouth, if there had been passion in his touch instead of the cool pleasantness with which he'd ended the evening? Her heart leaped at the thought, and her lips parted unconsciously. She wanted to know the taste of him.

Restlessly she turned on her side, forcing the thought away. Passion was one of the things she'd forced out of her life. Passion was dangerous; it made sane people suddenly turn into unreasonable maniacs. Passion meant a loss of control, and a loss of control ultimately led to terrible vulnerability. She was sometimes lonely, she admitted to herself, but loneliness was better than leaving herself open to the sort of devastating pain she'd barely survived once before. And she *was* afraid; that was another, more difficult thing that she admitted, lying there in the darkness. She lacked the self-confidence with which Martine faced every morning. She was afraid to let anyone get too close to her, because she might not be all they had expected, and she didn't know if she could bear the pain of rejection.

It was far better to be friends rather than lovers. Friends didn't risk as much; friendship lacked the intimacy that necessarily gave lovers the sure, deadly knowledge of where and how to inflict the most hurt when the relationship went bad.

And friendship was what Max wanted, anyway. If she threw herself at him, he would probably turn away in disgust. He didn't want passion, and she was afraid of passion. Daydreams—or nighttime fantasies—about him were a waste of time.

Chapter Three

Until she answered the telephone the next morning and heard his voice, Claire hadn't realized just how much she had been looking forward to seeing him again. Her heart gave a little leap of joy, and her eyes closed for the briefest moment as she listened to his cool, deep voice, and his clipped, exceedingly British upper-class accent that delighted her ear. "Good morning, Claire. I've realized that we didn't set a time for me to pick you up today. What would be good for you?"

"Noon, I think. Have you seen any likely prospects in the paper?"

"I've circled three or four. Noon it is, then."

It disturbed her that just the sound of his voice could affect her. She didn't want to miss him when he wasn't there, didn't want to look forward to seeing him again. Just friends. That was all they were going to be, all they could be.

But when she dressed, she once again found herself paying far more attention to her hair and makeup than usual. She wanted to look good for him, and the realization caused a small pain deep inside her chest. There had been times before when she'd hovered anxiously before her mirror, wondering if she would come up to par, if the Halseys would approve of her, if Jeff would look at her with desire in his eyes again.

The situations weren't the same at all; at that time she'd been desperately trying to hold together a disintegrating marriage, and now she was simply going to spend the day with a friend, helping him look for an apartment. If Max made her heart beat faster, that was something she would have to ignore and never, never let him see.

Telling herself that was one thing, but schooling her features to reveal only a pleasant welcome when she opened the door to him was another thing entirely. She'd seen him in a formal white dinner jacket and in a severely conservative gray suit and had thought at the time that nothing could make him look any better, but in casual clothes he was almost breathtaking. His khaki pants, crisp and neat, outlined his lean hips and belly. The emerald green polo shirt he wore had a double impact: it revealed the surprising muscularity of his arms and torso, and intensified, darkened, the shades of green in his eyes until they were the color of some paradise lagoon. Those eyes smiled down at her, and deep inside her something stirred.

"I'm ready," she said, picking up her lemon-yellow garden hat. It matched her yellow-and-white striped sundress, which Martine had persuaded her to buy more than two years ago, insisting that the sunny color suited her. Claire had to admit that Martine's taste, as usual, was impeccable. She didn't wear the dress often, preferring more businesslike attire, but the morning was so bright and warm that nothing else had seemed suitable.

He put his hand on her bare arm, his lean fingers gently curving around her elbow. It was only a polite gesture, but Claire felt her skin tingle under his touch. An instinct of self-protection told her to move away from him, but it was only a small voice, easily swamped by the disturbing rush of warmth generated by the light touch of his hand. Just walking beside him gave her pleasure.

He opened the car door for her, and when she was seated, he leaned down to tuck her skirt out of the way, another of his casually courteous gestures that disturbed the even rhythm of her pulse. Thank God he didn't have any romantic interest in her! If she responded to him this strongly when he was merely being polite, what would it be like if he were making an effort to charm her? With an almost helpless fear, she realized that she wouldn't stand a chance against him.

Lying on the seat between them was a newspaper, folded open to the ads for apartments for rent, and several of them had been circled. Max pointed to the first one. "This seems suitable. Are you familiar with the area?"

Claire picked up the newspaper and glanced at his choices. "Are you certain you want to look at these?" she asked doubtfully. "They're terribly expensive."

He gave her an amused glance, and Claire looked up in time to see it. She flushed suddenly; if she'd thought about it, she would have realized that he had no need to worry about money. He wasn't flashy, but the signs were there for anyone to read. He dressed well; his clothing was tailored instead of bought off the rack. All the trappings of wealth were there, from his Italian shoes to his impossibly thin Swiss wristwatch, as well as being evident in his speech and manner. Perhaps he wasn't rich, but he was certainly comfortable; companies would pay dearly for his services. She'd made a fool of herself by fretting about what he could afford to pay for an apartment.

"If I must travel so much, the people who pay me must be prepared to keep me in comfort," he said with a chuckle in his voice. "I need privacy, but enough space to entertain when it's necessary, and the apartment must be furnished, as I refuse to cart my furniture about the country."

She gave him stilted directions to the first apartment he'd circled, her cheeks still warm. He began to tell her amusing tales of the pitfalls he'd encountered when he first came to the United States, laughing at himself, and gradually Claire began to relax. She had a horror of making social gaffes, a fear that had been born in the early days of her marriage when it had seemed as if everyone was pressuring her to "live up" to her newly acquired position as Jeff Halsey's wife. As one of *the* Halseys, even by marriage, she'd been expected to be socially perfect; even the smallest mistakes had been so terribly public that every social function had become an exercise in endurance for Claire.

But Max didn't let her retreat into her shell. He talked to her easily, without letting awkward silences fall between them. He sprinkled small questions through his conversation, compelling her to answer them and in that way contribute, until the last traces of embarrassment had faded and she was smiling naturally again. He watched her carefully, gauging her reactions. He'd be damned if he would let her draw back behind those cool, blank barriers of hers. He had to teach her to trust him, to relax in his company, or he would never be able to get any information from her. This damned takeover irritated him. He wanted it out of the way so he could concentrate on Claire and discover more about the woman behind the defenses. He was becoming obsessed with her, and that knowledge irritated him, too, but he couldn't simply shrug it away. Her cool, distant manner attracted him even while it drove him mad with frustration. She had a habit of drifting away in her thoughts, those deep brown eyes revealing secrets that he couldn't read and she wouldn't share with him. His reaction to her confused him; he wanted to make love to her until all the shadows in her eyes were gone, until she burned for him, until she lay warm and helpless beneath him, her skin dewy from the heat and violence of his possession . . . and he wanted to protect her, from everything and everyone except himself.

She didn't want him in either capacity, as lover or protector. She wanted him only for companionship, which was almost as exciting as warm milk.

The first address he'd marked was a group of condominiums, turning their bland identical faces to the street. They were new and expensive, but they were nothing more than brick growths on the Texas soil. Claire glanced at Max, unable to imagine him living there. He surveyed the condos; then his aristocratic brows climbed upward. "I think not," he said mildly and put the car in reverse.

Absurdly pleased that she had been right in her estimation of him, Claire picked up the paper and studied the addresses of the other apartments he'd marked, trying to place them. Houston had grown so rapidly that she wasn't certain where two of the apartments were, but one address she did recognize. "I think you'll like the next one better. It's an older building, but the apartments are very exclusive."

Once again, she was right. Max looked pleased when he saw the mellowed building with the wrought-iron gate at the entrance and the brick-paved courtyard. There was private underground parking for the tenants. Max stopped the car before the office and came around to open the door for Claire. His fingers were warm on her elbow as he helped her from the car; then his hand moved to the small of her back. Claire didn't even try to move away; she was becoming used to his touch, to his more formal European manners.

Even in his casual clothing, Max had an air of authority that commanded the attention of the apartment manager. The man bubbled over with enthusiasm, showing them about the vacant apartment, pointing out the old-fashioned charm of the oak parquet floors and the high, arched ceilings. The windows were wide and tall, flooding the apartment with light, but the rooms were rather small, and Max politely thanked the man for his time.

When they were in the car, Claire said casually, "You do believe in being comfortable, don't you?"

He laughed aloud. "I'm fond of the creature comforts, yes. Being cramped is one of the things I hate most about hotels. Does that make me horribly spoiled?"

She looked at him. The bright sun was caught in the golden cap of his hair, framing his head in a gilt halo. He was relaxed, smiling, his vivid eyes sparkling, but still there was something about him, perhaps a natural sense of arrogance bred into him by the same aristocratic ancestors who had given him that hard, lean, graceful body and sun-god face. She had no doubt that he was spoiled; probably from the day of his birth, women had been dashing about to satisfy his smallest whim. What truly surprised her was that he had the ability to laugh at himself, as if he accepted his looks and the attention they brought him but didn't take them too seriously.

He reached out and took her hand. "What are you thinking? You're looking at me, but you've drifted away."

"That you *are* incredibly spoiled but rather nice in spite of it."

He threw back his head on a shout of laughter. "Aren't you worried that such lavish compliments will go to my head?"

"No," she said serenely. A warm sense of happiness was filling her again, making the bright spring day take on an incandescent glow. She let her hand lie in his, content with the touch.

"Direct me to the next apartment on the list while I still have a healthy ego."

The third apartment was being sublet by an artist who was taking a sabbatical on a Greek island. The decor was understated and sophisticated, from the black slate tiles in the entry to the peach-colored walls and the tracks of indirect lighting overhead. The rooms were large; Claire's entire apartment would have fit easily into the enormous living room. Max wandered into the bedroom to inspect the bed, and Claire knew that he was pleased. His tastes were sophisticated, but never avant-garde. The almost spare luxury of this apartment would appeal to him.

"I'll take it," he said easily, interrupting the manager's spiel. "Are the papers ready to sign now?"

They were, but there was the matter of references; Max squeezed Claire's shoulder, smiling warmly at her. "While I take care of this, will you look about the place and decide what extras I'll need to buy, other than linens?"

"Of course," she agreed, wryly aware that now she was spoiling him, too. He had been polite and logical in his request, but the simple fact was that he'd expected her to agree to do that chore for him. If she hadn't been there, he would have done it himself, but she *was* there, and therefore available to do his bidding. Max went with the manager down to the office, and Claire took inventory of the apartment, making note of what he would need.

She was bemused by the luxury that he took for granted. Her background was in no way deprived. She was the product of an upper-middle-class upbringing, used to a certain amount of luxury herself; she had been married for almost six years to a wealthy man and had lived in the center of the lap of luxury, yet she had transplanted herself without problem into a four-room apartment that could best be described as cozy. Having refused alimony, not wanting the link of financial dependence to tie her to Jeff, she had found a job and begun living on a budget, and not once had she missed the money that had enabled her to buy anything that took her fancy. Max's income was obviously far larger than hers, but still his attitude was an aristocratic expectation that his comfort be assured.

Sometime later he found her standing in the middle of the bedroom, her shoes off, her stockinged feet sunk into the thick dove-gray carpet. Her eyes were open, but that dreamy far-away look was in them again, and he knew that she was unaware of his presence. She was motionless, the tiniest of smiles on her face as she drifted in her thoughts. He stopped, watching her, wondering what dreams pleased her so much and if she wore that same look of contentment after lovemaking, when everything was quiet and dark and the frenzied heat had passed. Had she worn that look for her ex-husband or for another man? The sudden twist of jealousy in his gut was unwelcome and left a bitter taste in his mouth.

He crossed the room and put his hand on her arm, determined to draw her away from those dreams and back to him. "All finished with the paperwork. Are you ready to go?"

She blinked, and the dreams vanished from her eyes. "Yes. I was just enjoying the room."

He looked down at her bare feet. "Especially the carpet."

She smiled. "The colors, too. Everything blends together so nicely."

It was a mellow room, large and well lit, with the soothing gray carpet and peach walls. The bed was covered with a thick melon-colored comforter, and the melon was used again in a large ceramic urn in the corner that held an enormous philodendron. The bed was oversize, piled high with pillows; it was perfect for a tall man, and more than roomy enough for two people. He looked at the bed then at Claire as she bent down to slip on her shoes. He would have her in that bed before this was finished, he promised himself.

She gave him the list she'd made of what he would need to buy. He read it briefly then folded it and put it in his pocket. "We've certainly made short work of this; we have most of the afternoon left. Would you like to have a late lunch or an early dinner?"

She thought of inviting him home to eat dinner with her but hesitated; she had never before invited a man to eat at her apartment. The apartment was her place of privacy, and she had been reluctant to share it. But she didn't want the day to end, and somehow she didn't mind the thought of his presence in her home. "Why don't we go back to my apartment?" she offered a bit nervously. "I'll cook dinner. Do you like orange-glazed chicken?"

"I like food," he stated, glancing at her as they left the apartment and wondering at her obvious unease. Was cooking dinner for him such an ordeal? Both the invitation and the occasion were casual yet something about it bothered her. A woman with her social experience should be completely relaxed with such a simple evening, but nothing about Claire was as it should have been. He wondered if he would ever understand what went on in her mind.

The telephone began ringing as they entered her apartment, and Claire excused herself to answer it.

"Claire, guess what!" her mother said enthusiastically. Claire didn't even attempt to guess, knowing from experience that her mother wouldn't pause long enough to allow an interruption, and she was right. Alma rushed headlong into her next sentence. "Michael and Celia are being transferred to Arizona, and they've stopped to visit on the way through. They'll only be here this one night, and we're having a family cookout. How soon can you be here?"

Michael was Claire's cousin from Michigan, and Celia was his wife. Claire was fond of them both, but she had already invited Max to dinner, and she couldn't just throw him out now, even though Alma took it for granted that Claire would drop everything and rush right over. "Mother, I was just about to cook dinner—"

"Then I've called just in time! Martine and Steve are already here; I tried to call you earlier, but you were out."

Claire took a deep breath. She didn't want to tell her mother that she was entertaining, because she never did so, and Alma would immediately attach far greater significance to it than it warranted, yet she didn't see any way out of it. "I have company. I can't just rush over—"

"Company? Anyone I know?"

"No. I've invited him to dinner—"

Immediately Alma's maternal curiosity switched on. "Who?"

"A friend," Claire said, trying to evade any further questions, but knowing it was a hopeless maneuver. She looked up to see Max grinning at her, his turquoise eyes twinkling. He signaled that he had something to say, and she interrupted Alma's barrage of questions before her mother could get up speed. "Hold on just a minute, Mother. I'll be right back." She covered the mouthpiece with her hand. "My cousins have arrived from Michigan, and they'll only be here overnight, so Mother wants me to come over for a cookout," she explained.

"And you have already invited me to dinner," he finished, coming close to her and taking the phone out of her hand. "I have the perfect solution."

"Mrs. Westbrook," he said into the phone, "my name is Max Benedict. May I offer a solution and invite myself to your cookout, if it wouldn't be too much of an imposition on you? Claire really would like to see her cousins, but she has me on her hands, and she's too well mannered to withdraw her invitation to dinner, and I'm too hungry to do the polite thing and take myself off."

Claire closed her eyes, not having to hear the other half of the conversation to know that Alma had completely melted at the sound of Max's deep, smooth voice and that seductive English accent. Part of her was amused, but another part of her went into a panic at the thought of taking Max to meet her family. Everyone in her family was outstanding in some way, and she tended to fade into the background, overshadowed by their more exuberant personalities. Max perceived her as quiet; if he saw her with her family, he would realize that mousy was a more accurate description, and suddenly she knew she couldn't bear that. Something in her would die if he compared her to Martine, then looked back at her as if wondering what had gone wrong with the family genes.

"Thank you for taking pity on me," Max was drawling. "I'll have Claire there shortly." He hung up the phone, and Claire opened her eyes to find him watching her intently, as if wondering why she was so reluctant to attend her family's impromptu outing. "Don't look so frightened," he advised, winking at her. "Perhaps I don't have on my best bib and tucker, but I'll be on my best behavior."

There was still a residue of terror in her eyes as she turned away. "It isn't you," she confessed, trying to make light of it. "Family gatherings tend to overwhelm me; I'm not at my best in a crowd." That was a massive understatement, she thought, resigning herself to the bleak hours ahead of her. "Excuse me while I change clothes and—"

"No," he said, reaching out to take her hand and effectively halting her flight. "You look wonderful as you are. You don't need to change clothes, brush your hair, or freshen your lipstick. Waiting will only make you more nervous." He watched her thoughtfully, wondering at the sudden urge he had to protect her, but there

it was. There was something about her that made him
want to gather her close and keep everything hard and
hurtful away from her. The realization that he wasn't
being completely honest with her gave him a tight feeling in his chest; what would happen when she found out
who he really was? Would she withdraw completely
from him, her soft, dark eyes becoming cold and remote? A chill ran down his back at the thought, and he
knew he couldn't let it happen. Somehow, some way he
had to engineer the takeover without alienating Claire.

His eyes were narrowed and brilliant as he watched
her, and Claire felt uneasiness grow in her. He saw too
much, read her too well. The realization that she was so
vulnerable to him frightened her, and instinctively she
withdrew behind a quiet, polite, blank wall as he led her
back out to the car, his hand still clasping hers in what
would have been a comforting grip if she had noticed it,
but she paid no attention to his touch. Her mind was
already constructing painful scenarios in which Max fell
in love with Martine on sight and spent the entire afternoon staring at her with an adoring expression in his
turquoise eyes. He would be in pain, too, because Martine wouldn't return the emotion. Martine was deeply
in love with her husband and never seemed to be aware
of her devastating effect on the male sex.

Claire automatically gave directions, and too soon
Max was turning into the driveway of her parents'
home. The drive was already crowded with her father's
BMW and her mother's small Buick, Steve's Jeep
Cherokee, and a loaded-down blue Ford station wagon
with Michigan license plates. Max parked his car off to
the side, under a tree. Claire stared blindly at the roomy
Tudor-style house where she had grown up, almost
paralyzed with dread of what was to come. Everyone

would be in the large backyard, under the enormous
chestnut trees; it was too early in the year for the pool
to be uncovered, so the children would be running wild
on the grass instead of swimming. The adults would be
sitting lazily in the chairs grouped under the trees, and
her father would be guarding the steaks and hamburg-
ers slowly smoking on the grill. It would look like sub-
urban heaven, but everything in Claire shrank from the
ordeal of walking across the grass toward the small
group, knowing that everyone would be avidly staring
at the handsome man walking beside her, wondering
why on earth he was with someone as ordinary as she,
when he could obviously have any woman he wanted.
Oh, God, she couldn't do it.

Max opened the car door, and Claire got out. The
shouts and laughter of children at play came from the
backyard, and he grinned at her. "That sounds like
home. My nieces and nephews are hellions, every one of
them, but there are some days when my sanity slips
away and I miss their chaos. Shall we?"

His hand was warm on her back, and now she was
aware of his touch, because he'd put his hand between
her shoulder blades, and his fingers were resting on her
bare skin, revealed by the low back of the cheery yel-
low-striped sundress. As they walked through the gate
and came in view of her family, seated beneath the trees
just as she'd pictured them, his thumb rubbed gently
across her spine, and the sensation fractured the icy
dread that had gripped her stomach. She was helpless
against the surge of warmth that washed through her,
tightening her nipples and making her breasts feel
heated and full. That small touch had thrown her completely off balance; all her defenses had been raised
against the dread of having Max meet her family and

compare her to them, and she'd been totally unprepared to deal with the way she responded to him despite the caution of her common sense.

Then they were surrounded by her family, and Claire heard herself making the introductions automatically. Alma was practically beaming at Max, her beautiful face aglow with enthusiasm, and Claire's father, Harmon, was both dignified and warm as he greeted his new guest. There were hugs and kisses as Claire greeted Michael and Celia, conflicting exclamations, the noise of the children as Martine's two rowdy youngsters, followed closely by Michael's two children, charged into the group to hug and kiss Claire, who was their favorite aunt. Martine, who was unbelievably gorgeous in a dazzling white knit top and white shorts that hugged her lithe figure and exhibited the golden length of her long, perfect legs, began good-naturedly trying to bring some sort of order to her children; Celia did the same, but it was several minutes before things settled down. Through it all, Claire was aware of Max standing closely beside her, smiling and chatting with that incredible charm of his that already had everyone eating out of his hand.

"Have you known Claire long?" Alma asked, smiling at Max, and Claire tensed. She should have known that Max would be grilled on his life from birth to present. It was her own fault; since her divorce from Jeff, she'd stubbornly resisted the efforts of her family to plunge her back into the social scene, so it was out of character for her to show up with a man in tow. Virginia's party had been the only party she'd attended in years, except for small family get-togethers, and Claire had no doubt that Martine and Alma had discussed at length the fact that she'd finally given in to Martine's urgings. Their curiosity over Max would be running high.

His eyelashes had drooped over his brilliant eyes, as if he were a little drowsy. "No, I haven't," he said, his tone gentle and faintly amused. Claire wondered if she were the only one who heard that amusement, and she darted a quick look at her mother. Alma was still smiling, and she wore that slightly dazed expression Claire had seen before on women's faces when they saw Max for the first time. Suddenly Claire relaxed, no longer worried about any interrogation Max might face from her family; she sensed that he was perfectly at ease, as if he'd expected to be questioned.

"Max is new in town, and I've been showing him around," she explained.

Both Alma and Martine gave her intensely pleased looks then glanced at each other as if congratulating themselves for a job well-done in finally getting Claire out of her shell. Now that she was older, Claire often found this silent communication between her mother and sister amusing, though when she was a child it had intimidated her, making her feel left out. Her lips twitched in a smile; really, there was something comforting in knowing your family so well that you could almost read their thoughts. Martine looked back at Claire and saw her sister's amusement, and a sunny smile broke over her lovely face. "You're doing it again!" she said, laughing.

"What's that?" Steve asked, leaning toward his wife.

"Claire's reading my mind again."

"Oh, she's always done that," Alma said absently. "Harmon, dear, the steaks are on fire."

Claire's father calmly sprayed water on the flaming charcoal. "What type of work are you in, Mr. Benedict?'' he asked, keeping an eagle eye on the coals in case they flamed up again.

"Investments and real estate.''

"Real estate? That's a volatile profession.''

"Speculating in real estate certainly is, but I'm not in that area of the business.''

"When we get settled in Arizona, I'm going to begin studying for my real estate license,'' Celia put in. "It's a fascinating career, and now that the children are both in school I want to get back into it. I worked in a real estate office in Michigan,'' she explained to Max. "I was planning to get my license then, but two babies persuaded me to put it on hold until they were older.''

Martine leaned forward, her dark blue eyes sparkling as she leveled them on Max. "Do you have any children, Mr. Benedict?'' she asked sweetly, and Claire closed her eyes, wavering between horror and a bubble of laughter. Martine didn't believe in tact when she was engaged in protecting her younger sister, and right now that protection took the form of digging all the information she could from Maxwell Benedict.

Max threw back his golden head and laughed, a deep, rich sound that made Claire open her eyes. "No children, and no wives, either present or past, to the despair of my mother, who thinks I'm a disobedient reprobate for not providing her with grandchildren as my brother and sisters have done. And please call me Max, if you'd like.''

After that, everyone was eating out of his hand. Though she'd seen it before, Claire was still amazed at his talent for striking just the right note. His relaxed laughter and the fond references to his family had assured everyone that he was perfectly normal, not a con man, an ax-murderer or a heartless womanizer who would take advantage of her. Sometimes Claire thought that her family must consider her an absolute nitwit, incapable of taking care of herself, and she couldn't think what she'd ever done to deserve that opinion. She lived quietly, she worked and paid her bills, she never got into any trouble, and she handled the varied crises at work with serene aplomb, but none of that seemed to matter to her family. One and all, they seemed to think that Claire "needed looking after." Her father wasn't quite as obvious as Alma and Martine, but he still had a habit of regularly asking her if she needed any financial help.

Max lightly touched her arm, bringing her thoughts back to the laughing, chattering group, and his turquoise eyes were warm as he smiled at her. He never lost pace with the conversation swirling around them, and he promptly removed his hand, but that small touch told her that he was aware of her.

The afternoon was a revelation to Claire. Max was friendly and relaxed with her family, but he wasn't bowled over by Martine's classic golden beauty, as most men were. He was there with Claire. He sat beside Claire while they were eating at the redwood picnic table, he joined Claire in entertaining the restless children after they had been fed, and soon he was romping on the grass with all the aplomb of a man who was accustomed to being swarmed by his energetic nieces and nephews. Claire watched him playing with the children, this beautiful, elegant man who seemed to care not at all that his golden hair was tousled, or that his pants were now stained with grass. The setting sun made a gilt halo of his hair and caught the brilliant sea-colored sparkle of his eyes, and as she looked at him Claire felt her heart swell until it was almost on the point of exploding, and everything went dim for a moment.

I don't want to love him, she thought in despair, but it was already too late. How could she not love him? His laughter as he rolled on the grass, wrestling gently with the four giggling, shrieking youngsters, undermined her defenses far more quickly than any attempt at seduction would have.

She was still in a state of shock when Max drove her back to her apartment that night. It was almost ten o'clock, as everyone had been reluctant to let the day end.

"I like your family," Max said as he walked her to the door, rousing her from her thoughts.

"They liked you, too. I hope all those questions didn't make you uncomfortable."

"Not at all. I'd have been disappointed if they hadn't been interested in your well-being. They love you very much."

Startled, Claire paused with the key in her hand. Max took the key, unlocked the door and reached in to turn on the light then ushered her inside with his hand on her back. "They think I'm an idiot and can't do anything by myself," she blurted.

"That's not what I saw," Max murmured, cupping her bare shoulders in his warm hands. Claire's pulse suddenly throbbed, and she glanced down to hide the response that she couldn't control. "If you think your family is overprotective, I shudder to think how you'd react to mine. My entire family is so incredibly nosy that I sometimes think the KGB would have more finesse."

She laughed, as he'd meant her to, and the way her face lit suddenly made his loins throb. He clenched his teeth, restraining himself from grabbing her and grinding his hips against her soft curves. "Good night," he said, bending to press his lips against her forehead. "May I call you tomorrow?"

"Again? I mean, of course, but I thought you'd be tired of my company."

"Not at all. I can relax with you. If you have other plans...?"

"I don't," she said hurriedly, suddenly terrified that now he wouldn't call at all. The thought of a day without seeing him made her feel bleak.

"Then have lunch with me. Is there a restaurant close to your office?"

"Yes, just across the street. Riley's."

"Then I'll meet you there at noon." He touched her cheek briefly then left. Claire locked the door behind him, her eyes filling with unexpected tears and her throat clogging. She was in love with him, with a man who, by his own admission, wanted only the refuge of an undemanding friendship. What a stupid thing for her to do! She had known, by her unusual response to him, that he was a danger to her and the quiet, uncomplicated life she'd built for herself. By not making any demands at all, he'd taken far more than she would ever have offered.

Chapter Four

When Claire entered the office, she saw at once that Sam had spent the night there again. File drawers were open, the lights were on, and a pot of old coffee was scorching on the warming pad of the coffee maker. Wrinkling her nose, she poured out the old coffee and put on a fresh pot, then set about restoring order to the office. The door of Sam's office was closed, but she knew that he would either be sprawled on the sofa or slumped over his desk. He spent a lot of nights in the office whenever he was working on a new alloy; his delight was in the development of new metals, not in the day-to-day routine of running the business he'd founded. For all that, he was a cagey businessman, and nothing escaped his attention for long.

When the coffee was finished, she poured a cup and carried it through to Sam's office. He was asleep at his desk, his head resting on his folded arms. A legal pad crowded with numbers and chemical symbols lay beside him, and five Styrofoam cups with varying levels of cold coffee was scattered around the desk. Claire set the cup of steaming coffee on the desk and crossed to the windows to open the curtains, flooding the office with light. "Sam, wake up. It's almost eight o'clock."

He woke easily, yawning and stirring at her voice. Sitting up, he yawned again and rubbed his face, eyed the fresh cup of coffee with appreciation and drank half of it. "What time did you say it is?"

"Eight."

"Almost five hours' sleep. Not bad." Five hours' sleep was really a lot for him; he often functioned on less. Sam was something of an enigma, but she was fond of him and intensely loyal; he was lean and gray haired, and his face had lines that told of hard living sometime in his fifty-two years, making her suspect that he had quite an interesting past, but he never talked about it. She knew little about him other than that his wife had died ten years before and he still mourned her, having no interest in remarrying. Her photograph still sat on his desk, and Claire had seen Sam look at it with an expression of such pain and longing that she'd had to turn away.

"Have you been working on something new?" she asked, nodding toward the legal pad.

"I'd like to make that new alloy stronger, but so far all I've done is make it brittle. I haven't hit on the right combination yet without making it heavier, too."

The challenge was to develop a metal that was both strong and light, because the heavier a metal was, the more energy was required to move it. The advanced metal alloys had practical applications more far-reaching than simply making a long-lasting I-beam for construction; the sophisticated alloys were used in space and opened up new opportunities in land travel. After an alloy was developed, ways had to be found to produce it cheaply enough that industry could use it. When Claire had first begun working, it had seemed like a routine job to her, like working in any steel mill, but she'd soon discovered her error. The security was tight and the research fascinating.

She loved her job, and that morning she was especially grateful for it, because it took her mind away from Max and gave her some breathing space. He had occupied both her time and her thoughts since she had first met him Friday night, overwhelming her with his sleek sophistication and wry good humor, inserting himself into her life so neatly and firmly that even in her sleep she couldn't quite escape from him. Claire had slept badly the night before, waking to tell herself over and over that she didn't love him, she *couldn't* love him, but then her traitorous mind would form his image in her thoughts, and her body would react wildly, growing warm and heavy, and she was afraid. Loving him was both reckless and foolish, especially for a woman who prized the secure, even tenor of her life and never again wanted to risk the pain of loving. It was even more foolish because Max had told her from the outset that he only wanted to be friends. How awkward it would be if he guessed that she was just like all the others, mooning over him like a starstruck teenager! Goodbye friendship, goodbye Max.

Sam called her into his office late that morning to take letters, but dictated only a few. Leaning back in his chair, he steepled his fingers and peered at her over them, frowning. Claire sat quietly, waiting. Sam wasn't frowning at her; he was lost in his thoughts and probably didn't even see her. At last he roused himself and got to his feet, groaning a little as his stiff muscles protested. "Days like this remind me of my age," he growled, rubbing his lower back.

"Sleeping at your desk reminds you of your age," Claire corrected, and he grunted in agreement.

"I heard some rumors over the weekend," he said, walking to the window to look down at the roof of his laboratory. "Nothing concrete, but in this case I tend to believe them. Some foreign interest seems to be interested in buying up some of our stock. I don't like that. I don't like it at all."

"A takeover?"

"Could be. There's no active trading in our stock, no sudden surge in demand or price, so the rumor could be groundless. Still, there is something else that makes me uneasy. Another rumor is also circulating, about the new titanium alloy I'm working with now." His lined face was taut with worry.

They stared at each other in silence, both aware of the implications. Sam had developed an alloy so superior to its predecessors in strength and lightness that the possibilities for its use were so far-ranging they were almost beyond belief, though he still wasn't satisfied with the production process. That was still in the experimental stage, and security had been especially tight on its development. By necessity the lab people knew about it, though Sam was the only one in possession of all the information; the people in production also knew about it. Information, once leaked, took on a life of its own and spread rapidly.

"This is too sensitive," Claire finally said. "The federal government wouldn't allow a foreign-held company to buy access to this alloy."

"I've always tried to stay independent," Sam mused, staring out the window again. "This research should have been classified, and I knew it all along, but I was too much of a maverick to do the sensible thing. I thought we were too small to attract notice, and I didn't want the hassle of government security clearance. It was a mistake."

"Are you going to contact the government?"

He thrust his fingers through his gray hair. "Damn, I hate to! I don't want all that going on right now, distracting me. Maybe..."

Sam was a maverick all right, with his unorthodox genius and his impatience with boundaries and restraints. Claire watched him, already knowing what his decision would be. He would wait and watch. He wouldn't allow the alloy to fall into the wrong hands, but he was going to conduct his research in private for as long as possible.

"Any takeover attempt right now would probably fail. We have some property that has skyrocketed in value, but it hasn't been appraised in years. An offer wouldn't take that into account."

"I'll have it reappraised," Claire said, making a note.

"Tell them to rush it; I hope it'll be enough to keep us safe. I just want time to finish my research before I turn this over." He shrugged his broad shoulders, looking tired. "It was good while it lasted, but I've known for some time that we were getting too close to an important breakthrough. Damn, I hate to complicate things with bureaucratic nonsense!"

"I suspect it isn't nonsense, but you just hate for *anyone* to tell you what you have to do, bureaucrat or not."

He scowled at her, a look that Claire met with complete serenity, and a moment later the scowl faded into wry acceptance. That was one of the things she liked most about Sam. He had the ability to see the truth and accept it, even when it was something he didn't like. Whatever blows life had dealt him, he'd learned from every one of them. He was a genius, locked into his creative dreams, but he was also a cautious, scrappy street fighter. Sam would never be a nine-to-five button-down executive; paperwork and corporate decisions, as important as they were, didn't interest him, and he did them only out of duty. His ambition, his life, was in his laboratory.

Despite the distractions of the morning, Claire was always aware of the passage of time, bringing her closer and closer to lunch, when she would see Max again. At last it was time to leave, and she grabbed her purse and darted out of the office. Her flesh was burning and her heart was pounding as she crossed the street, and she took several deep breaths in an effort to calm herself. This would never do. This was a simple lunch date between friends, nothing more; she didn't dare let it appear to be anything else.

Max stood up as she wove her way through the maze of crowded tables. She was flushed from hurrying, and his eyes dropped momentarily to her mouth, parted because of her rapid breathing. Her lips were wide and soft, and his senses jolted. He wanted to taste her, not restrict himself to those chaste, monumentally unsatisfying pecks on her cheek or forehead. He wanted to strip off her clothes and *taste* her, from her head all the way down to her pink toes, with a hungry urgency that threatened to shred his self-control. Damn her, he couldn't get her out of his mind, but he didn't dare make a move on her. She was so skittish that she would retreat from him again, and he wouldn't be able to get any information from her at all. He didn't have a lot of time, anyway, and he was hampered by not knowing exactly what he was looking for, but Anson was certain that Bronson would have hidden assets, and Anson Edwards's hunches were never wrong.

The trouble was that when he looked at Claire, it was difficult to remember that business was supposed to be his primary reason for being in Houston. The entire thing was beginning to leave a bad taste in his mouth; corporate maneuvering was one thing, but he didn't like the idea of involving Claire, of using her. Only his loyalty to Anson Edwards kept him on this particular job, and for the first time Max felt that loyalty wavering. He didn't want to waste his time searching for information; he wanted to fold Claire in his arms and hold her so tightly that there could never be any distance between them again. A sharp longing knotted his insides as she finally reached his table and he stood to welcome her, but he schooled his features to reflect only the light, casual friendliness she seemed to prefer.

"Busy morning?" he asked, leaning down to kiss her cheek before seating her. His gesture was smooth and casual. He probably kissed every woman he met, Claire told herself painfully, but that didn't stop the surge of warmth that suffused her body.

"It's a typical Monday. Everything was in perfect order when I left Friday afternoon, but over the weekend it somehow turned into chaos."

A waitress appeared with the menus, and they were silent while they made their selections. They ordered, and Max turned his attention back to her. "I moved into the apartment this morning."

"That was fast!"

"All I had to relocate was my clothing," Max pointed out, amused. "I've stocked the pantry and bought new sheets and towels—"

The waitress whisked up with their coffee, sliding the cups and saucers in front of them with practiced ease. Riley's was famous for fast service, and today the waitress was outdoing herself. They tried several times to begin a conversation, but each time they were inter-

rupted as their coffee cups or water glasses were re-
filled. The restaurant was crowded and noisy, and the
clatter of plates and glasses was incessant, forcing them
to raise their voices in an attempt to be heard.

"Claire! And Mr. Benedict! I'm so glad to run into
you here!"

Max politely got to his feet, and Claire turned to see
who had addressed them. The pretty brunette beaming
at them was Leigh Adkinson, a member of the Houston social stratosphere to which Claire had belonged
when she'd been Mrs. Halsey. Leigh was cheerful and
lacking in malice, but they had been acquaintances
rather than friends, and after Claire's divorce she'd almost completely lost contact with all of the old crowd.
She could count on one hand the number of times she'd
talked with Leigh in the years since her divorce, but
there Leigh was, smiling at her as if they were the best
of friends. And how did Leigh know Max? she wondered.

"Do you remember me, Mr. Benedict? We met at
Virginia's party Friday night," Leigh chattered.

"Of course I remember. Won't you join us?" He indicated an empty chair, but Leigh shook her head.

"Thank you, but I have to run. I know it's short notice, but I wanted to invite you to a dinner party I'm
giving Saturday night. Actually, it begins as a dinner
party at my house; then we're moving it to the Wilt-
shire Hotel for dancing in the ballroom. Tony's kick-
ing off his candidacy for the governorship. Please say
you'll come, both of you. I noticed at Virginia's party
how well you dance together!"

Max glanced at Claire, his eyebrows uplifted.
"Claire?"

She didn't know what to say. Leigh had somehow assumed that they were a couple, but that wasn't the situation at all. Perhaps Max would prefer taking someone else to the dinner party, if he wanted to attend at all.

"It isn't a fund-raising dinner," Leigh said, laughing. "It's a party for friends. You've been hiding yourself away for far too long, Claire."

Claire hated it when anyone made it sound as if she'd buried herself in deep mourning after her divorce, which wasn't what had happened at all. She stiffened, withdrawing from them, and a refusal began forming on her lips.

Max put his hand on hers, stalling her. "Thank you, we'd love to attend."

"Oh, good. We're having an early dinner, at seven. Claire knows where we live. I'll see you Saturday, then. Bye!"

Max resumed his seat, and silence fell briefly between them. "Are you angry that I accepted for both of us?" he asked, forcing her to look at him.

"I'm embarrassed. Leigh assumed that we're an item, and you were too polite to tell her the truth."

His eyebrows arched, and suddenly the languid, cosmopolitan gentleman was gone, and in his place was a man with cool, almost ruthless eyes. "Do you really think I'd care about being polite if I didn't want to attend? I can be a bloody bastard on occasion."

Claire felt mesmerized, staring into his turquoise eyes and suddenly seeing someone else, but abruptly the ruthlessness was gone, and in its place was the familiar calm control, making her feel as if her mind and eyes were playing tricks on her.

"Why don't you want to go?" he probed.

"I don't belong to that social set any longer."

"Are you afraid you'll see your ex-husband again?"

"I'm certainly not interested in socializing with him and his wife!"

"You don't have to socialize with them," Max persisted, and Claire felt the steely purpose in him. "If they're there, simply ignore them. Divorce is too rampant nowadays for it to be practical to split friends and acquaintances into warring factions."

"I'm not at war with Jeff," Claire denied. "That isn't the issue at all."

"Then what *is* the issue? I'd like to take you to the dinner party and dance with you afterward. I think we'd have fun, don't you?"

"I'm monopolizing your time—"

"No, dear," he interrupted gently. "I'm monopolizing yours. I like being with you; you don't have emotional fits all over my jacket. I freely admit to being selfish, but I'm comfortable with you, and I like being comfortable."

Claire gave in, knowing that for her own emotional safety she should stay as far away from him as possible, but she simply couldn't. She wanted to be with him, see him, talk to him, even if only as a friend, and the need was too strong to be controlled.

After lunch he walked her across the street. While they had been eating, the sky had rapidly filled with dark clouds, promising a spring shower. Max glanced up at the sky. "I'll have to run to beat the rain," he said. "What time are we having dinner tonight?"

Claire turned to stare at him in disbelief. "Dinner *tonight*?" Three nights in a row?

"Unless you have other plans. I'll be the chef. After all, it'll be the first meal in my new apartment. You don't have other plans, do you?"

"No, no other plans."

"Good. Strictly casual tonight, too, so you can relax. I'll collect you at six-thirty."

"I'll drive," she said hastily. "That way you won't have to leave in the middle of cooking."

He gave her a cool, deliberate look. "I said I'll collect you. You're not driving home alone at night. My mother would disinherit me if I allowed such a thing."

Claire hesitated. She was beginning to learn how determined Max was to have things his way. He was unyielding once he'd made up his mind. Behind the pose of sophisticated indolence was pure steel, cold and unbreakable. She had glimpsed it a few times, so briefly that she had never been quite certain of what she'd seen, but she was too intuitive not to sense the strength of the man behind the image.

Max tilted her chin up with his finger, bringing his charm into play as his eyes twinkled at her. "Six-thirty?"

She glanced at her wristwatch. She was already late and didn't have time to argue over such an unimportant detail. "All right. I'll be ready."

He was an expert at getting his way, she realized some ten minutes later. If charm didn't work, he used that cold authority that appeared without warning, and vice versa, but usually the charm would be enough. How often had anyone refused him, especially a woman? Probably not in this decade, Claire thought ruefully. Even as wary as *she* was of handsome charmers, she hadn't been immune to him.

She rushed home after work, alive with anticipation. Quickly she showered and shampooed and was just beginning to blow-dry her hair when the telephone rang.

"All right, spill your guts," Martine drawled when Claire answered the phone. "I want to hear all about that gorgeous man."

When Claire thought about it, she realized that it was nothing less than a minor miracle that Martine had curbed her curiosity for as long as she did, instead of calling Claire at work.

Claire paused, and a tiny frown pulled at her brow. What did she know about Max? That he had three sisters and a brother, was from England, and dealt in real estate. Her family already knew that much, from the adroit answers he'd given them the day before. She knew that he had expensive tastes, dressed elegantly and had impeccable manners. Other than that his life was a blank. She remembered asking him questions, but oddly enough, she couldn't remember his answers. She didn't even know how old he was.

"He's just a friend," she finally answered, because she didn't know what else to say.

"And the *Mona Lisa* is just a painting."

"In essence, yes. There's nothing between us except friendship." He'd never even kissed her, except for those sexless pecks on the cheek and forehead, and it wasn't that he didn't know how to go about it. He simply wasn't interested.

"Ummm, if you say so," Martine said, her skepticism evident. "Are you seeing him again?"

Claire sighed. "Yes, I'm seeing him again."

"Aha!"

"Don't 'aha' me. We're *friends*, without the capital F that Hollywood uses so meaningfully. You saw him, so I'm sure you won't have any trouble imagining how he's chased. He's tired of it, that's all, and he feels comfortable with me because I don't chase him. I'm not after a hot romance."

On the other end of the line, Martine raised her expressive eyebrows. She readily believed that Claire wasn't after a hot romance, but she didn't for one minute believe that Max Benedict was seeing her sister merely because he was "comfortable" with her. Oh, he was probably used to being chased, all right, and every hunting instinct man possessed would have been aroused when Claire looked right through him as if he were sexless. Martine knew quite a lot about men, and one look had told her that Max was pure male, more predatory than most, smarter than most and possessed of a sexuality that burned so vividly she wondered how Claire, who was so unusually sensitive to other people, could fail to see it. But perhaps Claire was too innocent to recognize that energy for what it was; even though she'd been married to Jeff Halsey, there had always been a certain distance to her, a dreaminess that separated her from other people.

"If you're certain..."

"I'm certain, believe me."

She finally got off the phone with Martine and glanced anxiously at the clock. It was almost six. She hurriedly finished drying her hair, but she didn't have time to do anything with it except leave it loose. He'd said to dress casually, so she pulled on beige linen pants and topped them with a loose blue sweater with a deep neckline and a shawl collar. Was that too casual? Max was always so well dressed, and he had the English sense of formality. Another look at the clock told her that she didn't have time to dither over her clothes; she still had to do her makeup.

Just as she pulled a brush through her hair one last time, the doorbell rang. It was six-thirty exactly. She picked up her bag and hurried to open the door.

"Ah, you're ready, as usual," he said, and fingered the collar of her sweater. "You'll need a jacket. The rain has turned chilly."

Tiny raindrops glittered on his tweed jacket and in his golden hair as he leaned against the doorframe, waiting for Claire to get a jacket. When she rejoined him, he draped his arm over her shoulders in a friendly fashion.

"I hope you're hungry. I've outdone myself, if I do say so." His smile invited her to share his good humor, and when he hugged her into his tall body as they walked, she was content to lean against him. To be that close to him was a painful pleasure that she knew she should resist, but for the moment she simply couldn't pull away. She felt the heat of his body, the strength of the arm that lay so casually over her shoulders, and smelled the warm, clean scent of his skin. Her eyes closed briefly on the longing that welled inside her; then she pushed it away. It would do no good to pretend, even for a moment, that the way she felt could ever come to anything; all it would bring her was pain. She was destined to be Max's *buddy*, and that was all the arm around her shoulders signified.

"I hope you like seafood," he said as they entered his apartment. The gilt-edged mirror over the Queen Anne table reflected their movements as he took her jacket from her and shrugged out of his then hung both in the small coat closet in the foyer. Attracted by the mirror, Claire watched him in its reflection, noticing the grace of his movements in even that small chore.

"This is Houston; the Gulf is at our back door. It would be unpatriotic or something not to like seafood."

"Shrimp in particular?"

"I love shrimp in particular." She licked her lips.

"Would that include shrimp creole?"

"It would. Are we having shrimp creole?"

"We are. I got the recipe in New Orleans, so it's authentic."

"It's hard for me to imagine you puttering around in a kitchen," she said, following him into the narrow, extremely modern kitchen, where everything was built-in and at his fingertips. A delicious spicy aroma filled the air.

"I usually don't but when I develop a taste for a certain dish, I learn how to prepare it. How else could I have shrimp creole when I'm in England for a visit? It's a certain thing my mother's cook has never prepared it. Then again, I had to learn how to do Yorkshire pudding for the same reason; different continent. The table is already set; will you help me carry all this through?"

It was difficult for her to believe that he had moved into the apartment only that morning; he seemed so at home there, and the apartment itself bore no signs of unpacking. Everything was in place, as if it had all been waiting for him, and he'd simply strolled in. The table was perfectly set, and when they were seated, Max uncorked a bottle of white wine and poured it into their glasses. The wine was crisp and clean, just what she wanted with the spicy shrimp creole and wild rice. They were relaxed together, and Claire both ate and drank more than she usually did. The wine filled her with warmth, but pleasantly so, and after dinner they both continued to sip the wine while they cleaned up the dinner dishes.

Max didn't insist that she leave the dishes for him, and that amused her; he wasn't *that* domesticated. He saw no reason why she shouldn't help him. It was difficult for two people to maneuver in the narrow kitchen, and they were continuously bumping into each other, but even that was pleasant. The brush of his body against hers gave her such secret pleasure that a couple of times she deliberately didn't move out of his way. Such behavior was uncharacteristic of her, because it bordered on flirtatiousness, and Claire had never been a flirt. She wasn't good at it, like Martine. Martine could smile and bat her eyelashes and make teasing little innuendos, but Claire wasn't at ease with sexual games, even when they weren't meant to be taken seriously.

The wine had relaxed her even more than she had realized; as soon as they sat down in the living room, she felt her muscles begin to turn into butter, and she sighed drowsily. She took another sip of the golden wine, and Max took the glass from her hand to set it on the coffee table.

"I think you've had your limit. You're going to go to sleep on me."

"No, but I *am* tired," she admitted, leaning her head back. "It was a busy day, even for a Monday."

"Anything unusual?" He sat down beside her, his eyes shielded by lowered lashes.

"You might say that. Sam—that's Mr. Bronson, my employer—heard a rumor that we may be the target of a takeover attempt."

"Oh?" His attention was focused on her, his body tense despite his relaxed pose. "How did he hear that?"

"Sam has remarkable sources and remarkable instincts. What bothers him the most is the possibility that a foreign company may be behind it."

His face was expressionless as he reached behind her and began kneading the muscles of her neck and shoulders, his fingers making her give a quiet *mmmm* of pleasure. "Why is that particularly disturbing?"

"Because Sam is in the process of developing an alloy that could have far-reaching possibilities, especially in space," she murmured, then heard her own words echoing in her ears, and her eyes popped open. "I can't believe I told you that," she said in horror.

"Shhh, don't worry. It won't go any further," he soothed, resuming the massaging motion. "If the production of the alloy is that important to national security, why isn't it classified? That would protect him from a takeover by a foreign company."

"Sam is a maverick; he doesn't like rules and regulations or the strict supervision he knows would come with government intervention and protection. He wants to perfect the alloy first, do all of his research and experimentation at his own speed, under his own rules. He'll go to the government, of course, if the rumor turns out to be true. He won't let the alloy go to another country."

Spencer-Nyle had been buying stock in Bronson Alloys, but very quietly, in small amounts. Anson wasn't quite ready to make his move, but if Bronson had also heard the rumor that foreign interests were backing a covert takeover, that gave it a certain credence, and Spencer-Nyle might have to step in sooner than Anson had planned. The danger was that now Bronson would be on the alert for any movement of his stock, and Claire had confirmed that Bronson worked best on his own. He wouldn't welcome a takeover by Spencer-Nyle any more than he would by a foreign interest. The company, though publicly held, was his baby, and Sam Bronson was known as a tough, gritty fighter. Max made a mental note to call Anson after taking Claire home.

He eased Claire down on the couch, stretching her out full-length on her stomach. "What're you doing?" she asked, her eyes widening.

"Just rubbing your back," he said, keeping his voice low and soothing. He used the strength of his hands to find the kinks left by tension, and silence fell between them, except for the gentle sound of Claire's sighs. Max noticed her eyelids drooping again, and a smile tugged at his chiseled lips. She was actually going to go to sleep on him; that had never happened to him before, at least not this early in the evening. Women had gone to sleep in his arms, after the loving, but Claire seemed totally unaware of his sexuality. Even when their bodies had brushed in the kitchen, while they were cleaning up, she'd given no sign that she noticed it; it was as if she didn't even know sex existed.

He looked down at her, her honey-blond hair spread out across the couch, her lips soft and relaxed, those enormous, velvet-brown eyes closed. His hands looked big against her slender back; if he put his thumbs together on her spine, his spread fingers would reach around to the sides of her breasts. He could feel the fragile cage of her ribs beneath the soft fabric of her sweater and the even softer silk of her skin. She was asleep, in more ways than one; he wanted to wake her up and take her to bed, then wake her up sexually. He wanted to make her aware of him, so that she never again looked at him with that maddening distance in her eyes. But not yet. Not quite yet. He couldn't take the chance of frightening her off until he had found out all he needed to know for that bloody damned takeover. But then... then he would move, and Claire Westbrook would find out what it was like to be a woman in his bed.

His hands trembled as he looked down at her, and for the first time he wondered what she would say when she discovered his true identity. She would be angry, of course; he couldn't imagine her *not* being angry, but he thought he could handle her anger. It was the thought that she might be hurt that disturbed him. He didn't want to hurt her in any way. He wanted to hold her, make love to her, *cherish* her, damn it! It was insupportable that he might lose the trust he had so slowly earned from her, that she would no longer give him any of her slow smiles or quiet company. He'd met no other woman like Claire, no one so gentle or remote; he never knew what she was thinking, what dreams went on behind those dark eyes. Max was extraordinarily acute where women were concerned. Only Claire eluded him, and every smile, every thought, she gave him was like a treasure, because it allowed him closer to the secret woman behind her aloof facade.

Tenderness filled him as he watched her. She really was exhausted; if he couldn't take her to his bed, then she needed to be in her own. Gently he woke her, enjoying the way she blinked her dark eyes at him in confusion; then she realized where she was, and a blush of mortification spread over her cheeks. "I'm sorry," she apologized, scrambling to her feet. "I didn't mean to fall asleep."

"Don't worry about it; you were tired. What are friends for? I'd have let you sleep on the couch, but I

thought you'd be more comfortable in your own bed."
They walked to the foyer, and he held her jacket for her.
He was quiet on the drive back to her apartment, and
Claire was still too sleepy to be interested in talking, either. It was raining again, a slow drizzle that kept the
streets wet, and the chill made her huddle deeper into
her jacket.

He checked her apartment while she watched, knowing that he would get that arrogant look if she suggested that he didn't need to do it. "I'll call you
tomorrow," he said, coming back to her and cupping
her chin in his hand.

"Yes," she agreed softly, feeling that each hour until she saw him again would seem a year long. "Max?"

He lifted a brow at her hesitant tone, waiting.

"What I said about the alloy..."

"I know. I promise, I won't say a word about it. I
understand how sensitive that information can be." It
was a promise he felt safe in giving, since he had no
need to discuss the alloy with anyone. Anson already
knew about it. Their problem now was the possibility—no, the probability—that a foreign interest, almost certainly unfriendly, was working behind the
scenes to gain that technology through a takeover using a domestic company as a front. Bronson would
move swiftly to protect his company from such a threat,
and in doing so also protect it from other takeover at-
tempts.

She looked so incredibly soft and sleepy, her defenses down. He tilted her chin up and bent to kiss her
lightly, his mouth closing over hers before she realized
he wasn't going to give her another brotherly peck on
the cheek. He kept the contact light and swift, but almost immediately she stiffened and backed away from

him, that damned blank look coming over her face. He dropped his hand and stepped away from her, as if he hadn't noticed anything, but a primal rage burned in his gut. Damn her, someday soon he'd make her see him as a man!

"I'll call tomorrow," he said again. "I have to investigate a few details, so I'll be busy until early afternoon, but I'll call you before you leave work." Without waiting for her agreement, he let himself out and walked away.

_____ *Chapter Five*

"Claire, dear, I don't see why you're being so stubborn about this," Alma argued gently. "It's just a small party to repay some social favors, and I'd like for you to come. Your father and I would both like you to come; we don't see enough of you. Martine and Steve will be there."

Knowing it was useless, because when Alma used that gentle voice it meant that she'd dug in her heels and wasn't budging an inch, Claire tried again. "Mother, I don't like going to parties."

"Well, I don't like giving them. They're too much trouble, but I do it because it's expected and helps your father."

Which meant that Alma was doing her duty, Martine and Steve were doing their duty by showing up as the supporting cast, and Claire, as usual, was failing to come up to par, by refusing to do her part. Claire winced inside.

"You can leave early; I know you have to work tomorrow," Alma soothed, reading her victory in Claire's silence. "And bring Max Benedict with you; from the rumor flying around town, Harmon and I think we should be better acquainted with him."

"What rumor?" Claire asked, horrified.

"That things look pretty serious between you. Really, you could at least have warned me, so I wouldn't have to act as if I knew what everyone was talking about."

"But we *aren't* serious! We're just friends." Claire had repeated that statement so often that she was beginning to feel like a parrot who knew only one phrase.

"You haven't been seeing him regularly?"

Only every day, but how could she tell Alma that without it sounding as if there was a passionate romance going, when it wasn't a romance? It was…well, it was almost like a partnership. They provided each other with companionship, simple, undemanding companionship. "I've seen him, yes."

"Leigh Adkinson saw you having lunch with him on Monday; Bev Michaels saw you having dinner with him on Tuesday; Charlie Tuttle saw you with him last night in a mall, shopping. Every day! That's pretty regular, dear. Now, I'm not pushing you; let the relationship develop at its own pace. But, really, it would be so much more comfortable if Harmon and I were better acquainted with him."

"I'll be at the party," Claire said quietly. She might as well capitulate and get it over with, because Alma wasn't about to give up.

"With Max."

"I don't know. I haven't talked to him about today. He may have a date."

"Oh, I don't think so," Alma chuckled. "Thank you, dear. We'll see you both tonight."

Claire hung up, biting her lip in consternation. What a way to begin the morning! Alma's call had come mere seconds before Claire's alarm clock had gone off. Well, her mother might be certain that Max didn't have a date, but Claire wasn't. Max was too much of a man not to have a love life, and since he didn't have that sort of relationship with Claire, nor did he seem interested in developing one, it followed that he would be seeing other women. If not tonight, then soon. A rest from strenuous pursuit was one thing, but a healthy man wouldn't let it go on too long. Max had a man's needs, and Claire had seen how women followed him with their eyes.

He couldn't have made it more obvious that he wasn't physically attracted to her; he hadn't kissed her again after that brief kiss on Monday night. As light as it had been, it had sent tingles of electricity shooting all through her body, and she had had to force herself to step away from him, to keep him from seeing how it had affected her. That one small touch and she had been ready to throw herself at him, just like all those other women. She had cried herself to sleep that night, certain she'd made a fool of herself and that he would never come near her again, but he'd called her the next day as promised and didn't seem to have noticed what had happened. Perhaps she had covered it well enough that he didn't suspect.

It didn't seem possible that it had been only a week since she'd met him. She had seen him every day, usually twice a day, when he met her for lunch, and after work, too. She sometimes felt as if she knew him better than she'd ever known anyone before, even Jeff, but at times Max was like a stranger. If she looked up quickly...she would occasionally catch him watching her with an unreadable expression in his eyes. If crossed, he could be a hard man, but he always kept himself under strict control, and it was that control that made her trust him.

She thought of not even asking him to go to her mother's party; she could go by herself, stay long enough to be polite then plead tiredness and go home early. That would satisfy Alma. But it would also mean that Claire wouldn't see Max that day, and emptiness filled her at the thought. Before she could talk herself out of it, she pushed herself up on the pillows and punched out his number on the telephone.

It rang only once before he answered it, his voice deep and a little husky with sleep. As always, Claire's heart gave a tiny leap at hearing him speak.

"It's Claire. I'm sorry to wake you," she apologized.

"I'm not sorry you woke me," he said and yawned. "I had planned to call you as soon as I woke, anyway. Is something wrong?"

"No, nothing like that. Mother just called; she's giving a cocktail party tonight and insists that I be there."

"Am I invited?" he asked with that smooth, cool self-confidence that often amazed and disconcerted her. Max was always so certain of what he was about. It was as if he knew Alma had insisted that Claire invite him and as if he was equally aware that Claire, being herself, would find it difficult to ask him. The more he seemed to see inside her mind, the more Claire tried to keep him from doing just that. She was in love with him; he wasn't in love with her. If he knew that... he would pity her, and he would also stop seeing her.

"You don't mind?"

"I like your family. Why should I mind?"

"People are talking about us."

"I don't give a bloody damn what people say," he said calmly then yawned again. "What time is the party?"

"Seven."

"Of course. Everything starts at seven. I'm going to be a bit tight on time, darling. I have to go out of town today, and I'll be shaving it down to a whisker if I drive all the way to my apartment, then to your apartment, then to your parents' house. Would it inconvenience you terribly if I simply got ready at your apartment? It would save almost forty-five minutes in driving time."

Her heart gave that stupid little leap again at the thought of his using her bathroom to shower in and then dressing in her bedroom. "No, it wouldn't be a bother," she managed to say. "It's a good idea. What time will you be here?"

"About six. Will that give you time?"

"Yes, of course." She would have to hurry, but she thought she could make it. It usually didn't take her long to get ready, and she had time to wash her hair before going to work. That would help.

"I'll see you tonight, then."

It was a horribly busy day; Alma's phone call had set the tone for the entire day. No matter how she hurried, Claire seemed to be a step behind all day long; even routine tasks developed aggravating complications. Part of her job was to shield Sam from unnecessary interruptions, which meant that she had to handle them herself, and there were some things that simply couldn't be put off to the next day. She worked through lunch, trying not to wonder where Max was and wishing that she were with him, wherever he was.

It was midafternoon when the emergency reappraisals arrived by special delivery, and a slow smile moved across Sam's face when he read them. With a gesture of supreme satisfaction he tossed the reports on his desk and leaned back in his chair, linking his hands behind his head. "Even better than I'd hoped," he told Claire. "The real estate values have quadrupled in the past year. We're safe, and I was really beginning to sweat it. Trading has picked up in our stock, though no pattern has developed yet. Someone's definitely after this company, but they're not going to get it. Take a look at that reappraisal."

Claire read through the documents, amazed at the way the value of the land had skyrocketed. Once again Sam's instincts had been right. It was really uncanny, the way his long shots all seemed to pan out. He had bought that land as a hedge against inflation, and now the land would probably be what saved the company from an unfriendly takeover attempt, and Sam wouldn't have to entangle himself in government regulations before he was finished with his research.

Of all days, she was almost twenty minutes late leaving work. It was fifteen to six when she let herself into her apartment, and she pulled off her clothes as she dashed to the bedroom. She jumped in and out of the shower, and had just dried off and pulled on her robe when the doorbell rang. She pressed her hands to her clean face, wishing that she had at least had time to put on her makeup, but there was nothing she could do about that now.

"I had to work late," she stammered in explanation when she opened the door to Max. "Let me get fresh towels and the bathroom is yours."

He carried a fresh suit and shirt and a small traveling kit. A shadow of beard darkened his jaw, but his smile was relaxed. "Don't worry, we'll be on time," he assured her, following her into the bedroom. He placed his clothing on the bed and carried the kit into the bathroom while she got fresh towels for him. Coming back out of the bathroom, he shrugged out of his suit jacket and tossed it across the bed, then began tugging at his tie. Her breath caught in her chest, and she turned away to sit down at her dresser, picking up a brush and pulling it through her hair without having any realization of what she was doing. She tried not to watch him, but the edge of her mirror caught him, and there was no way she could look away. He pulled his shirt free of his pants then unbuttoned it and pulled it off. For all his leanness he was unexpectedly muscular, his torso roped with long, smooth muscles that rippled when he moved. Dark brown curls grew across his chest, fascinating her with the discovery that his body hair was dark instead of blond, though she should have guessed, because his brows and lashes were dark brown, creating a striking contrast with his golden hair and framing his brilliant eyes.

To her relief he didn't take his pants off, though she wouldn't have been surprised if he had. Max was probably very comfortable with being nude in front of a woman, and he had no reason to be ashamed of his body. He was beautiful, even more beautiful than she'd dreamed, his body rippling with fluid strength that was usually hidden by his clothing.

He took his fresh pants off the hanger and took them into the bathroom with him. It wasn't until she heard the shower start that Claire recalled the need to hurry. She forced herself to begin applying her makeup, but her hands were shaking and she botched her eye makeup twice before she got it right. The shower stopped, and her mind immediately supplied a picture of Max standing there naked, drying himself on her towels. Hot color surged into her cheeks. She had to stop thinking about him! She was making a nervous wreck out of herself, when she should be concentrating on getting ready.

"Bloody hell!" he muttered clearly, then raised his voice. "Claire, I forgot my razor. Do you mind if I borrow yours?"

"No, go ahead," she called back. He was shaving; she would have time to dress before he came out. Jumping up, she got out fresh underwear and pulled it on, not taking the time to savor the sensation of cool silk on her skin as she usually did. She smoothed hosiery on her legs, not daring to hurry with that task or she would put a run in the delicate fabric. Now, what to wear? She opened the closet door and hurriedly surveyed the contents; she didn't have that many dresses suitable for a cocktail party. The water had stopped running in the bathroom; he would be out any moment. She jerked a cream-colored jersey dress off the hanger and pulled it over her head just as the bathroom door opened. Hidden in the folds of material, her face flamed red at the spectacle she was making of herself, with her head and upper torso fighting to emerge from the garment, while her lower body was exposed in only skimpy panties, a garter belt and hosiery. Turning her back on him, she tugged the dress into place and began fumbling with the back zipper.

"Allow me," he said, his voice very close. His warm hands brushed hers aside, and he efficiently pulled up the tab of the zipper then hooked the tiny hook at the top. His hands dropped. "There."

Keeping her face averted, she muttered a stiff thanks and returned to the dresser to repair the damage she'd just done to her hair. He was whistling under his breath as he finished dressing, and for a moment she envied his casual attitude, which was a measure of how accustomed he was to that type of situation. She leaned toward the mirror to apply her lipstick and saw him unzip his pants to tuck in his shirt. Her hand was shaking, and she had to take extra care with the lipstick to keep from smearing it.

Then he appeared in the mirror, standing behind her and bending down to check his hair, an abstract frown on his face. "Is everything in place?" he asked, standing back for her inspection.

She had to look at him then, and her eyes drifted over him. Again his charcoal-gray suit was ultraconservative but extremely well tailored. He knew what looked best on him; with his looks, trendy clothes would have made him too overpowering, like a neon light. The plain, unadorned clothes he chose enhanced rather than challenged his golden Viking beauty. Perhaps the lean, high-cheekboned beauty of his face had a Celtic origin, but there was something, perhaps that touch of ruthlessness that she had sometimes sensed in him, that made her think again that many generations back he might have had a Viking ancestor who had gone raiding on English shores and left behind a reminder of his visit. "No, you're perfect," she finally said, and he couldn't guess how much she meant those words.

"Let me look at you." He took her hand, drew her from the chair and turned her for his inspection. "You're just right—wait, you need earrings."

She'd forgotten them. Quickly she slipped pearl-drop earrings into her ears, and Max nodded, checking his watch. "We have just enough time to get there."

Perhaps it was just a small cocktail party, but the driveway was already choked with cars when they arrived at her parents' house. Alma and Harmon were both popular and outgoing, drawing people to them with the magnetism of their personalities. Inevitably Claire felt herself tensing as she walked up to the door with Max close beside her.

The door opened before they reached it, and Martine stood laughing at them, resplendent in an emerald-green dress that showed off her beautiful figure and made her glow with color. "I knew you'd be here," she said in triumph, hugging Claire. "Mom has been in a dither that you wouldn't come."

"I told her that I would," Claire said, reaching deep inside herself for the composure that she kept like a shield between herself and others, even her family.

"Oh, you know how she has to fret over something. Hello, Max, you're looking as beautiful as ever."

He laughed, a deep sound of true amusement. "You really must work to get over that shyness."

"That's what Steve tells me. Oh, here come the Waverlys. I haven't seen Beth in ages." She waved past them to the approaching couple.

"Is there anything I can do to help?" Claire asked.

"I don't know. Ask Mom, if you can find her. She was in the den, but that was five minutes ago, so it's anyone's guess where she is now."

Max put his hand on her waist as they walked into the crowded living room, and Claire immediately felt the impact of everyone's eyes as they turned to survey the new arrivals. She knew their thoughts, knew that everyone had heard the rumors and was looking them over, trying to decide if the rumors were true.

"You did make it!" Alma beamed, sailing across the room to kiss Claire's cheek. She turned that thousand-watt smile on Max, whose mobile lips twitched into a devilish grin. Before either Alma or Claire could guess what he was about, he took Alma in his arms and kissed her lips, then did it again. Alma laughed, but she was blushing when he released her.

"Max, what are you doing?" she exclaimed.

"Kissing a pretty woman," he replied blandly, the tone of his voice belied by the wicked twinkle in his eyes. He reached out and brought Claire back into the circle of his arm. "Now Claire and I are going to find something to eat; I'm starving, and she didn't have time for dinner, either."

Claire felt frozen as she walked beside him to the kitchen, feeling the eyes boring into her back like knife blades. He'd kissed Alma twice, which meant that he'd kissed her mother more than he'd kissed her. She had stood to the side, envying the brilliant, easy charm that both Max and Alma possessed, wishing that she had the gift of laughter. Martine could do it, too, have people eating out of her hand within moments of meeting them. All her life she'd been surrounded by beautiful, charming people, but none of that magical self-assurance had rubbed off on her.

The breakfast bar in the kitchen was crowded with hors d'oeuvres and finger sandwiches, and Max raided it shamelessly, but Claire only nibbled at a sandwich. Automatically she replenished the trays as Max depleted them and finished the condiment tray that Alma had been in the middle of preparing before she had rushed off to greet her guests. Alma rushed back into the kitchen, her glowing smile bursting over her face when she saw that Claire had completed the preparations. "Bless you, dear. I completely forgot what I was doing. You always did keep your common sense; I can't count the times Harmon has told me to slow down and think before I do something, but you know how deep an impression it's made."

Claire smiled quietly at her mother, thinking that she did love her very much even though it had never been easy, growing up in the shadow of a beautiful mother and an equally beautiful sister. Both Alma and Martine were warm and outgoing people, without an ounce of maliciousness. It wasn't their fault that Claire had always felt overshadowed by them.

She picked up the heavy tray, and Max promptly relieved her of the burden. "Show me where you want it," he said firmly when Claire turned to him with her brow raised in question. "You're not to try to carry these trays yourself." He looked at Alma as she began to lift one of the trays, and the cool warning in his eyes made her drop her hands and step back.

"Masterful, isn't he?" Alma whispered to Claire as they followed Max's broad shoulders back into the living room.

"He has set ideas on what's proper," Claire said in understatement.

Max carried all the trays in, then became immersed in a conversation with Harmon, Steve and several other men. Periodically his eyes sought out Claire, wherever she was in the room, as if reassuring himself that she wasn't in need of him.

Claire sipped on a margarita and surreptitiously checked the time, wondering when they would be able to leave. The cocktail party wasn't as bad as she'd feared, but she was tired. The pressure of the hectic day, the hectic *week*, was telling on her. Bracing herself, she tried to concentrate on the conversation around her.

Someone turned on the stereo, but since Harmon was an ardent blues fan, the selection was limited. The smoky, mournful wail of a saxophone lured several people into dancing. Claire danced with Martine's law partner, then with her father's best friend, then with an old friend from school. She was on her second margarita when it was taken from her hand, placed on the table, and Max turned her into his arms.

"You're tired, aren't you?" he asked as they swayed to the low music.

"Exhausted. If tomorrow weren't Friday, I don't think I could make it."

"Are you ready to leave?"

"More than ready. Have you seen Mother lately?"

"She's back in the kitchen, I think. The nation's dairy farmers would be in ecstasy if they could see the amount of cheese that has been consumed tonight," he said dryly.

"You ate your share, I noticed."

His mouth quirked. "I burn off the calories."

Sighing, she stepped back from his embrace. "Let's find Mother. I think we've stayed long enough to be polite."

Alma was indeed in the kitchen, dicing cheese into another heap of small squares. She looked up when they entered, and a mixture of dismay and resignation crossed her features. "Claire, you can't be leaving!" she protested. "It's still early."

"I know, but tomorrow's a working day." Claire leaned forward to kiss her mother's cheek. "I've enjoyed myself. Really."

Alma looked at Max for reinforcement. "Can't you get her to stay a little longer? She has that stubborn look, and I know she won't listen to me."

Max's arm went around Claire's waist, and he, too, bent to kiss Alma's cheek. "That isn't a stubborn look; it's a tired look," he explained easily, employing his charm as he smiled at Alma, pacifying her. "It's my fault; I've had her out every night this week, and the lack of sleep is catching up with her."

It worked, but then, Claire had never doubted him. Alma was beaming at him. "Oh, all right, take her home. You must come back with her; we haven't really had a chance to get to know you."

"Soon," he promised.

It was a silent drive back to Claire's apartment, but when she offered him coffee he came inside with her. After making the coffee and carrying the cups into the living room, they sat on the couch and sipped quietly. Claire kicked off her shoes, sighing in relief and wiggling her toes.

Max's gaze was on her slender feet, but his mind was on other matters. "What happened that you had to work late today?"

"Everything. It was just one of those days, and it didn't help that Sam was so edgy. He's almost certain there's going to be a takeover attempt, and soon; there's been increasing trading in our stock. Even though he has an ace in the hole, the waiting and wondering are nerve-racking."

"What's his ace in the hole?" Max asked, his voice sleepy, almost disinterested.

It was a new situation for Claire, actually being able to sit down and discuss her day at work with someone. She had never talked about her day before; she couldn't remember if anyone had ever asked. Small talk was a subtle sort of intimacy, letting someone into her mind by sharing the details of her life with them, and she had always instinctively kept to herself. But it was so easy to talk to Max; he listened, but he didn't make a big deal of it.

"Real estate," she said, smiling a little. His lashes lifted to reveal a lazy gleam of interest. "I thought that might interest you."

"Ummm," he said, an indistinct sound of agreement.

"Sam invested in some property that has quadrupled in value. The reappraisal came in today, and it was even better than he'd hoped."

"Land values can do that. They go up and down like a roller-coaster. The trick is to buy just before the price bottoms out, and sell just before it goes over the top. The value must really be astronomical to be enough to protect him against a takeover." He sat up more alertly and finished his coffee.

"I'll get you a refill," Claire said, getting up and going into the kitchen before he could refuse. She reappeared almost immediately with the pot, and Max watched her walk toward him, her slender body moving gracefully. She looked so quiet and restrained, but he knew what was beneath that ladylike dress. He'd seen the satin panties, the shockingly sexy garter belt and filmy hosiery. A garter belt, for God's sake! His body jolted with response now just as it had then, and he clenched his teeth. He'd had a difficult time keeping his mind off her underwear and his hands off her body; he kept seeing her with that dress over her head, baring her slender hips and legs to his view. The need to take her to bed was growing out of control, fed by frustration that she was so unaware of him as a man and by anger that she would freeze up on him if he tried to change the situation. He wasn't accustomed to abstinence, and he didn't like it one damned bit.

Claire picked up the conversation where they had left off, sitting down beside him again. "I wouldn't call the land value astronomical, but we're a small enough company that it doesn't have to be. Anyone making a bid for the company is going to come short by several million dollars.''

He jerked his thoughts back to what she was saying. Damn it, she was practically handing him the information he needed on a silver platter, and he couldn't keep his mind on the conversation. He wanted very much to stretch her out on the couch and lift that dress over her head again, to run his hands over her and feel the softness of her skin, but that would have to come later.

"How much was the appraisal?" he asked. He watched her closely, wondering if she would answer him. It was a bold move, asking outright for the information he needed, but she had already given him the major part of it, and the actual appraisal would only fill in the details. He kept his face carefully blank, hiding his intense interest in her answer.

"Almost fourteen million."

Damn, that *would* make a difference! "What did they do? Find oil on it?" he muttered.

She laughed. "Close."

Mingled satisfaction and relief filled him; the job was done. It hadn't taken long, and had been relatively easy. The difficult part had been restraining himself from making a move on Claire and scaring her off, but now the job was out of the way and he could concentrate on her. She could try hiding behind that shell of hers, but he was free to pursue his own interests now, and Claire was his interest. He wanted her; he had no doubt that he would have her. He was a master at seduction, and no woman had ever resisted him for long when he made the effort to charm her into his bed. But with Claire, he'd been handicapped by his professional concerns, forced to restrain himself. She was already accustomed to his company, and she had come to accept his casual touches; it wouldn't be long before she was also accepting the most intimate touches between a man and a woman.

His hunger, his *need*, for her were becoming more urgent. It wasn't just the physical need for release, though that was strong enough; he wasn't accustomed to celibacy. No, his strongest need was the primitive urge to bind her to him *now*, before she found out the truth, but he found himself uncharacteristically hesitant, his usual self-assurance fading. What if this wasn't the right time? What if she rebuffed him? What if she retreated completely? He would have lost even her friendship, and to his surprise he wanted her friendship very much, as much as he wanted her physically. He wanted all of her, her mind as well as her body.

She smothered a yawn, and he laughed, reaching out to massage her shoulder, the light touch filling him with pleasure. "You need to be asleep. Why haven't you told me to leave?"

Claire curled up on the couch, tucking her feet under her, and sipped her coffee contentedly. It was so peaceful, sitting there together and drinking their coffee, making desultory conversation. Her heart was beating in that slow, heavy way it did whenever she was with him, and in that moment she was happy. "I'm comfortable with you," she replied, and knew that she was lying. Her nerves were alive and acutely tuned to him, her senses assailed by his nearness. She could smell him, feel his warmth, look at him, and her flesh ached to be even closer to him. How foolish she was to love too fast, too much, but it was out of her control and perhaps had been from the very beginning.

He reached out and took her hand, folding her fingers in his and rubbing his thumb over her silky skin. "Claire," he said in a quiet voice, drawing her gaze to him. Her eyes were dark pools, soft and velvety. "I want to kiss you."

He felt the way her hand jerked in his, and he tightened his grip just enough to hold her. "Do I frighten you?" he asked, amused.

Claire looked away from the laughter in his face. "I don't think it would be a good idea," she said, her voice going stiff. "We're just friends, remember, and—"

He got to his feet, laughing at her as he pulled her up and took the coffee cup from her free hand to set it down. "I'm not going to bite you," he said and kissed her.

It was a light, swift touch, exactly the way he had kissed her before. "There, did that hurt?"

His vivid eyes were dancing. He was teasing her, and she relaxed. She had thought that he meant a different kind of kiss, and she didn't dare let him kiss her deeply. She wasn't certain of her control; if he kissed her with any degree of passion, she felt that she would explode in unbridled response. He wouldn't have any doubt then about the way she felt. He was too experienced, had been with too many women who were desperate to hold him, not to recognize the same lovesick symptoms in her. It was far better that he tease her rather than feel sorry for her.

Then he kissed her again.

It was an admirably restrained kiss, but it lingered, and he opened his lips over hers. Automatically she parted her own lips to adjust the fit. His taste filled her mouth, his lips firm and warm. Pleasure rose in her, and for a moment she almost melted against him, almost raised her arms to twine them around his neck. Then panic twisted her stomach; she didn't dare let him know, or she would never see him again! Swiftly she turned her head away, breaking the contact of their mouths.

He pressed his lips to her temple, and his strong hands rubbed up her back in a long, slow sweep. He didn't want to push her too far; just for a moment she had responded to him, and the taste of her had gone to his head like a potent wine. His body was responding strongly to her nearness; he didn't dare hug her to him the way he wanted, because there was no way he could hide his arousal. Reluctantly he let her go, and she immediately took a protective step away from him, her face set in a blank mask. Suddenly he was determined not to let her retreat, as she had done so many times before. He was a man; he wanted her to see him as one. "Why are you so uneasy whenever I touch you?" he asked, tipping her chin up with his finger so she couldn't hide her face from him; she was too good at hiding her thoughts, anyway, and he needed every little clue he could get. He wanted to be able to see her face, her eyes.

"You said you wanted to be friends," she replied stiffly.

"Friends aren't allowed to touch?"

His whimsical tone made her feel as if she were making far too much of things, and perhaps she would have been—if she hadn't felt far more for him than just friendship. But she was in love with him, and even his most casual touches tormented her with mingled pleasure and longing.

"You told me that you wanted a friendship without sex."

"Surely not. I don't believe I've taken leave of my senses." Gently he rubbed his thumb over her bottom lip. "What I said was that I was tired of being pursued simply as a sexual trophy."

Claire was both astounded and alarmed. Had she so completely misread the situation? He was looking down at her with amusement, and she began to tremble. "Don't look so frightened," he soothed, moving his hand down to stroke her bare arm. "I'm attracted to you, and I'd like very much to kiss you occasionally. Is that so alarming?"

"No," she stammered.

"Good, because I intend to continue kissing you." His lashes veiled his eyes, allowing only a thin glittering line of turquoise to show, but Claire sensed his burning triumph and satisfaction, and she became even more uneasy. It was just like those times when she had glimpsed something ruthless in him, as if he weren't what he seemed at all. It didn't help that his look of triumph was immediately gone, because it left her feeling disoriented, not knowing anything for certain.

He bent and kissed her again, then left, and Claire stood staring at the door long after it had closed behind him. He seemed to have decided that he wanted more than simple friendship from her, and she didn't know how to protect herself. She was without any emotional defenses and so terribly vulnerable to any hurt he might give her. She loved him, but she felt that she didn't know him at all.

_____ *Chapter Six*

Max placed a call to Dallas as soon as he got back to his apartment, wanting to pass along the information Claire had given him as soon as possible. He knew that Anson would take action on it first thing in the morning; by Monday, the takeover would be in motion. His job wasn't finished, of course; he would have to oversee the transfer of ownership and negotiate the endless details that were always so important to the anxious personnel of the acquired company, but the major hurdle had been cleared. Max Benedict could become Max Conroy again, and he could turn his attentions on Claire.

Claire. She was the most complex, elusive woman he'd ever known; she kept herself hidden away, not letting anyone get close enough to really know her, but that was about to change. The irritating restraint he'd placed on himself was at an end. He would take it slow with her, gradually getting her accustomed to his touch. As torturous as this past week had been, it had had a positive side in that she was already used to his company. She was relaxed with him, and despite his frustration, the undemanding companionship he'd shared with her had had its own charm. Claire wasn't a chatterbox, and the time he spent with her had been punctuated by peaceful silences. He wanted her more than he'd ever wanted any other woman, and he didn't know why.

She wasn't the most beautiful woman he'd ever known; she was quietly pretty, with a fragile bone structure and eyes as dark as midnight pools, eyes that were full of dreams. She wasn't voluptuous; her body was almost reed slender, yet undeniably feminine. There was a softness to Claire that he found very appealing. He wanted to take her in his arms and make love to her, get behind the blank wall that she kept between herself and other people; he wanted to know her thoughts, what she felt, what dreamworld she drifted away to when those dark eyes turned shadowy and faraway.

Added to that, he liked her as a person. Max was passionately fond of women in general, but his intense sexuality sometimes got in the way of friendship; a woman was in his bed before they had a chance to know each other as people. The restraints that had been necessary in his relationship with Claire had allowed liking and friendship to grow. He liked talking to her; she was thoughtful and never malicious, and she wasn't uncomfortable with occasional silences. It would be extremely pleasant to wake up next to Claire, to spend lazy mornings with her, reading the newspaper and lingering over breakfast, talking if they felt like it and simply being silent if they didn't.

There had been only one other woman he had *liked* in the same manner, and he thought about her for a moment. Sarah Matthews, his friend Rome's wife: she was incredibly gentle, and incredibly strong. Max had been on the verge of loving her, and in fact did love her for the very special person she was, but she had made it plain from the beginning that Rome was the only man in the world for her, and the way Max felt about her had never grown into the area of intimacy. Now she and Rome were his closest friends, and their marriage was stronger than ever, more passionate than ever.

He would like to have that with Claire.

The thought jolted him. He kicked his shoes off and stretched out on the bed, staring at the ceiling. The scenario he had just imagined had a powerful charm to it, too powerful. Claire tugged at something in him. He wasn't certain that he liked what he felt, but he was completely certain that he had to do something about it. Claire Westbrook was going to be his.

The next night he took her to the symphony, which she loved, and afterward they ate at a tiny Japanese steakhouse. Claire had been nervous at first, and because she was nervous she became quieter, more remote, but the music had helped to relax her. Max seemed just as he always had: cool and controlled, watching the world with lazy amusement. She felt safe when he was like that.

She had slept restlessly the night before, her imagination picturing again and again the way he had kissed her, what he had said, like a loop of film on a projector that ran continuously. Every time she woke it was to find her heart racing with excitement, her body warm and yearning for him. She'd had no lovers since the divorce; she had drawn so deeply into herself, trying to build strength and recover from the shattering emotional blow of losing her baby and watching her marriage disintegrate, that there had been nothing left, no passion to give to a man. But without her being aware of it, time had worked its healing process, and she was alive again. Her nature was warm, passionate, and she trembled inside with need whenever she remembered his mouth on hers.

It hadn't even been a passionate kiss, but she had wanted to lace her arms around his neck and stand on tiptoe to press herself against him. She had wanted to lose herself in him, to give him everything that she was. It was a primitive, unconquerable urge, the need to lie in his arms, to mate, an urge that was inborn. Just as strong was the need to protect herself, and the two needs were warring inside her. Claire's capacity to love was so enormous that she was instinctively wary, backing away from any threat to her emotions. Because she loved so deeply, she was acutely vulnerable to him. He had the power to hurt her so badly that she might never recover.

The safe thing to do would be to run, to simply stop seeing him. She had lain in her bed and turned the idea over and over in her mind, but when morning had come she had admitted to herself that she couldn't do it. She loved him, and perhaps he was coming to care for her a little. There had been something hot and a little frightening in his eyes before he'd masked his expression, an almost predatory look of hunger. A man didn't look like that if he wasn't interested. That look gave her hope.

Now she came out of her thoughts to find him watching her with wry amusement, and color tinted her cheeks. Had he been able to tell the direction of her imaginings?

"You aren't eating at all; you're dreaming," he said, taking the fork from her hand and placing it on the mat. "Shall we go?"

On the drive home he asked quietly, "Claire, I didn't intend to make you uneasy with me. I apologize for putting you in a difficult spot. If you aren't attracted to me, I understand; we'll simply continue being friends—"

"Oh, please," she sighed, interrupting him. "Do you honestly believe I'm not attracted to you?"

He glanced sharply at her then returned his attention to his driving. "You've made it fairly obvious that you don't want me to touch you; in fact, at first you didn't want to have anything to do with me at all. I all but begged to get you to accept me as a friend."

She was silent. She couldn't tell him that she had been afraid of his charm, afraid that she would fall in love with him, because she'd done exactly that. Finally she turned her head to look at him, his perfect profile etched in silver against the darkened window, and her heart gave that funny little leap that she'd come to expect. Was he asking her to believe that dreams came true? It was hard for her to trust, to let anyone get behind the emotional barriers that protected her from hurt. She didn't think she was the type who could recover from one heartache after another, bouncing right back to take another try at true love, trusting that eventually everything would work out. Claire loved too deeply; it took her too long to recover from heartbreak.

She wasn't a gambler, but she didn't see that she had much choice. She couldn't walk away from him now; her heart had known it almost from the beginning, and now she acknowledged it in her mind. She had to try again; she had to reach out or despise herself for the rest of her life. Max was worth the risk, and perhaps she might win.

"I'm very attracted to you," she finally said, her voice so soft that he wasn't certain he'd heard her. His head jerked around, his eyes narrowing, and she steadily met his gaze.

"Then why have you held me away?"

"It seemed safer," she whispered, tightly knotting her hands together in her lap.

His chest expanded as he drew in a deep breath. They were near her apartment building, and nothing more was said as he parked the car. The silence extended; then he reached out and gently drew her into his arms. She didn't see his head coming down, but she felt the warmth of his body close to her, the controlled strength of his arms wrapping around her, and then his mouth was on hers. Her head tilted back to fully accept him, and her lips parted softly, her response slow and tender. He took her mouth in the same way, taking his time about it, not bruising her soft flesh. The way was open for his tongue, and he probed her mouth, feeling the quiver of her body at the deepening intimacy of the kiss. He held her closer, arching her to him, and another quiver ran along her body at the sweet, heated pleasure of feeling her breasts pushing against his chest. A small groan rose in his throat. With a sure, experienced motion he covered her breast with his hand.

Her hands clenched his sleeves, her fingers shaking. Max lifted his mouth from hers and began nuzzling her jawline, seeking the delicate fragrance of her skin. He tasted her flesh as he went, discovering some of the soft places that had been driving him wild for a week: the small hollow below her ear; the length of her neck; the ultrasensitive hollow above her fragile collarbone. And all the time her small, firm breast nestled in his palm, the nipple already peaked, inviting a more intimate touch.

"Put your arms around me," he said, his voice one of quiet demand. He wanted to feel her clinging to him, all weak with wanting. She fit into his arms as if no other woman had ever been there; he wanted it to be the same way for her. He wanted her to hold him, feel how perfect it was, their two bodies pressed together. Slowly her fingers released his sleeves, and her arms slid upward. One twined around his neck and the other around his shoulder. A shuddering breath eased out of her.

Slowly he massaged her breast, taking care not to hurt her or to scare her by losing control and grabbing at her. His own breathing didn't sound quite steady, and he knew that he had to stop or lose control. He wasn't accustomed to celibacy, and since he had met Claire, his only lovelife had been in his imagination. Reluctantly he eased away from her, his body on fire with a burning hunger that bordered on violence. He would have to get himself under control before he dared make love to her. She was so soft, so fragile; he didn't want to take the chance of hurting her, and he was very much afraid that he would.

"It's time to call a halt to this, while I still can," he admitted ruefully, his sharp, knowing gaze taking in the dazed look of passion on her face. Delight filled him that Claire wasn't a cold woman, merely a deeply reserved one, and she was finally responding to him.

His words recalled her from the warm, drifting world of physical pleasure where he had carried her, and she sat up straighter, her glance darting away from him, her hands going up to smooth her hair, as if by tidying herself she could deny what had just happened. Max took her hand and carried it to his lips. "Don't," he whispered.

He got out of the car, walked around to open the door for her and helped her out, his hand under her elbow as she maneuvered the long skirt she'd worn to the symphony. His arm went around her waist as they entered her apartment building and remained there during the short elevator ride to her floor; some of Claire's distress at herself began to fade. His attentiveness was doing something to her, slowly making her feel more certain of herself, and it was like the first hesitant flutterings of a butterfly's new wings.

He checked her apartment then came back to her. The usual lazy, good-humored smile was on his lips, but his eyes were vivid and intent as he bent down to kiss her again. "I won't stay, not tonight. I want you to be comfortable with me, and frankly, my self-control is wavering. I'll see you tomorrow night. How formal is Mrs. Adkinson's dinner party?"

Claire remembered Leigh's inclinations well. "Very."

"White dinner jacket?"

He had been wearing a white dinner jacket when she had met him exactly a week ago, and her senses gave a brief whirl as she recalled the way he had looked, with the lights caught in his golden hair like a halo, his eyes as brilliant and glowing as gemstones, the white jacket molded to his broad shoulders. She hadn't been the same person since that night.

"That would be perfect," she said. He didn't know how perfect.

He kissed her again and left, and Claire went through the motions of getting ready for bed, but her mind was drifting, floating, recalling every sensation, every moment of his kisses, his touch on her breast. Her natural human need to be touched had been suppressed for a long time by her driving need to prove to herself that she could be independent, but now her body was aching and burning as it came alive after being dormant for so long. She lay in bed, and she dreamed of him.

The gown she wore to Leigh's dinner party the next night was almost nine years old, but she had seldom worn it before, and it was one of those simple styles that couldn't be dated. It was black velvet, with only a little fullness to the skirt, and the bodice hugged her lovingly. It wasn't particularly lowcut, revealing only a hint of the beginning curve of her high breasts, but it was held up only by two thin straps, leaving her shoulders and back bare. Jet earrings dangled from her ears, and she wore no other jewelry. Her mirror told her that she had never looked better, and her fingers loved the soft, lush feel of the velvet. All her senses seemed to be more alert, and she was achingly aware of her own body in its casings of silk and velvet. When she opened the door to Max, his pupils expanded until the black almost swallowed the sea-colored irises, and the skin seemed to become taut across his cheekbones. Tension hummed from his body.

But if he thought of reaching for her, he controlled the impulse. "You're lovely," he said, his eyes never leaving her, and she felt lovely.

Claire enjoyed the dinner party more than she had expected, even though her pleasure was dimmed by the presence of Virginia Easley. It would be a long time before she'd forget Virginia's maliciousness in inviting Claire and Jeff to the same party. Max felt Claire's slight stiffness and glanced at her in question. Then he saw Virginia, too, and his eyes narrowed. "Don't let her bother you. She isn't worth the effort."

Leigh Adkinson sailed up to greet them and hug Claire, exclaiming how glad she was to see Claire again.

Max stood close to Claire, a little behind her, his presence like a solid wall of strength in case she needed him. He had met several of the other guests at Virginia's party, so people drifted over to speak to him and Claire, but most of the guests were strangers to him. For a time he and Claire merely stood still, like royalty holding court, surrounded by people who hugged and kissed Claire and told her how much they had missed her. The women would glance slyly at him, waiting for an introduction, but there was no hint of flirtation in his manner. As he had before, he made it perfectly clear that he was with Claire and had no intention of straying from her side.

Virginia came up, all smiles and dripping sweetness. "Rumors about you two are all over town," she cooed. "Why, I hear you're practically *living* together! I'm so proud that you met at my party!"

Claire's smile went brittle, and Max stepped forward, his hand touching her arm. He pinned Virginia with a narrowed, deadly look that made her smile fade, and a waiting silence descended over the guests nearest them. "Rumors have a way of turning on those who repeat them," he said in a tone laced with contempt. He was furious, and he had no compunction about letting others see it. "Especially jealous bitches who lack both breeding and manners."

Virginia went pale, then beet red. Leigh, sensing a budding scandal, came up to hook her arms through both Max's and Claire's. "There's someone you just have to meet," she chattered gaily as she led them away. Her quick action defused the situation, and the party resumed its normal buzz of conversation. After dutifully introducing them to someone, she darted away to make certain Virginia wasn't seated close to them at the table.

Except for that one scene, it was an enjoyable dinner. Claire found that she wasn't as upset as she would have expected; she was with Max, and that was the most important thing. When she remembered how difficult she had found dinners like this when she was married to Jeff, she wondered at the difference. She had proved to herself that she was capable of managing her own life, and somehow it no longer seemed so important if she accidentally picked up the wrong fork.

The woman on Max's other side leaned across to get Claire's attention. "Do you still play tennis? We miss you at the club, you know."

"I haven't played in years. I was never any good at it, anyway; I didn't keep my mind on the game."

"Dreaming?" Max teased.

"Exactly. My mind wanders," she admitted, laughing at herself.

"I concentrate as hard as I can, and I'm still not any good," the other woman admitted with a chuckle. Claire couldn't remember her name but had often seen her at the country club where the Halseys had belonged. The woman sipped her wine then set the glass down, but it caught the edge of her bread plate and toppled over, sending her wine splashing over Max's white jacket.

The woman blushed crimson. "Oh, Lord, I'm so sorry. Now you see why I'm not any good at tennis. I'm too clumsy!" She grabbed her napkin and began trying to blot the wine from his jacket.

"It's only a jacket," he soothed, his face calm. "And you're drinking white wine, so it won't stain. Please, don't let it upset you."

"But it's all over you!"

He took the woman's hand and kissed it. "It isn't important. Claire and I will stop by my apartment on the way to the hotel and I'll change."

His manner was so unruffled that it reassured the woman, and the meal continued without further mishap. When dinner was finished, he quietly made his excuses to Leigh, and he and Claire left.

"I always had a horror of spilling my wine on someone," she mused in the car. "It never happened, but I was always terrified that it would."

He was philosophical about it, and there was a slight smile on his lips. "I poured my wine in a lady's lap on one occasion. Her dress became transparent when wet, so it was truly memorable. Then, too, I've dandled my nieces and nephews when they were babies, and everyone knows what complete barbarians babies are, no shame or manners at all, so in comparison wine is definitely preferable."

At his apartment, he went into the bedroom to change while Claire checked her appearance in the gilded mirror in the foyer, reapplying her lipstick and tucking a strand of hair away from her face. Max took only a moment, reappearing in a stark black evening jacket that intensified his golden beauty. Looking at him, Claire caught her breath. Dressed all in black, except for the snowy expanse of his tucked dress shirt, he was overpoweringly male. His eyes drifted over her as she returned the tube of lipstick to her tiny evening bag. "We're a matched pair," he said.

Claire glanced down at her black gown as she preceded him to the door. "Yes, we are. Perhaps it was a happy accident at that."

He paused with his hand on the door handle, giving her another appreciative look. Releasing the handle, he turned to face her, tilting her chin up with his hand. His lips brushed lightly over hers; then he lifted his head and their eyes met, hers wide and dark, his brilliant, narrowed. He kissed her again, molding her lips with gentle pressure. She responded, returning the kiss, standing quietly before him. As if he were cupping a fragile flower, he put both hands on her face, his thumbs meeting under her chin, and continued to kiss her with long, slow, leisurely kisses, their tongues meeting in play. His taste filled her mouth, and with a sigh of pleasure Claire put her hands on his shoulders.

He murmured something unintelligible, moving his hands from her face and putting his arm around her to pull her closer. With that utter assurance of his, he put his free hand on her breast, the warmth of his fingers heating her through the velvet of her gown.

She trembled, and shivery desire began to grow inside her. Lifting herself up on her toes, she pressed against him, needing to feel his hard body and the strength of his arms enfolding her. Their mouths clung together, the contact hungry, his tongue thrusting into her mouth. His hand delved inside her bodice and cupped her naked breast, his thumb rubbing over the sensitive nipple and sending heated sparks racing along her nerves. She whimpered a little, unprepared for the sudden flood of passion that swept over her flesh. Her body arched against him, and she felt his hardness, and suddenly they both exploded with need, fierce and uncontrolled.

His mouth ground into hers, his lips hot and firm, his arms straining her to him so tightly that she couldn't take a breath. Her senses spun wildly, overwhelmed by the sudden excess of pleasurable messages that were ricocheting along her nerves. She could feel his steely strength in the muscles of his shoulders, taut under her clenched fingers; he was boldly, obviously, aroused, his flesh pushing against her. An insidious weakness began to creep through her bones and muscles, and deep inside her there was heat and a burning, writhing need.

She hadn't expected this wild hunger in him, or in herself, and she was helpless to stop it. She hadn't been prepared for the intensity of his touch, or the way in which she was responding to him, as if her body had taken charge, and she could no longer control it. He moved his hands down to cup her buttocks and bring her against him in a movement so blatantly sexual that she couldn't stop the moan of pleasure that broke from her throat. She loved him, she wanted him, and nothing else mattered.

"Claire," he muttered, his breath rasping as it left his chest. The thin strap had drooped off her right shoulder, letting her bodice slip, and he brushed the strap completely down until her breast was exposed. He stared down at her naked flesh, and she felt seared by his gaze. His face was hard, taut, like that of a man on the verge of agony. She was a doll in his grasp, completely helpless against his strength, as he bent her back over his arm and arched her breast up for his mouth. He wasn't gentle now; his mouth closed hotly over her nipple, suckling at her and making her cry out.

His hand was under her skirt, smoothing over her thighs, her bottom, between her legs. A thin, wordless cry broke from her lips, but it wasn't a cry of protest. She was beyond protesting. His touch intensified the torrent of sensation inside her; she felt afire, literally molten with need, and he was wild with the need to get at her. His hard fingers closed on her panties and garter belt and jerked them down with one movement, tugging them off; then she felt the hard edge of the table behind her, and he lifted her onto it. His hand was there now, touching her intimately, stroking and rubbing and probing, doing things to her that pushed her intolerably close to the edge. She cried out again, clutching at him, so empty and aching that she couldn't stand it any longer and tears seeped out from under tightly closed lids.

"Claire," he said again, his voice no longer recognizable. It was rough, raspy, and as her name left his lips, he was tearing at his clothing. In a fever, he pushed her skirt to her waist then spread her legs and put himself between them. For a frozen moment in time she felt the shock of his naked flesh against her, then he drove into her, and her body jolted from the impact. She ceased to exist as a person; she was only heat and need, her bare legs wrapped around his waist, her arms around his shoulders, crying out and twisting to meet his thrusts. He caught her mouth with his, and her breathing stopped, taken away by his wildfire. The pressure and aching need were building inside her, and it was more than she could stand. It was going to kill her, shatter her into a thousand tiny pieces.

"Max, stop," she moaned, tearing her mouth from his. "I can't . . . I can't bear it."

His teeth clenched, and an animal sound rose from his throat. "I—can't stop. Not now, not now—"

The need exploded, and she did shatter, her body heaving in his arms. He held her and surged into her and met his own shattering, blind with the unbridled fury of what had just happened between them. Claire was limp in his arms, drooping against him, her head on his shoulder. He let his own head drop, resting on the curve of her neck and shoulder, her sweet, female scent rising to his nostrils as he gulped in air. Her skin was fevered, and he felt the way she was shaking, like a leaf in a storm.

It was a long time before either of them could move, could gather enough strength to do anything except cling to each other for support. Then she began to move, trying feebly to free herself from him, to pull her bodice up and cover her naked breast. She kept her head down, her face averted, unable to face him. She couldn't believe that she had acted like an animal in heat, moaning and writhing against him, out of control and lost to every thought except the need to satisfy her body.

"Stop it!" he ordered in a fierce whisper, finally stepping back from her, but instead of being freed she found herself swept into his arms, held high against his chest. He carried her swiftly through the darkened apartment and into the bedroom, with only the small light from the foyer to show him the way. Without bothering to turn on a light even then, he laid her on the bed and stood over her as he tore out of his clothes, popping buttons from his shirt in his haste to get out of it. He was naked before she could control her quaking limbs enough to get off the bed, and by then it was too late. He bent to pull the gown off her, leaving her bare on the melon-colored satin comforter. The satin was cool on her overheated skin; then he was on her, and in her, and she was no longer aware of the coolness beneath her. He was slower this time, the urgency gone, his body moving against her with long, slow movements that rubbed his hair-covered chest against her breasts, and she began to move with him.

She hadn't realized that such a degree of sensuality even existed, but he revealed to her a new side of her nature, the potential of her woman's body for pleasure. And he reveled in her, holding her and kissing her endlessly, taking her to the peak of pleasure, letting her rest then doing it again before it all became too much for him, and he began surging wildly as he reached for his own sweet madness.

She lay in his arms, and he smoothed the sweat-dampened hair back from her face. He took small kisses from her lips, her cheek, her temple. "I've been going half-crazy, wanting you," he muttered rawly. "I know this was too fast, that you weren't ready for it, but I don't regret it. You're mine. Don't try to run away from me, love; stay with me tonight."

She was incapable of running from him, her strength gone, her legs like water, and at the moment she couldn't think of why she should want to run. He pulled the comforter back and put her between the sheets, resting her head on the pillow. He lay beside her, his body warm and hard, his arm draped over her waist, and exhaustion claimed them. Claire went to sleep right away, sinking into the enveloping blackness and welcoming it. She didn't want to think, didn't want to dream. She just wanted to sleep....

She woke in the darkened room and lay staring through the darkness at the blank ceiling. Max still slept beside her, his breathing deep and easy, his strong body relaxed. Until that night she hadn't realized just how strong he was, but now her body ached in ways that testified to his strength. For all his sophistication and cosmopolitan manners, he made love savagely, as if civilization hadn't touched him. Perhaps his smooth urbanity was only a veneer, and the real man was the one who had taken her with primitive urgency.

And perhaps she wasn't the woman she had always thought herself to be. If he had been wild, so had she. If he had been hungry, so had she.

He had asked her to stay, but she didn't know if she could face him in the morning. Every instinct in her wanted to find a place that was quiet and private, where she could come to terms with this new part of herself. A lifetime of reserve hadn't prepared her for the wildness that had surged within her; it frightened her that he had such power over her. She hadn't known that this could be a part of love.

Moving slowly, her body protesting, she slid out of the bed and groped around on the floor until she found the crumpled velvet heap of her gown. At the door she paused, looking back at his barely visible form on the bed, but he still slept deeply. Tears welled in her eyes; was it wrong to leave him now? What would happen if she woke beside him in the morning light, without the shield of darkness to protect her from the possibility that he might see too much? She wanted to creep back to his side and curl up in his arms, but she turned away.

"Come back here."

His voice was low, rough with sleep. She stood there with her back to him. "It's better that I leave now," she whispered.

"No, I won't let you." She heard the rustle of the bed as he left it; then he was behind her, his naked body hot against her back. His arms circled her waist, and the gown slipped from her fingers to the floor.

"Have I frightened you?" he asked, his mouth against her neck. "Is it because I hurt you?"

Her head moved slowly from side to side in denial. "You didn't hurt me," she said.

"I was on you like a rutting bull, love, and you're so soft." His lips moved to her shoulder and found the tender hollow there. His hot breath wafted over her skin like a caress, and she felt her breasts tighten in automatic response. "So delicate. Your skin is like silk." His hands were on her breasts now, and her head dropped back against his shoulder, her eyes closing as delight spiraled in her again.

"Come back to bed," he urged softly. "I know you're uneasy, but everything will be all right. I promise. We'll talk in the morning." Sometime during the next day he would tell her who he really was, and he was glad that this night had happened. It bound her to him, gave him an advantage in handling her. She would be angry, of course, but he didn't think it would be anything he couldn't handle.

She went to him, allowing herself to believe that it really would be all right. And a small while later, lying beneath him with the now-familiar fire burning inside her, she forgot why she had ever been uneasy.

The shrill ringing of the telephone woke her. Beside her, Max uttered an obscenity and sat up in the bed, reaching for the receiver to halt the intrusive noise. Bright sunlight filled the room, and she pulled the sheet higher under her chin then closed her eyes again. She didn't feel quite ready to face the morning yet, and she wished the phone hadn't rung.

"It's too bloody early in the morning to be funny," Max snarled into the receiver, running his fingers through his tousled hair. He listened a moment then said, "I don't give a damn what time it is, whenever I've just woke, it's too early. What is it?"

When he hung up the phone a few minutes later, he cursed under his breath before rolling over to look at her. Claire opened her eyes and stared at him, uncertainty plain on her face.

"I have to go to Dallas," he said, putting out his hand to finger her hair. "This morning."

She swallowed and tried for a casual tone. "It must be urgent; this is Sunday."

"It is. Bloody hell, what timing! I wanted to spend the day with you. We badly need to talk about what's happening between us, and there are some other things I wanted to tell you, but now they'll have to wait."

"It can wait," she whispered.

Chapter Seven

But could it? After hurriedly taking her home, Max had left, and Claire hadn't heard from him since. She hadn't really been surprised when Sunday passed without a call; his business in Dallas must have been urgent to require him on a Sunday, but she had expected to hear from him on Monday. In such a short length of time he had insinuated himself so deeply into her life and her heart that now things didn't feel right without him. She hurried home after work on Monday, afraid that she might miss his call, but her telephone sat in silence, and the longer the silence stretched, the more she became convinced that something was wrong. She didn't know what it might be, but there was a sense of unease growing inside her. What was it that he had wanted to talk about? She knew it had to be important; his expression had been too serious, even a little grim. But it had all gone unsaid, and it shouldn't have; whatever it was, that had been the time for it, and now that time had passed.

She slept badly, too worried to rest, her awakened body reminding her of the pleasure he had given her, the things he had taught her. It was amazing that she had been married to Jeff for years without learning that she could go mad with desire, that a man's touch could turn her into pure molten need. No, not just a man. One man. Max.

Why didn't he call?

Lack of sleep left shadows under her eyes the next day, and when she looked in the mirror, the sense of impending doom intensified. She stared at the fathomless dark pools of her eyes, trying to see beyond them into the woman she was, deep into herself where she sensed these things without really knowing what they were. Had he found her lacking somehow? Had she been clumsy? Had he been appalled to find that she was just like all the others, easy to bed and easy to forget? Had he done just that, forgotten her?

But he had been wild to have her, so wild that he hadn't even taken her to the bedroom, hadn't even removed their clothing. A hot blush colored her cheeks at the memory. In the foyer, of all places, like savages in evening clothes. Her reserve had been shattered, his control destroyed, and they had merged together with primitive force. It had to mean something to him.

But he was so sophisticated, while in many ways she was not. Had that night been normal for him? Was it nothing to him but more of the same?

There were no answers in the mirror.

It was after lunch when the call came at work, and Sam spent a long time in his office. When he came out, he was pale.

"I've just been notified of a takeover attempt," he said quietly.

Claire looked up at him, waiting.

"It's Spencer-Nyle, in Dallas."

It was an enormous corporation, spreading out into diverse fields, and the chairman of the board was legendary for his crafty moves. Sam and Claire looked at each other, knowing that it was really only a matter of time. Had the takeover attempt been by anyone closer to Bronson Alloys in size, they would have had a good chance to fight, but Spencer-Nyle could swallow them whole and never even strain. Sam might win the first round, because of the real estate values, but the war would go to Spencer-Nyle.

"They can't be foreign-backed," Claire said, shocked and puzzled.

"No. It seems we were being threatened on two fronts, but I didn't see it. I was too worried about keeping my research secure."

"When will they make their offer?"

"That's up to them, but I'd better use however much time we have left to strengthen our position."

"Can we possibly win?"

"Anything is possible." He grinned suddenly. "If we put up such a fight that the takeover would be more trouble than we're worth, they might pull out of it."

"Or you could find a white knight."

"White knight or hostile takeover, the end result would be the same: the company would belong to someone else. I suppose I could give in gracefully, but hell, I've always liked a good fight. Let Anson Edwards and his team of hatchetmen work to get us."

Now that the moment was actually there, Sam seemed to relish the thought of a fight. Claire wondered a moment at his mentality; he actually enjoyed conflict. But there were people who thrived on challenge; Martine was one of them. Put a mountain in front of her and she climbed it; it was as simple as that. Claire preferred to go around it; she approached a challenge head-on only when the other paths were blocked.

There was a lot to be done; the board of directors had to be notified, and proper action had to be discussed. Until a firm offer was received, they had little to go on. As the principal stockholder and chairman of the board, Sam's opinion carried a lot of weight, but he was still answerable to the board.

The phone rang off the hook. Claire worked late and was even grateful that the pressure kept her mind off Max, at least a little. She was almost afraid to go home, afraid that he wouldn't call and she would have to spend another night with that silent telephone. At least this way she didn't know.

But eventually she had had to go home, so she put a stack of records on the stereo to fill the apartment with noise. Odd, but the silence had never bothered her before; she had welcomed it, enjoying the peace and solitude after the hectic pace of her job. Max had changed that, had turned her interests outward, and now the silence grated on her nerves. The stereo abolished the quiet outside but couldn't touch the stillness inside.

He wasn't going to call. She knew it, sensed it.

Had she been only the last warm body in a long line of warm bodies in his bed? Was that all she had been to him, a challenge, so that once she capitulated the challenge was gone? She didn't want to think that; she wanted to trust Max completely, but more and more she remembered those tiny jarring moments when she had seen the hardness beneath his perfect manners, as if the cosmopolitan gentleman were only a veneer. If that were so, then the image he projected was just that, an image, and she didn't really know him at all. Several times she had thought that, but now she was terrified that it was true.

* * *

Max brooded in his office, wishing that he could call Claire, but things were in motion now, and it would be in the best interests of both sides if he had no more contact with her until the takeover was settled. To see her now would put her in an awkward position, possibly subject her to undeserved hostility. Damn Anson for calling him back so soon, before he had a chance to talk to her and explain things! He wasn't worried about making her see reason; he was very experienced, and he knew the power of the weapon he had over her, the power of sensuality. Beneath that aloof, ladylike exterior was a woman who burned for his touch, whose own sensuality exploded out of control during his lovemaking. No, he could handle Claire's anger. What worried him was the pain and confusion she must be feeling because he had seemingly walked out of her life after that unbelievable night they had shared. He didn't want anything or anyone to hurt her, but he was very much afraid that he had, and that thought caused a tightening in his chest. Damn this bloody takeover to hell and back! It wasn't worth hurting Claire.

The senior vice president, Rome Matthews, entered his office. It was late and they were both in their shirtsleeves, and they were friends as well, so Rome didn't bother with the formality of knocking.

"You've been glaring at that file for the past hour," Rome commented. "Is something bothering you about Bronson's?"

"No. We won't have any trouble," Max said, assured on that point, at least.

"You've been edgy since you got back from Houston."

Max leaned back in his chair and hooked his hands behind his head. "Isn't Sarah waiting for you?"

Rome's black eyes glittered the way they did when he was on to something, and he had the determination of a bulldog. Sprawling his big frame in an office chair, he watched Max through narrowed eyes. "Well, I'll be damned," he drawled. "You're acting just like I did when Sarah used to drive me crazy. God, I love it! It's poetic justice. You, my friend, have woman trouble!"

Max scowled at him. "Funny, is it?"

"Hilarious," Rome agreed, a wolfish grin lighting his hard, dark face. "I should've guessed sooner; hell, you were in Houston a week. Something would have been seriously wrong if you *hadn't* found a woman."

"You have a perverted sense of humor," Max said without heat, but also without smiling.

"Who is she?"

"Claire Westbrook."

Because Rome had studied the file on Bronson Alloys, he knew the name and knew her connection with the company. He also knew that the vital information needed for the takeover to be successful had come from her. One brow lifted. "Does she know who you are?"

"No," Max growled, and Rome gave a soundless whistle.

"You're in trouble."

"Damn it, I know that!" Max got to his feet and paced the expanse of his office, shoving his fingers through his hair. "I can handle that, but I'm worried about her. I don't want her hurt by this."

"Then call her."

Max shook his head. A call wouldn't work; he knew that. He had to be where he could hold her, soothe her with his touch, reassure her that what was between them was real.

"You're going to be back in Houston in a couple of days; Anson is really pushing this. She'll have to know then who you are."

"I intend to tell her before anyone else knows." Frowning, he stared out the darkened window at the myriad lights and angles of the Dallas skyline. He wanted to be with Claire now, lying in bed with her and stroking the intoxicating softness of her skin. He wasn't sleeping well, wanting her, tortured by his aching loins. If he had had difficulty getting her out of his mind before, it was damned impossible now.

Claire tried to eat the sandwich she had brought for lunch, but it was tasteless, and after a few bites she rewrapped it in cellophane wrap and tossed it into the garbage can. She hadn't had much appetite, anyway. The office was empty; Sam was at lunch, as was almost everyone else. It was Friday, almost a week since she had seen Max or heard from him. A small eternity. She had stopped expecting the call, but something inside her was still marking time. Two days. Three. Four. Soon, a week. Eventually it would be a month, and perhaps someday the pain would be a little duller.

The most important thing was to keep her time filled, to stay busy. She began typing a stack of letters; correspondence had doubled this week in direct relation to the notification Spencer-Nyle had given that it was interested in Bronson Alloys. It really couldn't have happened at a better time, she told herself; it left her less time to brood.

It was amazing how happy Sam seemed to be. He was preparing for this like a football coach preparing his team for the annual game against an arch rival, with almost unconcerned enthusiasm. He was actually enjoying it! The stockholders were coming out pretty well, too; the price of the stock had shot up as soon as the news got out.

Sam had been doing some research into Spencer-Nyle in general, and Anson Edwards in particular, and had come up with an impressive array of articles on the man. His desk was littered with them when Claire carried the letters in to leave them for his signature. A business magazine lay open on his desk, folded to an article on Spencer-Nyle, and Claire curiously picked it up. A color picture of Anson Edwards was on the first page; he didn't look like a corporate shark, she thought. He was trim and nondescript, with no outstanding features, the sort of man who blended into a crowd, except for the sharp intelligence obvious in his eyes.

The article was surprisingly interesting and went into some depth. She carried the magazine back to her desk to finish reading it. Then she turned the page, and Max's face stared up at her.

She blinked, stunned, and tears blurred her eyes. She closed her eyes, willing the tears away. Just a picture of him stirred up a whirlwind of pain and memories and aching love. If only she knew what had happened!

Opening her eyes, she looked at the picture again. There was another picture beside it of a dark man with penetrating dark eyes, and beneath both photos was the caption: "Roman Matthews, left, and Maxwell Conroy, are Anson Edward's handpicked lieutenants, and corporate America generally considers Spencer-Nyle to have the nation's best team of executives."

They had his name wrong. He was Maxwell Benedict, not Maxwell Conroy. Her hands shook as she held the magazine, her eyes skimming to find the text concerning him. There it was; she read it then reread it, and finally the truth sank in. He was Maxwell Conroy, not Benedict at all, and he had romanced her so intensely in hopes of getting information about Bronson Alloys from her. Perhaps he'd even planned to snoop in her papers, but that hadn't been necessary. She had *given* him the information he needed; she had a vivid memory of herself talking to him, trusting him, never dreaming that he was a spy for another corporation! After he had what he wanted, he had left. It was that simple, and that terrible.

Slowly, painstakingly, Claire reread the entire article, some tiny part of herself hoping against hope that she had misunderstood, but the second reading was even worse, because the details she had skipped the first time only supported the facts. Maxwell Conroy was an Englishman who had emigrated first to Canada, where he had been employed at a branch of Spencer-Nyle and had swiftly climbed the corporate ladder. He had been transferred to the Dallas headquarters four years ago, gained American citizenship, and was acquiring a reputation for engineering lightning-fast takeovers, moving in and taking control before the target company could be warned and devise any sort of defense.

She felt numb all over, as if paralyzed; even her face was still, and it was an effort to blink her eyes, to swallow. Lightning-fast takeovers. He moved in; he took control; he walked away. Yes, he had done exactly that. She hadn't had a chance. He had played her like the expert he was, reeling her in so gently that she hadn't even realized she'd been hooked. She thought of her gullibility in swallowing that line he'd fed her, about how tired he was of being pursued as a sexual object, how he just wanted a friend. She had actually believed it! How had he kept from laughing in her face?

She couldn't have been much of a challenge to him, she thought, cringing inside at how stupid she'd been. She had fallen in love with him almost immediately and fell into bed with him the first time he'd made the effort. He hadn't had to make love to her, she thought painfully. She had already told him about the land reappraisal. That must have been the icing on his cake, to see how easily he could topple her into bed.

Her eyes were dry, burning, and her throat hurt. She realized that she was breathing in quick, hard rasps, and a hard chill shook her. Betrayal burned like acid inside her.

The magazine had slipped from her cold, numb fingers, and she sat there in numb shock; that was how Sam found her when he came back from lunch.

Her face was white and still, and she didn't seem to see him, even though she was looking straight at him as he came in the door. Sam frowned, walking toward her. "Claire?"

She didn't answer, and he squatted down in front of her, lifting her hand in his and chafing her cold fingers. "Claire, what's wrong? Has something happened?"

Her lips barely moved, and her dark eyes were black as she stared at him. "Sam, I've betrayed you."

Slowly, like someone who was old and feeble, she leaned down and picked up the magazine. With great care she leafed through it until she came to the article on Spencer-Nyle and folded the pages back to Max's photograph. "I've been seeing him," she whispered, pointing to him. "But he told me his name was Max

Benedict, not Max Conroy, and he... he knows about the property."

Sam took the magazine from her, his face set, and Claire wondered if he hated her. He should; he'd probably fire her on the spot, and it was nothing less than what she deserved. She had cost him his company with her stupidity, her incredible, inexcusable stupidity.

"How did it happen?" he murmured.

She told him, sparing her pride nothing. Max had made a fool of her, and she had fallen for every word he'd said. Tears began to slide down her pale cheeks, but she didn't notice them. Sam reached out and held her hand, and when it was over he did something incredible. Gently he took her in his arms and held her head to his shoulder. His tenderness, when he should have hated her, when he should have railed at her, broke what little control she had left, and sobs began tearing from her throat. She cried for a long time, rocked in Sam's arms, and he stroked her hair and whispered soothing words to her until at last her body stopped shaking from the force of her crying, and she raised her wet, tear-swollen face from his shoulder.

"I'll get my things and leave," she whispered, wiping her face with the heel of her hand.

"Why?" Sam demanded calmly.

"Why?" she echoed, her voice cracking. "Sam, I've lost you your company! You can't possibly want me around now; I've proved that I can't be trusted."

"Well, now, that's where you're wrong," he said, taking his handkerchief out of his pocket and offering it to her. "It's true that the property was our ace in the hole, but it's also true that if Spencer-Nyle really wants us, we don't have a prayer. They're just too big, too powerful. The best I hoped to do was make them pay more than they'd wanted to. As for trusting you—" he shrugged "—I'd say you're the most trustworthy employee I have. You made a mistake, and I think you'd walk over live coals to keep from making another."

"I don't see how you can possibly forgive me, because I'll never forgive myself." She dried her eyes then knotted the handkerchief in her hands.

"You're only human. We all make mistakes, some of them more serious than others. Examine your mistake from another point of view. Will any jobs be lost because of what you told Conroy? Probably not. Spencer-Nyle will need our expertise; they won't run in a whole new set of employees. Did your mistake affect the outcome of the takeover attempt? I don't think so. I think they have us, one way or the other, and to tell you the truth, I almost feel relieved. The only thing that's changed is the timetable." A ghost of a smile touched his hard mouth, and his eyes took on a certain faraway look. "I wish that the mistakes I've made were no more serious than that."

"He used me," she whispered.

"That's his loss," Sam said. "He'll be back, Claire; this is his baby. He'll be here, negotiating, supervising the takeover. You're going to have to see him, work with him. Can you handle that?"

Part of her said no, shrinking from the idea of seeing him again. How could she bear to look at him, knowing that he had used her, lied to her, betrayed her, and knowing deep inside that she still loved him, because love didn't die easily for her? But if she ran, where would she run to? She had to have a job, and running wouldn't change anything. She would still have to face herself in the mirror in the morning; she would still

:arry inside herself the knowledge that it had all been a
.ie.

She should have known better. How could she ever
have been blind enough to really think a man like Max
would be interested in her? He would want someone
:leek and sophisticated and beautiful, someone who
wore experience like a luxurious mink on smooth, sun-
tanned shoulders. Her only attraction for him had been
that she gave him an inside contact in Bronson Alloys.

But she had loved him and trusted him.

She had spent the past five years slowly and painfully rebuilding her life, her sense of worth and self-
respect. If she ran now, it would all be for nothing; she
would be a rabbit, hiding from herself. No, not again.
Never again. She would *not* let Max Benedict—no, Max
Conroy—destroy her.

"Yes, I can handle it," she told Sam.

"Good girl," he said, patting her shoulder.

She got through the day... and the night. The night
was the worst; at least during the day she was distracted by the necessity of doing her job, but at night
there was nothing, and she was alone with herself. She
lay awake, as she had done every night since Max had
left, trying to marshal her strength for the grueling days
that lay ahead. She tried to plan the future, because she
knew that, despite Sam's effort to cheer her up, there
would be changes made at Bronson Alloys. Sam would
almost certainly leave management entirely and devote
himself to his research. That would suit him; he was
happier in his laboratory, anyway. Where would that
leave her? Would he need a secretary then, even taking
for granted that he would want her if he did? Would the
new CEO want her for a secretary? Would Spencer-Nyle
allow her to work in any position where she would have

access to sensitive information? After all, she had already proved herself untrustworthy! All a man had to do was pay attention to her and she would tell everything she knew! She thought bitterly that they would be justified in taking that position.

Alma called over the weekend, inviting Claire and Max to dinner. Claire accepted, but calmly told Alma that she hadn't seen Max lately. It was inevitable that then Martine would call, trying to find out what had happened.

"I tried to tell you and Mother that there wasn't anything serious between us," Claire pointed out. How true that was! But her voice was even, almost casual, and she was proud of herself.

"But he acted so...so wild about you; he hardly took his eyes off you. Did you have a fight or anything?"

"No, no fight. There was just nothing there." On his part, at least. It was just like Martine that she had hit on the crux of the entire situation: Max had been *acting*, and he was so good at it that he had fooled everyone.

Late Sunday night, just as she was finally dozing off to sleep, the telephone rang. Sleepily she propped herself on her elbow and reached for it, thinking it would be a wrong number. None of her family ever called that late, and Claire wasn't the type to think that every late-night call meant an emergency. "Hello," she sighed, pushing her tangled hair out of her face.

"Claire. Did I wake you, darling?"

She froze, horrified, that familiar deep voice with the crisp-edged accent making chills run down her body. She didn't think; she simply reacted, replacing the receiver in its cradle so gently that it didn't even click. A soft whimper rose in her throat. How dare he call her after what he'd done? Was he back in Houston? Sam had warned her that Max would be back, but she hadn't thought that he would have the arrogance to call her.

The ringing began again, and she reached out to turn on the lamp, staring at the telephone with pain and indecision etched on her face. She had to cope with him sometime, and perhaps it would be better to do it over the phone rather than in person. It was cowardly of her, but she had endured a lot of pain; she wasn't certain how much more she could take, and pride demanded that he not know how badly he'd hurt her. If she broke down in front of him, he would be able to see how horribly foolish she'd been.

"Hello," she said again, picking up the phone and making her voice brisk.

"The connection must have been bad," he said. "I know it's late, darling, but I need to see you. May I come over? We have to talk."

"Do we? I don't think so, Mr. Conroy."

"Damn it, Claire—" He stopped, realizing what she had called him. "You know," he said, his voice changing as tension edged into it.

"Yes, I know. By the way, the connection wasn't bad. I hung up on you. Goodbye, Mr. Conroy." She hung up again, as gently as before. Crashing the receiver down would be too mild to even begin to express the way she felt, so she didn't waste the effort. She turned off the lamp and made herself comfortable on her pillows again, but her former drowsiness was gone, and she lay awake, her eyes open and burning. The sound of his voice reverberated in her mind, so deep and smooth and so well remembered that it hadn't been necessary for him to identify himself. She had known who it was, from the first word he'd said. Had he really thought he could take up where he'd left off? Yes, probably so. She had been such a pushover for him the first time that he wouldn't have foreseen any difficulty in seducing her again.

Why did she still have to love him? It would be so much easier if she could hate him, but she couldn't. She was hurt and angry and betrayed; she had trusted him, only to have that trust thrown in her face. But she didn't hate him. There wasn't a night that she didn't cry for him, that her body didn't ache with an emptiness that wouldn't go away. Well, if she couldn't hate him, she could at least protect herself by never, never letting him get close enough to hurt her again.

In his apartment, Max cursed viciously and threw the telephone across the room in a rare fit of violence. The instrument jangled crazily then lay on its side with the receiver beside it. Damn it. *Damn it!* Somehow she'd found out who he really was and probably put the worst possible connotation on it. He'd intended to tell her that night rather than walk into the offices of Bronson Alloys the next day and hit her with it cold, but at least then he would have been with her, able to hold her and love her out of her anger. Now it would be hell getting through her door again; she'd probably slam it in his face.

The telephone began a raucous beeping to signal that it had been left off the hook, and he swore again, stalking over to pick it up and crash the receiver down on the button. This damned job had been nothing but trouble. It had brought Claire into his life, but it had also been between them from the start, and now he had to get the merger negotiations out of the way before he could approach her again. He sat down, frowning at the carpet. He missed her more than he'd ever missed anyone in his life.

She looked up from the computer terminal when the office door opened, and her heart stopped. Max stood there, flanked by two men who carried bulging briefcases. His face was expressionless, his turquoise eyes guarded. There was no point in playing games, so he said bluntly, "I'd like to see Sam Bronson."

Claire didn't betray her feelings by even a flicker of emotion. "Yes, Mr. Conroy," she said neutrally, as if there were nothing unusual in his presence there, as if she had never lain naked in his arms and burned with desire. She got to her feet without another glance at him and knocked briefly on Sam's door, then entered and closed it behind her, leaving Max and his associates to wait. She came out after a moment. "Go in, please," she said, holding the door open for them.

His gaze lingered on her face for a fraction of a moment as he passed her, and there was something hard and threatening there, something that frightened her. She kept her face blank; he might have been a stranger to her. When the door closed behind them, she sat down at her desk again and clasped her shaking hands to still them. Seeing him had been like taking a knife in the chest, a sharp, brutal pain that almost doubled her over. Odd, but she'd forgotten how handsome he was, or perhaps that had been blanked out. The lean, chiseled planes of his face had stunned her anew, and underlying that was the memory of how he'd looked in the throes of passion, his hair damp with sweat, his eyes burning in his taut face. He'd braced himself above her, and the muscles in his torso had rippled with power—

Stop it! she ordered herself, biting down on her lip

hard enough to bring blood. Wincing, she grabbed a tissue and blotted the tiny drop of blood away. She couldn't let herself keep thinking about him. There was no point in it, no use in tormenting herself with memories of that one night. She had a job to do, and if she concentrated on it she just might get through the day.

But the day was a nightmare. She was called in to take notes, and it was almost more than she could bear to sit so close to Max, feeling his eyes on her as she scribbled page after page. Sam was a hard-nosed negotiator, and he was determined to win everything he could. An emergency meeting of the board of directors was called, and the office hummed with activity.

Finally they went out for lunch. As soon as the office was empty, Claire collapsed into her chair, her eyes closed in relief. She hadn't known how hard it would be to see him again. He hadn't said a personal word to her, but she had been vividly, painfully aware of him.

She heard a sound at the door and hastily opened her eyes. Max stood there with his hand on the knob. "Get your bag and come with us," he said curtly. "You haven't had lunch, either."

"I brought my lunch, Mr. Conroy, but thank you for the invitation." She kept her voice even as she uttered the careful courtesy, her face a blank wall that hid her thoughts. His mouth tightened, and she knew that her answer had angered him. Without another word he turned and left the office.

It was a lie that she had brought her lunch; she put on a pot of fresh coffee and ate a pack of crackers that she found in her desk, telling herself that she had to start eating better. She wasn't going to let herself lapse into a decline like some Victorian maiden. She was going to get through this somehow.

Her first instinct was to quit her job and get as far away from Max as she could. She wanted to be safe; she wanted to get her emotions back on an even keel and forget about him, if that were possible. She even typed up a letter of resignation, but when she reread it, she knew that she couldn't do that and tore the letter into little strips. She wasn't going to let this take command of her life. She was going to continue just as she always had. She would get on with the everyday business of living; she wasn't going to run. Running and hiding was a childish reaction. It wouldn't be easy, facing Max and doing her job without letting him see how he affected her, but she really had no choice if she wanted to face herself in the mirror every morning.

She had changed a lot in the past few years, changes that hadn't been easily attained. She was more self-confident now. She would never be as bold and eager for new experiences as Martine, but she had found a quiet inner strength that she'd learned to trust. No matter what it took, or how painful it was, she was going to do her job and ignore Max Conroy as best she could.

They came back from lunch, and the negotiations resumed. Max somehow maneuvered things so that he was sitting next to her while she took notes, forcing her to concentrate on getting the notes right and not letting him know how his nearness affected her. Whenever she glanced at him, she would find his eyes on her, narrowed and intent, and she knew that he wasn't going to let the subject of their relationship drop gracefully. She stopped looking at him even when he spoke. That was the only way she could keep her composure; to pretend that he didn't exist.

Max watched her, trying to read her expression, but her quiet face was a total blank. If she had been aloof before, she was totally unreachable now, and her distance from him made him furious. She was ignoring him, and that was the one thing he didn't intend to allow. He was hampered now by the job at hand, but it wouldn't last forever. When it was finished, he was going to smash down those damned defenses of hers and never let her build them again.

Chapter Eight

It took two long weeks for the negotiations to be hammered out; it was a hard fact for Spencer-Nyle to accept, but Sam Bronson still had a card they couldn't trump: himself. He was, in effect, the most valuable asset of Bronson Alloys. It was his genius, his instinct, his research, that produced the alloys. They were trying to buy the man as much as the company, and Sam knew it, they knew it, and they knew he knew it. To keep the man, they had to keep him happy, and keeping him happy meant making concessions. The job security of his employees was guaranteed; no one would be brushed aside in the usual house cleaning that came with a takeover. Benefits were sharply increased and raises were given, and even though the overall structure of the company would be changed, the employees would be happy because they would be very well taken care of.

Yet in the end Max still managed to work out an agreement that cost Spencer-Nyle less than what Anson had feared. He did it with cool, relentless negotiating, not giving in on anything he thought was excessive, and inch by inch working Bronson into a position they both found acceptable. He had to give Bronson credit; the man was as tough as nails, fighting as hard as he could for his company, even though the end had been inevitable from the first.

And Claire was there every day, calmly taking notes, her very presence controlling the tempers that threatened to flare. There was something about her cameo-smooth features and velvety dark eyes that made people control their anger and their language. Max watched her closely without appearing to, so hungry for just the sight of her that he couldn't stop himself. He hadn't tried to call her again; not only would she probably accuse him of trying to get information from her, but he preferred to wait until he could devote himself completely to making her see reason. Time would work in his favor to blunt the edge of her anger. He watched her closely, incessantly, trying to read the thoughts behind that smooth blank face. She had to be furious with him, but there was no hint of it in her speech or actions. She was as remotely polite with him as she would be with a stranger, as if he meant nothing to her, as if they had never made love with frantic, explosive need. After a week Max decided that he would rather have her scream curses at him—anything—than treat him with that immense indifference. He could handle anger and tears; it was her mental distance that frustrated him to the point of madness.

Claire knew that Max watched her, though she never reacted to it in any way. The only way she could function was to push all her pain and sense of betrayal into a small part of her mind and lock them away. She didn't think about them; she didn't agonize over what might have been. She had survived the destruction of the life she'd built once before, and she was determined to do it again. The end of every day marked a small victory for her: a day that she had gotten through without breaking down. She couldn't wallow in self-pity; she had to complete the task she'd set for herself, getting through the days one at a time. She couldn't guess how long the negotiations would continue, so she didn't try to make plans or look forward to the day when Max was gone. It could be days, or weeks, or even months, if he remained to oversee the changeover to Spencer-Nyle ownership.

Sam hadn't discussed Max with her, and he acted as if he had forgotten that she had been involved with him. In actuality, there was little chance for them to talk; it seemed there was never a spare minute, and someone was always in the office. Max and his associates were going over the books, which meant they were constantly underfoot, and Sam, like Claire, guarded his words.

The final meeting was long and exhausting, the boardroom filled with stale smoke and the stench of old coffee. Tempers were frayed and voices hoarse from hours of talking. Claire took notes until her fingers cramped, and her back felt as if it were breaking in two from sitting for so long. The odors in the closed room made her stomach roll threateningly, so she hadn't been able to eat lunch when sandwiches and fresh coffee were brought in. All she wanted was to escape into the fresh air and listen to the silence. Late in the afternoon a thunderstorm hammered the city, washing the streets with a deluge of rain. Sam, with an understanding glance at Claire's pale face, got up and opened the window to let in a gust of cool, fresh, rain-sweetened air. The heavy purple clouds had completely covered the sky, and the streetlights came on as premature dusk settled over the city. With the breaking of the storm there seemed to come a break in the negotiations; ev-

eryone was tired and sleepy, and the pounding of the
rain against the windows had a soporific effect. Points
that had been crucial just that morning no longer
seemed so important; what was important was reaching agreement, getting it over with and going home.

At last it was done, and men in rumpled shirt-sleeves
wearily shrugged into their coats, shaking hands and
smiling. Claire gathered her notes together; she had a
few more chores before her day was ended. Quietly she
slipped from the boardroom and walked to her office;
she planned to type the final agreement that night. She
was exhausted, her body aching, but she wanted to finish the documents while her notes were still fresh. The
contracts would be needed first thing in the morning, so
it was either do them immediately or come in to work
early; she elected not to put the chore off. It was much
more peaceful now than it would be tomorrow morning. The building was empty, except for the weary men
who had negotiated the details of the takeover; there
would be no phone calls, no interruptions, no series of
small crises to handle. All she had to do was finish her
work and leave.

She had barely begun typing the documents on the
computer terminal when the office door opened. She
glanced up inquiringly, and an expressionless mask
slipped over her face when she saw it was Max. Without a word she went back to work.

He strolled with indolent grace to her desk and leaned
his arm on top of her computer terminal. A frown
knitted his brow as he saw what she was doing. "That
doesn't have to be done tonight," he said.

"I have to do it now, or come in early in the morning." She kept her gaze on her work. Why didn't he go

away? His presence made her tense and started that dull ache in her heart that she had briefly forgotten.

"Let it wait." It was a crisp command, and he reached down to flick off the power switch to the terminal. The screen went blank, wiping out everything she had put into the machine. "You're exhausted, Claire, and you haven't had anything to eat today. I'm going to take you to dinner; then we're going to talk. You've put me off long enough."

She looked at him now, sitting back in her chair and raising cool eyes to his. "I can't think of anything we could talk about, Mr. Conroy. I don't have any more corporate secrets you'd be interested in."

Dark fury washed over his face. "Don't push me," he said in a voice like splintered ice. "I've let you hold me off for two weeks now, but that's at an end."

"Is it?" she asked indifferently and reached to turn on the terminal again. "Excuse me, I have work to do." She couldn't let herself respond to him, couldn't react to him in any way, or she would slide out of control. For the past two weeks she'd been holding on by a thread; it wouldn't take much to snap it.

Max turned the computer off again, punching the switch with controlled violence. His eyes were blue-green fire, burning like lasers. "You're coming with me. Get your bag—and don't turn on this bloody damned machine again," he snarled as she reached for the switch.

Claire stared straight ahead at the blank screen. "I'm not going anywhere with you."

His eyebrows lifted. "Do you want me to force you? You forget that you're an employee of Spencer-Nyle now."

"I've forgotten nothing, but my job doesn't require me to associate with you away from the office. I've gotten very particular of the company I keep." She faced him calmly, determined never to let him see the desolation inside her. Staring at him, she saw an entirely different man from the one she had thought she knew. He wasn't the epitome of a controlled, reserved, rather old-fashioned Englishman, after all. He was a fire behind mirrors that reflected the image he chose, a ruthless, determined man who let nothing stop him. His facade was that of an even-tempered and sophisticated man of the world, civilized to his fingertips, but it was a lie. He was an elegant savage, a shark cutting through opalescent seas, dazzling people with his beautiful image before he attacked.

He was very still, his eyes glittering the way they did when something displeased him. His mouth was a grim white line. "I know you're angry, but you'll still listen to me if I have to carry you to my apartment and tie you to the bed."

"I'm not angry," Claire pointed out, and she wasn't. She hurt too much to be angry. She could feel a tiny trembling beginning deep inside her as her exhaustion grew, and she knew she couldn't handle this scene right now. "As you pointed out, I'm your employee now; if you don't want me to work tonight, I won't. But I won't go anywhere with you, either. Good night, Mr. Conroy." She reached for her bag and stood, and Max lashed out, catching her arm in a grip that bruised.

"Don't call me Mr. Conroy," he said evenly.

"Why? Is that an alias, too?"

"No, and neither is Benedict; that's my middle name."

"How appropriate. Benedict Arnold was a spy, too."

"Damn you, I didn't spy," he rasped. "There were no papers gone through, no conversations taped. You *gave* me that information without any urging on my part."

Her dark eyes didn't even flicker. "You sought me out at Virginia's party because you knew I worked here."

"That's not important! Yes, I deliberately introduced myself to you. It was possible that you had some helpful information about Bronson Alloys." He shook her lightly. "What does that matter?"

"It doesn't, not at all." She glanced down at his hands, and her voice was cold. "You're hurting me."

He released her, something shadowy moving in his eyes as he watched her rub her upper arms. "That was business; it has nothing to do with us."

"How nice for you, to be able to put areas of your life in tidy little compartments and not let them touch! I'm not like that. I think that if a person is dishonorable in one thing, he will be in another."

"Don't be so damned unreasonable—"

"That was quite a blitzkrieg you put on," Claire interrupted, her voice rising as she felt her control slipping. Fiercely she groped to regain it. "Does Anson Edwards know what a prize he has in you? Has any woman ever resisted you when you turn on the heat? I fell for it completely, so you can give yourself a pat on the back. Poor man," she breathed, her eyes burning. "So handsome that women only treated you like a body without a soul, you were tired of meaningless sex and wanted someone to be a real friend. I must have the word 'fool' stamped on my forehead, because you knew just what line to feed me. You turned on the charm, forced yourself into my life and got the information you wanted, then waltzed out again. Fine. I was a fool once, but don't expect me to be a fool again! I'm not really stupid; I don't have to have my face rubbed in it!'' Breathing hard, she turned away, rubbing her forehead with a trembling hand. Perhaps she was stupid, at that; she hadn't learned all that much from Jeff's betrayal. It had made her cautious, but not cautious enough. In the end she'd walked back into the vicious trap of loving a handsome, charming man who could have anyone he wanted and had dreamed the fool's dream that he might love her in return.

"I didn't 'waltz out'!" he yelled, glaring down at her. Max rarely lost his temper. It was seldom necessary; he usually got what he wanted without having to put out that much effort, simply by using his charm and sensuality. But his reactions to Claire had been extreme from the beginning, and the cold contempt in her eyes triggered something fierce inside him. "I was called back to Dallas. You should know. You were in bed with me when the call came!"

The little remaining color washed out of her face, and she gave him an uncontrolled look of such naked pain that he halted. "Claire..." he began, reaching out for her, but she recoiled from him so violently that she bumped into the edge of the desk and sent papers flying.

"How kind of you to remind me," she whispered. Her eyes were black in her paper-white face. "Get away from me."

"No. It was good between us; I want to have it again. I won't let you push me out of your life."

She was visibly shaking, and he wanted to put his hands on her to support her but didn't dare. All of a sudden her icy reserve had shattered before his eyes, leaving a woman who was almost staggering with pain. The realization struck him like a blow to the chest, taking his breath. She wasn't an aloof, controlled woman, a little unfeeling, a challenge to his male sexuality. She put a buffer between other people and herself in an effort at self-protection because she felt too much and was too easily and too deeply hurt by life. He hadn't understood her at all, casually counting on his sex appeal and charm to smooth things over as he'd always done, and so intent on getting her into bed that he'd overlooked all of the small signals she'd given him. God, what had he done to her? How deeply had he hurt her to put that look on her face?

"You don't have any choice about it," she said jerkily. "Do you really think I'd be stupid enough to trust you again? You lied to me, and you used me. It was all in a good cause, though, so that makes it all right in your eyes. The end justifies the means, right? Please, just leave me alone."

"No," he said harshly, feeling a sudden, intense twist of pain in his gut at the thought that he might have lost her forever. He couldn't accept that; he *wouldn't* accept that! For reasons he couldn't analyze, Claire had become increasingly precious to him, filling his thoughts during the day and his dreams at night. The night he'd spent with her had made him want more, a lot more.

"I'd say you're going to have to, at least for now," Sam interrupted from the doorway, his voice as cool as the look in his eyes. "Stop badgering her; she's worn out."

Max didn't move a muscle except to turn his head to look at Sam, but suddenly there was something wild about him, a fine tension in his lean, deceptively muscled body, his eyes icy and lethal. "This doesn't concern you," he said, and he was every inch the predatory, aggressive male, with the primitive instinct to fight whenever another male approached the woman he'd marked as his.

"I'd say it does. After all, it was my company that you took, using the information Claire gave you."

Max froze, then looked sharply at Claire. "He knows?"

Dumbly she nodded.

"Claire told me right away," Sam said, leaning against the door. "As soon as she realized who you were. Her sense of honor is too strong for corporate games; she wanted to quit right then, but I talked her out of it." At Max's lifted brow, he added, "I knew she'd never let herself make that mistake again."

Claire couldn't stay and listen to them talk about her; she felt exposed and raw, her deepest secrets laid out for the world to examine and chuckle over. A small sound of distress escaped her as she walked past Max, keeping her head averted.

"Claire!" He moved swiftly, catching her arm again and pulling her to a halt. Desperately she wrenched at her arm, trying to twist it from his grip, but he caught her other arm and held her still in front of him. Biting her lip, she stared fixedly at the knot of his tie and struggled for control. Why did he have to hold her so close? She could feel his warmth, smell the exciting male muskiness of his skin. His nearness reminded her of things she would have to forget in order to survive. Her body felt the touch that had driven her to such feverish heights of pleasure and reacted wildly, independent of her control. Her nipples hardened, wanting the touch of his hands, his mouth; her legs quivered, wanting to wrap about his hips, and the emptiness in her wanted to be filled.

"Let me go," she whispered.

"You're not in any shape to drive; you haven't eaten all day, and you look as if you might faint at any moment. I'll drive you home," he insisted.

"I wouldn't go with you to a dogfight," she said, using her last ounce of defiance. His grip slackened, and she pulled free, taking the chance to walk out of the office without him. It might be the only opportunity she had, and she was too upset to tolerate any more. Another minute and she would be weeping, completing her humiliation.

Her hurried steps carried her out of the building and to the parking lot; it was still raining lightly, but gusts of wind battered her, and flashes of lightning in the low-hanging purple clouds lit the darkness with momentary brilliance. The storm intensified the darkness, making the efforts of the streetlights seem ineffective. Her heels tapped sharply on the wet pavement as she ran to her car. She reached it and stopped to unlock it and only then heard the footsteps behind her. Cold terror washed down her spine, and tales of rape and robbery flooded her mind. Grasping her keys like a weapon, she whirled to face any assailants, but there was no one close to her. On the other side of the parking lot Max walked to his car and got in, and Claire sagged with relief.

Her hands were shaking as she opened the car door and slid behind the wheel, cautiously locking the door again. What if it had been a mugger or a rapist? How many articles had she read that warned women against going to their cars alone at night? She'd been foolish to let her emotions push her into a dangerous situation, and she drew a deep breath. She had to get control of herself.

She was still shaky, and the rain made the street-lights reflect dizzyingly on the wet streets; she drove with extra care, not wanting to risk an accident. She didn't notice the car behind her until she turned down the street to her apartment building and the other car turned, too. Nervously she peered into the rearview mirror, trying to tell what kind of car it was, but the headlights were right in her eyes, and she couldn't see anything. Was she so on edge tonight that she was becoming paranoid? Quickly she found a parking place and pulled into it, deciding to wait until the other car had gone on before she got out.

But the other car slowed and pulled into the empty parking space beside her. It was a black Mercedes, and the man driving it had golden hair that gleamed like a halo in the silvery artificial glow of the streetlight.

Still shaking, Claire leaned her head on the steering wheel. He was determined to talk to her, and she was beginning to realize that he didn't give up once he'd decided to do something. How had she ever thought him civilized? He was as ruthless as any Viking, and she feared him as well as loved him because he would destroy her if she didn't find a way to keep him at a distance, to protect herself with indifference.

He tapped on the window, and she jerked her head up.

"It's raining harder," Max said, his voice muffled through the glass. The rain beaded and ran down the windshield, emphasizing his words. "Let's go in, dear. You're going to get soaked if you wait much longer; I think a new storm is coming in."

She flinched at the endearment, amazed at how easily it rolled off his tongue. How many other women had been fooled by his glib lies?

He wasn't going to give up and go away, and she was too tired to sit out in the car indefinitely. Gathering her wavering strength, she got out of the car and carefully locked the door, then hurried up the sidewalk without looking at him. .

He stretched out his arm and opened the door for her and was right beside her in the elevator. Claire clutched her keyring, keeping it ready. Damn him, why wouldn't he give up? What did it matter to him, anyway?

Catching her wrist firmly, he relieved her of the keys and opened the door, stepping inside to turn on the lights and pulling her in with him. He released her wrist to close the door, and tossed her keys onto the small table that stood by the door, her catchall table that she had found in a flea market and refinished. Fixedly she stared at the table; it wasn't a Queen Anne, like the one in his foyer. She remembered the way he had lifted her onto that elegant Queen Anne table and moved between her thighs, and for a moment she thought she really might faint, after all. Her legs felt wobbly, and there was a faraway roar in her ears. She sucked in a deep breath, hoping the extra oxygen would steady her.

"Sit down," Max said roughly, propelling her toward the couch. "You look dead white. Are you pregnant?"

Stunned, she stared helplessly at him, sinking down onto the cushions as her legs folded beneath her. "What?" she gasped.

"You haven't eaten. You're pale. You've lost weight, and cigarette smoke is making you ill." He enumerated all the things that had been haunting him since that explanation had first blasted into his mind. "Did you think I wouldn't notice that Sam opened the window for you this afternoon? Why would you tell him and not me?"

"I haven't told him anything," she protested, thrown off balance by his line of questioning. "I'm not pregnant!"

"Are you certain? Have you had your period this month?"

For the first time that night color flooded her cheeks. "That isn't any of your business!"

His face was grim as he stood over her. "I think it is. I didn't protect you that night—*any time* that night— and I don't think you're on the pill. Are you?" Her expression was answer enough. "No, I didn't think so."

"I'm not pregnant," she repeated doggedly.

"I see. You're simply on a diet, is that it?"

"No. I'm exhausted; it's as simple as that."

"That's another symptom."

"I'm not pregnant!" she yelled, then buried her face in her hands, aghast at her loss of control.

"Are you certain?"

"Yes!"

"All right," he said with sudden calm. "I apologize for upsetting you, but I wanted to know. Now sit there while I get something for you to eat."

The last thing she wanted was something to eat; she wanted him to get out of her apartment so she could fall facedown on her bed and sleep. But she couldn't chase him out, because her legs were lead weights, and suddenly it wasn't worth the effort of getting up. She sat there staring blankly in front of her, wondering how she could have been so stupid as not to have considered the possibility of a pregnancy, but the truth was that it hadn't entered her thoughts at all. Nature had assured her that she wasn't pregnant, but she hadn't thought of it even then. It was a good thing, because she wasn't sure she could have borne the added stress. What if she had been pregnant? Would it have been all right this time? Would she have held her own baby in her arms? Max's baby, with golden hair and eyes like the sea. Suddenly pain shot through her, because it wasn't to be, and she wished it could have been.

She was so completely exhausted that to continue sitting upright was asking too much of her body. With a quiet little sigh she sank back against the cushions of the couch, her eyelashes sinking down as if pulled by a force she couldn't withstand. With the suddenness of a black curtain dropping down, she was asleep.

When Max came back into the living room with a tray loaded with a selection of sandwiches, a glass of milk for Claire and a cup of coffee for him, because he was hungry too, he was braced to receive all her hurt accusations, but he was also ready to stay there all night, if necessary, to explain his side of it and convince her that they had something special between them. Then he saw her curled against the cushions, one arm folded in her lap and the other hanging to the side in that limp way that indicated deep sleep. Her hand was lying palm upward, her fingers curled slightly, and he stared down at the peculiar, innocent vulnerability of her open palm, so soft and pink. Memory seared him. Sometime during the night they had spent together, during one of those frantic, greedy matings, he'd taken her hand and carried it down his body, and every muscle in him had jerked in reaction to her gentle fingers closing around him. He jerked now in reaction to the memory, his body growing hard and sweat popping out on his brow.

He swore soundlessly and set the tray down, bringing his surging appetite under iron control. Now wasn't the time to seduce her, assuming that he could even get her to wake up. He looked at the tray of food, then at Claire, sleeping so deeply. She needed both food and rest, but evidently her body had taken over and given sleep the highest priority. The kindest thing now would be to let her sleep, even though it meant postponing that talk once again.

Bending down, he gently slid his arms around her, one under her knees and the other around her back, and lifted her easily. Her head fell sideways against his shoulder, her gentle breath warming his flesh through his shirt, and he stood still for a moment with her clasped in his arms, his eyes almost closed as he drank in her nearness, the softness of her body in his arms and the faint, elusive sweetness of her skin. Until then he hadn't realized quite how much he'd missed her, but now the delicious agony of holding her again almost made him groan aloud. She fit into his arms in a way no other woman ever had. Max had held many soft, trembling bodies against him and beneath him, but now he couldn't recall any of the others. Only Claire. She made him feel oddly complete, and the thought disturbed him, because that meant he was incomplete without her.

He carried her into the bedroom and eased her down onto the bed. She was so soundly asleep that she didn't even murmur but lay exactly as he'd placed her. With the expertise of a man who had undressed many women, Max removed the short lightweight jacket she wore, then pulled her blouse free of the skirt. It was a thin silk blouse, and beneath it he could see the lacy edge of her camisole, reminding him of the marvelously sexy underwear she wore. Reminding him? He wiped his perspiring forehead. His problem was forgetting.

Reaching beneath her, he unbuttoned and unzipped her skirt then worked the garment down her legs. She wasn't wearing a camisole, but a full-length slip, all silk and lace. His hands began a fine trembling as he pulled off her shoes and set them aside. He didn't dare go any farther. Not only would she not appreciate being stripped naked, but he was suddenly afraid that his control would snap if he continued. He thought of the satin and lace garter belts she wore, and the filmy underpants, and his body flooded with heat. Bloody hell! He swore furiously, silently, forcing himself to his feet. Her penchant for sexy underwear was likely to give him a fetish.

With effortless strength he lifted her and turned the cover back, then placed her between the sheets. She looked so tired, he thought, pushing back a strand of hair from her temple. Her face was pale and strained, with dark shadows under her eyes, but it was a relief to know that it was only exhaustion instead of the strain of early pregnancy that had put those marks there. He had never before lost control like that, not only of his body, but of his mind; he had always made certain that his partner was protected and been more than willing to assume responsibility if she hadn't taken care of it herself. Then, and only then, would he unleash his sexuality, lose himself in the sensual pleasures of the flesh. But with Claire, he hadn't even thought of it. He had had only one thought, to penetrate, and had been blind to everything else. Even now he was stunned by the driving urgency he'd felt, the simple and powerful animal instinct to mate that had taken control. He didn't like the feeling. He'd always thought that the power of his mind could control the lusty appetites of his body. His icy, superlative intelligence had *always* been in control ... until Claire had responded to him, and the restraints he'd been placing on himself had shattered under the violent surge of desire.

He hadn't even had the control, the consideration, to take her to bed. He had simply lifted her onto the table in the foyer, pushed her velvet skirt to her waist and thrust into her. She was such a delicate woman, as finely made as the finest porcelain, and he'd taken her with all the finesse of a conquering warrior. The only thing that kept him from being completely disgusted with himself was the memory of her response, the way she had clung to him, twisted against him, the little whimpers in her throat as she met his thrusts, the way she had cried out and the sweet inner clenching that had signaled her peak of satisfaction. Behind her distant manner was a capacity for passion that overwhelmed him and made him hunger for her. He wanted her all for himself.

Realizing that he was shaking with the need to take her again, he turned away from the bed while he still could. Where Claire was concerned, his self-control was almost negligible.

He went into the living room, wolfed down several of the sandwiches and drank the pot of coffee he'd made, not worrying about the effect of the caffeine on his system so late at night. A deep frown furrowed his brow as he considered the situation with Claire.

Until that night he hadn't doubted his ability to talk her around eventually. Never in his life had he been denied anything he really wanted; nature had given him an enormous advantage in coupling his face and body with a superior intellect. But for the first time he wasn't certain that he would win. He had seen behind Claire's shield and, for the first time, seen the vulnerability of the real woman and realized the necessity for that shield. She felt too much, loved too deeply, gave herself too completely...and betrayal would strike a crippling blow at that too-tender heart.

Whatever happened, he had to make certain that she couldn't hide from him, and he knew her well enough to realize that would be her first form of defense. She would do whatever she could to put distance between them, mentally if not physically. Time was on her side. Soon he would have to return to Dallas, and they would be separated by more than two hundred miles; he would be traveling to other cities, putting even more distance between them. He considered his options, and a plan formed in his mind. The thing to do was to take her to Dallas with him; the problem was in getting her there.

He cleaned up after himself then went into the bedroom to check on her, to assure himself that she was really all right. She was still sleeping soundly, and a healthy pink color was beginning to return to her cheeks as she rested. Thoughtfully he looked at her alarm clock, then picked it up to make certain the alarm was turned off. Let her sleep as long as she needed. He wrote a short note and propped it on the clock, then let himself out of the apartment. He had plans to make, and it wasn't too late at night to set them in motion.

A faint grin relieved the grimness of his expression as he drove through the rainy Houston night. It wouldn't hurt Rome to be jarred out of a sound sleep by a telephone call; after all, it had been Rome's call three weeks before that had pulled Max out of the bed he'd been sharing with Claire. Fate had a way of evening things out.

Chapter Nine

When Claire woke the next morning she felt rested for the first time in weeks, and she lay in drowsy relaxation, waiting for the alarm to go off. The minutes ticked by without the alarm, and finally she opened a curious eye to check the time. The first thing she noticed was that the room was very light for so early in the morning, and the second thing she noticed was that it was almost nine-thirty. "Oh, no!" She hated being late to anything, even by a few minutes, and she was more than a few minutes late. She should have been at work an hour-and-a-half ago!

She scrambled out of bed, still a little disoriented from sleeping so long, and stared down at herself in confusion. Why was she wearing a blouse and slip instead of a nightgown? Then memory flooded back, and her face heated. Max! She'd gone to sleep on the couch; Max must have put her to bed. At least he hadn't stripped her; she couldn't have borne that. It was bad enough that he'd handled her so easily while she'd been asleep, undressing her and putting her to bed as if he had every right to be so familiar with her. She would have preferred that he let her sleep on the couch.

But that explained why she had slept so late; he hadn't set her alarm. She looked at the clock then noticed the note beside it. She didn't even have to pick it up to read it; the handwriting was a series of bold slashes written with a strong hand. *Don't worry about being late. You need the rest. I'll handle it with Bronson—Max.*

She grabbed the note and crumpled it with a despairing cry. That was just what she needed, for him to "handle" it with Sam! What would he say? That he'd left her in bed, and she was so tired that he was going to let her sleep late? Sam would have to pull one of the other secretaries in to handle the office, and the reason why she was late would spread through the office like wildfire.

Her stomach rumbled, and she realized that she was both very hungry and very grungy from having slept in her clothes and makeup. She was already so late that she would gain nothing by hurrying to work. She decided to take her time; after a long shower, a shampoo and a leisurely breakfast, she would feel better. She wouldn't go to work looking thrown-together; she would be professional if it killed her.

It was almost noon when she walked into the office, but her stomach was pleasantly full, her hair washed and pulled back into an attractive chignon, and she wore her favorite dress, a navy-blue blouson with white piping. Her efforts to bolster her spirits had worked, or perhaps it was the extra sleep she'd had; for whatever reason, she felt almost calm. There was indeed another secretary at her desk, a young woman who had been with the company only a few months, and whose eyes widened with surprise when she saw Claire. "Miss Westbrook! Are you feeling better? Mr. Bronson said you fainted last night and wouldn't be working today."

Bless Sam for covering for her! Claire said calmly, "I'm feeling much better, thank you. I was very tired, nothing else."

She relieved the young woman and sent her back to her own job; when she sat down at her desk, Claire felt more normal, as if things were settling back into their rightful place. Then the door to Sam's office opened, and someone stood there watching her. It wasn't Sam; she had never felt that tingle of awareness sweep over her from Sam's gaze. Without looking at Max, she gathered her notes on the documents that needed typing.

"Leave those," he ordered, coming to stand behind her. "I'm taking you to lunch."

"Thank you, but I'm not hungry. I've just had breakfast."

"Then you can watch me eat."

"Thank you, no," she repeated. "I have a lot to do—"

"This isn't personal," he interrupted. "It concerns your job."

Her hands stilled. Of course. Why hadn't she thought of that? Sam would no longer need a secretary, so she would no longer have a job. The guarantees that applied to the others could hardly be expected to apply to her. She raised shocked eyes to Max, trying to cope with the idea of being so abruptly unemployed. There were other jobs, of course. Houston was a boomtown, and she would find other work, but would she enjoy it so much and would it pay so well? Though her apartment wasn't an expensive one like Max's, it was nice and in a good section of town; if she had to take a large cut in pay, she wouldn't be able to afford it. For a terrible moment she saw herself losing not only her job but her home.

Max reached down and pulled her to her feet. His eyes were gleaming with the success he'd had in putting his plan into motion. "We'll go to Riley's; it isn't quite noon, so we should get a good table away from the crowd."

Claire was silent as they left the building and crossed the street. It was a hot spring, with the daytime temperatures already climbing into the low nineties, and though the sky was a deep, clear blue now, the forecast was for more thunderstorms in the afternoon. Even on the short walk to Riley's her navy-blue dress began to feel too warm. Worry ate at her. How much notice would she be given? Two weeks? A month? How long it would take to move Sam completely into research?

They just beat the lunch crowd at Riley's and got one of the secluded booths in the back. Claire ordered a glass of iced tea, earning a hard look from Max. "You might eat a little something; you've lost weight, and you had precious little to spare."

"I'm not hungry."

"So you said. The point is, you should eat even though you aren't hungry to gain back the weight you've lost."

Why did he keep harping about her weight? She had lost only a pound or two, and she had always bordered on thinness, anyway. She had other things to worry about. "Are you firing me?" she asked, keeping her expression blank.

His eyebrows lifted. "Why should I fire you?"

"I can think of several reasons. The most immediate is that my job is being phased out, since Sam won't need a secretary in research, and whoever takes over as CEO will probably bring his own." She met his gaze squarely, her dark eyes fathomless and a little strained, despite her efforts to keep all expression from them. "There's also the fact that this would be a good opportunity to get rid of a bad security risk."

Swift anger darkened his eyes. "You're not a bad security risk."

"I leaked confidential information. I trusted the wrong person, so I'm obviously a terrible judge of character."

"Damn it, I—" He interrupted himself, glaring at her from narrowed, brilliant eyes. "You aren't being fired," he finally continued in a clipped voice. "You're being transferred to Dallas, to Spencer-Nyle headquarters."

Stunned anew, she opened her mouth to say something then closed it when nothing came to mind. Transferred! "I can't go to Dallas!"

"Of course you can. It would be foolish of you to refuse this opportunity. You won't be executive secretary to the CEO, of course, but there will be a substantial increase in salary. Spencer-Nyle is much larger than Bronson Alloys and pays its employees well."

Panic edged into her eyes, her voice. "I won't work for you."

"You wouldn't be working for me," he snapped. "You'll be working for Spencer-Nyle."

"In what capacity? Shoved into a closet sorting paper clips, so I can never get my hands on any valuable information?"

He leaned over the table, rage turning his eyes dark green. "If you say another word about being a security risk, I'll take you over my knee wherever we happen to be, even if it's the middle of the street—or in a restaurant."

Claire sank back, warned by the look and the barely controlled ferocity in his face. How had she made the colossal mistake of thinking him civilized? He had the temperament of a rampaging savage.

"Now, if you're through with the sarcastic remarks, I'll give you your job description," he said icily.

"I haven't said I'll take the job."

"It would be foolish of you to turn it down. As you pointed out, your job at Bronson Alloys will no longer be there in a short while." He named a figure that was half again as much as she was currently making. "Can you afford to turn down that much money?"

"There are other jobs in Houston. My entire family is here. If I moved to Dallas, I'd have no one."

His jaw tightened, and his eyes went even darker. "You could visit on weekends," he said.

Claire sipped at her tea, not looking at him. It *would* be foolish to turn down that much money, even though it meant moving to Dallas, but her instinct was to turn it down, anyway. If she relocated to Spencer-Nyle's headquarters she would be in Max's territory, seeing him every day, and he would have authority over her. It wasn't a decision she could make immediately, even though logic said she should jump at it.

"I'll have to think about it," she said with the quiet stubbornness that her family had learned to recognize.

"Very well. You have until Monday."

"That's just three days, counting today!"

"If you decide not to take the job, another person will have to be found," he pointed out. "Your decision can't be very complicated; you have to relocate or join the unemployment lists. Until Monday."

She saw no sign of relenting in his eyes, even though three days seemed like no time at all to her. Claire didn't hurry toward change; she liked to do things gradually, becoming used to changes by slow increments. She had lived all of her life in or near Houston, and to move to another city was like asking her to change her entire life. Things were difficult enough now without being lost in a totally new environment.

Max's prime rib was served, and he devoted himself to it for a few minutes while Claire nursed her tea and turned the idea of moving over and over in her mind. At last she pushed it away; she couldn't decide now, and she had other things she wanted to ask him.

"What did you tell Sam?"

He looked up. "Concerning what?"

"Last night. The fill-in secretary said that Sam told her I'd fainted and wouldn't be working today."

"Embellishment on his part. When he asked me this morning what the hell I was doing following and harassing you last night, I told him to mind his own bloody damn business and that it was a good thing someone made certain you got home safely because you collapsed."

"I didn't collapse."

"Really? Do you remember when I undressed you?"

She looked away, her cheeks heating. "No."

"I didn't cheat; I don't take advantage of unconscious women. When I make love to you again, you'll damned well be awake."

She had noticed that the more irritated he was, the more crisp his accent became, and he was practically biting off his words now. "If I don't go to Dallas," she whispered, getting up from the booth, "it will be because of you, because I can't stand being near you." Then she walked off before he could say anything, fleeing back across the street to the relative safety of the office.

Max watched her go, his face stiff. He hadn't thought that she would reject the job offer, but now it seemed that she might, and he was afraid that if he lost track of her now he might lose her forever. Damn it, after all the strings he had pulled, she *had* to take the job!

Rome hadn't been pleased by the late phone call the night before. "Damn it, Max, this had better be good," he'd growled. "Jed is cutting teeth and raising hell about it, and we'd just gone to sleep after getting him settled."

"Kiss Sarah good-night for me," Max had said, amused by Rome's grouchiness.

Rome told him where he could go and how he could get there, and in the background Max had heard Sarah's laughter. "This is important," he'd finally said. "Is there a job opening in the office? Any job?"

They worked so well together that Rome hadn't wasted any time asking unimportant questions, like for whom, and why. They trusted each other's instincts and plans. Rome had been silent for a moment, his steel-trap brain running through the possibilities. "Delgado in finance is being transferred to Honolulu."

"Good God, what strings did he pull to get that?"

"He understands money."

"All right, who's taking his place?"

"We've been talking about bringing Quinn Payton in from Seattle."

Max had been silent in his turn. "Why not Jean Sloss in R and D? She has a degree in business finance, and she's done a damned good job. I think she's executive material."

By that time Rome had seen a pattern in all this moving around. "Who do you suggest to replace Jean Sloss? I agree that she deserves a promotion, but she's good enough that replacing her won't be easy."

"Why not Kali? She'd love to work in R and D, and it would be a chance for her to eventually move into a managerial position. She knows the company."

"Damn it, she's *my* secretary!" Rome had roared. "Why don't you move your own secretary?"

Max had considered that, but didn't think Claire would take the job; on second thought, being Rome's secretary would be too close and make working difficult, too. "Forget Kali, then. Caulfield, the general office manager... what's his secretary's name? Her qualifications are good, and she's ambitious. Carolyn Watford, that's it."

"I'm taking all this down. We're not in the habit of playing musical offices. Who takes Carolyn Watford's place?"

"Claire Westbrook."

After a long pause of silence Rome had said, "I'll be damned," and Max had known he didn't have to make any further explanations.

"I'll see what I can do. It won't be easy, moving this many people around on such short notice. When can I let you know?"

"Sometime before lunch tomorrow," Max had said.

"Hell!" Rome had snorted, and hung up, but he had been on the phone before ten o'clock with the all-clear. Rome Matthews was a mover and a shaker; when he decided something would be done, it was better not to stand in his way, and Anson Edwards generally gave him a free hand.

Max hadn't considered that he would have more trouble convincing Claire to move than Rome had had in shaking up an entire office, but he should have known. He had made enough mistakes in dealing with her, mistakes that had come back to haunt him, that he should have been expecting it. If he could just get her to Dallas, he would have plenty of time to convince her that he wasn't a complete bastard after all. If it took time to rebuild her trust in him, he was willing to take that time. He had hurt her, and the knowledge was eating away at him. It had been true when Claire accused him of compartmentalizing his life. He hadn't allowed for the possibility that Claire would think he had used her solely for the purpose of getting that information. Now he couldn't get her to listen to him, and he had the cold feeling inside that even if she did, she wouldn't believe him. He had destroyed her trust in him, and only now was he realizing how rare and precious that trust was.

Claire did her usual Saturday morning chores, finding comfort in the routine while she tried to get her thoughts in order and make a logical decision. She scrubbed and waxed the kitchen floor, cleaned the bathroom from top to bottom, did her laundry, and even washed the windows, trying to burn up the anger that consumed her. With a shock she realized that she was not just angry, she was furious. She was usually calm; she couldn't even remember the last time she had been truly angry, so angry that she wanted to throw something and scream at the top of her lungs. Damn him, how *dare* he! After using her as callously as he had, now he actually expected her to uproot herself and change her entire life, agree to move to another city and

in doing so throw herself into continuous contact with
him. He had said she wouldn't be working for him, but
she would be in the same building, in the same city, and
he had made it plain that he didn't consider things over
between them. How had he said it? "When I make love
to you again, you'll be awake." *Again.* That was the key
word.

His gall made her almost incoherent with anger, and
she muttered to herself as she cleaned. It was odd, but
she couldn't remember being angry when Jeff had left
her for Helene; she had been tired and grief-worn over
the baby, and bitterly accepting that Jeff should want
someone else, but she hadn't been angry. Only Max had
touched her deeply enough to find the core of passion
inside her. He brought out all the emotions and feelings she had spent a lifetime controlling and protecting: love, fierce desire, even anger.

She still loved him; she didn't even try to fool herself
on that score. She loved him, she burned for him, she
wanted him, and the flip side of the coin was her deep
anger. It was nature's decree that for every action there
should be a balancing reaction, and that was also true
of emotions. If she hadn't loved him so deeply, she
would have been able to shrug away his betrayal and
accept it as a lesson in trusting the wrong person. But
because she loved him, she wanted to shake him until
his teeth rattled. She wanted to scream at his arrogant
assumption that she was his for the taking, and she
wanted to show him just how wrong that assumption
was.

She could tell him to keep his job, turn her back on
him, and walk away; that would show him that he
couldn't use her and expect her to fall back into his bed
whenever he beckoned. That would show him that she

was perfectly capable of living without him…or would it? Wouldn't it instead be admitting that he had hurt her so badly that she *couldn't* face seeing him every day? She had to admit that joining the unemployment line when she had the offer of a good job was a drastic, illogical move. He would know how much he had hurt her, and her pride demanded that she put up a good front. It was somehow essential to her self-esteem that she prevent him from knowing that his betrayal had hurt her so deeply that the wound was still bleeding.

But what other choice did she have? If she went to Dallas, she would be playing right into his hands, dancing to his tune like a marionette on a string.

Claire straightened from her dusting, her mouth set firmly and her eyes deeply thoughtful. What she had to do was not allow Max to be a factor in her decision at all; this was her job, her financial future, and she shouldn't allow anger to cloud her judgment. Even if she went to Dallas, she wouldn't *have* to dance to Max's tune; when it came down to it, she was a woman, not a marionette. The choice, and the decision, were hers.

Looking at it like that, from a logical point of view, she knew that she would take the job. Perhaps that would be the best way of putting up a good front. If she went on about her life as normal, it would seem as if Max hadn't made such a disastrous impact on her heart, and only she would know the truth.

Once the decision was made it was as if a weight had lifted. The difficult part would be telling her family, and Claire chose to tell Martine first. That afternoon she drove out to Martine's house in the suburbs, a ritzy location that accurately reflected Martine's and Steve's dual success. Martine's house wasn't cool and picture-perfect, though. It reflected Martine's warmth and outgoing personality, as well as her joy in her children. A tricycle was parked next to the first step, and a red ball lay under a manicured shrub, but most of the cheerful tangle of toys was in the fenced backyard that surrounded the pool. Because it was a warm, sunny Saturday, Claire directed her steps toward the back. As she rounded the corner of the house, the tapping of her heels on the flagstones warned Martine of someone's presence, and she lazily opened her eyes. Just as Claire had expected, her sister was stretched out on a deck chair, lazing in the sun in a diminutive white bikini that had to make Steve choke whenever he saw it. Even wearing no makeup and with her golden blond hair pulled back in a haphazard ponytail with an ordinary rubber band, Martine was gorgeous and sexy.

"Pull up a chair," she invited lazily. "I would hug you, but I'm slimy with suntan oil."

"Where are the children?" Claire asked, sinking onto a deck chair and propping her feet up. The sun did feel good, all hot and clean, and she turned her face up to it like a flower.

"Skating party. It's Brad's best friend's birthday. It's an *all-day* skating party," Martine said gleefully. "And Steve is playing golf with a client. This may be the only day I have alone again until both children are in college, so I'm making the most of it."

"Shall I go?" Claire asked teasingly.

"Don't you dare. With our schedules, we don't see enough of each other as it is."

Claire looked down, thinking of the decision she'd made that morning. She was only now beginning to realize how close-knit her family was, without living in each other's pockets; moving away from them was going to be a wrench. "What if you saw even less of me? What if I moved to Dallas?"

Martine shot upright in the deck chair, her blue eyes wide and shocked. "What? Why would you move to Dallas? What about your job?"

"I've been offered a job in Dallas. I won't have my job here much longer, anyway."

"Why not? I thought you and Sam got along like a house on fire."

"We do, but Sam—the company has been taken over by Spencer-Nyle, a conglomerate based in Dallas."

"I've been reading about the possibility in the papers, but I had hoped it wouldn't happen. So it's final, then? When did it happen, and what does that have to do with you, anyway? They certainly aren't going to get rid of Sam; he's the brains behind Bronson Alloys. Aren't you going to stay on as his secretary?"

"The final agreement was signed yesterday." Claire looked down at her hands, surprised to see that her fingers were laced tightly together. She made a conscious effort to relax. "Sam is going completely into research, so he won't need a secretary any longer."

"That's bad; I know how much you like him. But it's also good that you've already had a job offer. What company is it?"

"Spencer-Nyle."

Martine's eyes widened. "The corporate headquarters! I'm impressed, and you must have impressed someone else, too!"

"Not really." Claire took a deep breath. This wasn't getting any easier, so she decided to just get it said. "Max Benedict's real name is Maxwell Conroy, and he's a vice president with Spencer-Nyle."

For a full five seconds Martine merely stared at Claire with a stunned expression; then hot color flooded her cheeks and she surged to her feet, her fists clenched. She seldom swore, but it was due to choice, not lack of vocabulary. She used every bit of that vocabulary now, pacing up and down and damning Max with every invective she could think of, and inventing new combinations when she ran out of the ones she already knew. She didn't need to hear all the details to know that Claire had been hurt; Martine knew Claire well, and she was fiercely protective of her sister, as she was of everyone she loved.

When Martine showed signs of running down, Claire interrupted quietly. "It gets more complicated. I gave him confidential information that he needed for Spencer-Nyle to engineer the takeover; that was why he was down here, and that was why he was showing so much interest in me. I blurted it all out like an idiot."

"I'll tear his face off," Martine raged, beginning to pace up and down again like a caged tigress. Then she stopped, and a peculiar expression came over her face. "But you're going to Dallas with him?"

"I'm going to Dallas for the job," Claire said firmly. "It's the only logical thing I can do. I'd have to be an even bigger idiot than I already am if I deliberately chose unemployment over a good job. Pride won't keep the bills paid."

"Yes, it is the logical thing to do," Martine echoed, and sat down. She still had that peculiar expression on her face, as if she were trying to think something through and it didn't quite tally up. Then a slow smile began to crinkle the corners of her eyes. "He's transferred you so you'll be with him, that's it, isn't it? The man is in love with you!"

"Not likely," Claire said, her throat going tight. "Lies and betrayal aren't very good indicators of love. I love him, but you already knew that, didn't you? I shouldn't love him, not now, but I can't turn it on and off like a faucet. Just don't ask me to believe that he ever saw anything in me except the means to an end."

"But when I think about it, he always watched you... oh, I can't describe it," Martine mused. "As if he were so hungry for you, as if he wanted to absorb you. It gave me the shivers, watching him watch you. The *good* shivers, if you know what I mean."

Claire shook her head. "That isn't likely, either. You've seen him," she said, feeling her body tense up again. "He's beautiful; it stops my breath to look at him! Why should he be interested in me, except for the information he needed?"

"Why shouldn't he? In my book he'd be a fool if he didn't love you."

"Then a lot of men have been fools," Claire pointed out wearily.

"Fiddlesticks. You haven't *let* them love you; you never let anyone get close enough to really know you, but Max is more intelligent than most men. Why *wouldn't* he love you?" Martine asked passionately.

It was hard for Claire to say, almost impossible. Her throat tightened. "Because I'm not beautiful, like you; that seems to be what men want."

"Of course you aren't beautiful like me! You're beautiful like *yourself*!" Martine came over to Claire and sat down on the deck chair with her, her lovely face unusually serious. "I'm flamboyant, but that isn't your style at all. Do you know what Steve once said to me? He said that he wished I were more like you, that I would think before I leaped. I punched him, of course, and asked what else he likes about you. He said that he likes your big dark eyes—he called them 'bedroom eyes'—and I was about ready to do more than punch him! Blue-eyed blondes like me are a dime a dozen, but how many brown-eyed blondes are there? I used to die with envy, because you only had to turn those dark eyes on a man and he was ready to melt at your feet, but you never seemed to know that, and eventually he gave up.'' Suddenly Martine caught her breath, her eyes widening. ''Max didn't give up, did he?''

Claire was staring at her sister, unable to believe that beautiful Martine had ever found anything about her to be jealous of. Distracted, she said, ''Max doesn't know those two words are ever used together.'' Then she realized what she had just admitted, and she flushed. She wasn't used to talking so frankly to anyone, even her sister, but she was learning some things about herself that she'd never suspected before. Was it true that she held people away from her, that she didn't let them get close enough to care? She hadn't looked at it from that angle before; she had thought that she was keeping a distance between herself and other people so *she* wouldn't care, without considering the person who was being held at arm's length.

''Max won't leave me alone; he insists that it isn't over. He was called back to Dallas,'' she explained steadily. ''By the time he returned to Houston, I had already found out his real name and what he was doing here. He called, but I refused to go out with him again. So now I've been transferred to Dallas.''

''To his own territory. Smart move,'' Martine commented.

"Yes. I know all that. I know how he reacts to challenges, and that's all I am to him. How many women do you suppose have ever refused him?"

Martine thought, then admitted ruefully, "You probably stand alone."

"Yes. But I have to have a job, so I'm going." Even as she said the words, Claire wondered if there had ever been anything else she could have done. "What would you do in my place?"

"I'd go," Martine admitted, and laughed. "We must be more alike than you think. I know I'd never let him think that he'd made me run!"

"Exactly." Claire's dark eyes turned almost black. "He makes me so angry I could *spit*!"

Martine raised a militant fist. "Give him hell, honey!" Seeing the anger in Claire's face made Martine want to dance around the yard. Too often Claire held her emotions in, hiding her vulnerabilities from the rest of the world. Even when she had lost her baby, Claire had been pale and quiet; only Max had ever jostled her out of her composure. Claire might not think that Max cared for her at all, but Martine had seen Max watching her sister, and thought Claire was seriously underestimating the strength of his attraction to her. There was no doubt that he loved a challenge; he had that sort of fire in his eyes, that self-confident arrogance. But Claire didn't realize that she was an ongoing challenge, with her silences and perceptions, and the depths of her personality. If Martine read him correctly, Max would be fascinated by the complexity of Claire's character. And, damn him, if he hurt Claire again, he'd have to answer to Martine for it!

Claire felt as if she had made a momentous decision, but she was calm, even though the thought of changing her life so completely was a wrenching one. She had lived in her quiet, cozy apartment for five years, and it hurt to think of leaving, yet she knew that she had made the only logical choice. It was just that she preferred changes to come slowly, so she could adjust to them, rather than in a confusing rush.

She sat in silence that night, looking around and trying to accustom herself to the idea of a new apartment, a different city. She wasn't in the mood for either television or music, and she was too disturbed to find refuge in a book. There were plans to be made, work to be done; she had to find another apartment, get the utilities turned on, pack...say goodbye to her family. Martine already knew, but Alma would be the difficult one. It wouldn't really be goodbye, but it would be the end of easy access to her family. The distance between them would be great enough that she couldn't just get in the car and drive over whenever the whim took her.

Her doorbell rang, and she answered it without thinking. Max filled the doorway, looking down at her with a peculiarly intense glitter in his eyes. Claire tightened her hand on the doorknob, not stepping back to allow him entrance. Why couldn't he leave her alone? She needed time by herself to get accustomed to the sweeping changes she was making in her life.

The glitter in his eyes intensified as he realized that she wasn't going to invite him inside. He put his hand on hers and gently but forcefully removed it from the doorknob, then stepped forward, crowding her back into the apartment. He shut the door behind him. "Are you sitting here brooding?" he asked shortly, glancing around the silent apartment.

Claire moved away from him, her face closed. "I've been thinking, yes."

Strong habits had been established in the short time they had been together; Claire went automatically to the kitchen and put on a pot of coffee, then turned to find him leaning in the doorway, still watching her in a way that made her want to check all her buttons to make certain they were fastened. She would have to brush past him to get to the living room, so she opted for retaining the relatively safe distance between them and remained where she was. "You might as well know," she said, throwing the words into the silence between them. "I've decided to take the job."

"Is that what you've been brooding about?"

"It's a major change," she replied coolly, using every ounce of self-control she possessed. "Didn't you have any doubts when you relocated from Montreal to Dallas?"

Curiosity sharpened his gaze even more. "Ah, yes, I've been meaning to ask you about that. Exactly how did you discover my last name?"

"I read a magazine article on Spencer-Nyle. It had a picture of you."

He strolled into the kitchen, and Claire turned away to get two mugs out of the cabinet. Before she could turn around again, he was behind her, his arms braced on the cabinet on either side of her, effectively trapping her. "I had intended to tell you that morning, when we woke up," he said, bending his head to take a little nip at her ear. Claire sucked in her breath and twisted her head away, both alarmed and angered by the way his slightest touch made her pulse race. He ignored her movement of rejection and nuzzled her ear again, continuing his explanation whether she wanted to hear it or not. "But that phone call interrupted everything, and by the time I got back to Houston, you'd already found out, damn my luck!''

"It doesn't matter," she protested tightly. "What could you have said? 'By the way, dear, I'm an executive with a company that has targeted your company for takeover, and I've been using you to get information'?'' She mimicked his clipped accent and saw his hands clench on the cabinet in front of her.

"No, that wasn't what I would have said." He pushed himself away from her, and Claire turned, clutching the coffee mugs to her chest, to find him staring at her with barely restrained violence in his eyes. "I wouldn't have said anything at all until you were in bed with me; trying to reason with you has turned out to be a waste of time.''

"Oh?" she cried. "I think it's terribly *un*reasonable of you to think you could just waltz back into my life and pick up where you'd left off, after what you did!'' She slammed the mugs down onto the cabinet, then stared at them in horror. What if she'd broken them? She never lost her temper, never screamed or threw things or slammed them down, but now it seemed as if her anger was so close to the surface that Max could bring it out every time he spoke to her. She was reacting in a way that was totally unlike herself. Or maybe, she thought grimly, she was simply discovering facts about herself that she'd never before suspected. Max had a talent for drawing intense reactions from her. Grimly she sought control again, taking another calming breath. "Why are you here?"

"I thought you might want to know more about the job before you made your decision," he muttered, still looking furious. He admitted to himself that he was lying. He had wanted to see her; he had no other reason.

"I appreciate the thought," Claire said, as distant as the moon. She poured coffee into both mugs and extended one to him, then took a seat at her tiny kitchen table, which was just big enough for two. Max took the chair opposite her, still scowling as he drank his coffee.

"Well?" she prompted a few minutes later, when he still hadn't said a word.

His frown deepened. "You'll be secretary to the general office manager, Theo Caulfield. The departments of payroll, insurance, general accounting, data processing, maintenance, office supplies and equipment, as well as the secretarial pool, are all under his control, though each department has its own manager. It's a demanding job."

"It sounds interesting," she said politely, but she was being truthful. A job that diverse had to be interesting, and challenging.

"You'll need to work late occasionally, but the extra hours won't be excessive. You have two weeks to get settled. I would give you a month but the office is in an uproar with a lot of transfers, and you're needed on the job." He didn't add that he was the reason the office was in an uproar. "I'll help you look for an apartment. You helped me, so I owe you a favor."

Claire's face stiffened at the mention of his apartment; it was only an expensive prop, a part of his hoax. That apartment had given him the appearance of stability and permanence. "No, thank you. I don't need your help."

His face turned dark, and he set his mug down with a thump. "Very well," he snapped, getting to his feet and hauling her up with a strong grip on her arm. "You're determined not to give an inch, not even to listen to my side of it. Be safe, behind those walls of yours, and if you ever think of what you might be missing, think of this!''

His mouth was hot and strong. His arms crushed her against him, as if he couldn't get her close enough. His tongue went deep, reminding her.

Claire whimpered, tears burning her eyes as the wanting curled in her again, as hot and alive as it had ever been.

Max pushed her away, breathing hard. "If you think that has anything to do with business, you're a damned fool!'' he said harshly and slammed out of the apartment as if he couldn't trust himself to stay a minute longer.

_____ ***Chapter Ten***

To her surprise, Claire was too busy during the following two weeks to feel much anxiety over her move to Dallas. Finding an apartment wasn't easy; she spent hours inspecting and rejecting, getting lost time and again in the unfamiliar city but somehow having fun doing it. Alma, once she'd gotten over the shock of one of her daughters moving out of her immediate reach, threw herself into the apartment search with all her typical zest and spent days touring Dallas with Claire, ruthlessly hunting out any potential trouble spots in an apartment. Claire let her mother go on, amused by that overflow of energy. It was odd that the older she became, the closer Claire grew to her family. At some point, their beauty and self-confidence had ceased to intimidate her. She loved them and was proud of their accomplishments.

Even Martine was dragged into the apartment hunting, and together they made a list of the most suitable locations then began narrowing the choices. Claire didn't like the ultramodern condos, despite their conveniences, and though she hadn't really considered a house, in the end it was a tiny, neat house that won over the apartments. The rent was remarkably reasonable because of its size. Getting it ready for Claire to move in became a major family project. Claire and her father repainted the rooms in white to make them seem larger, while Alma and Martine bought material and sewed curtains to fit the odd-size windows. Steve put new dead-bolt locks on the doors and locking screens on the windows, then sanded and polished the old-fashioned wooden floors. Brad and Cassie, the children, romped in the postage-stamp yard and appeared periodically with demands for sandwiches and Kool-Aid.

On the day she moved in the entire house was in chaos, with the movers carting furniture and boxes in, while she and Alma and Martine tried to put everything in some sort of order. Harmon and Steve kept out of the decision-making, simply standing by to provide muscle if needed. Claire was headfirst in a box of books when a cool voice said from the door, "Would another pair of hands be welcome?"

Claire straightened abruptly, her face still as she tried to deal with the way the sound of his voice affected her. For two weeks Max had been as polite as a stranger, and she had been tormented by a lingering sense of loss. The tumult of moving, with its mingled moments of hilarity and frustration, and her pure physical exhaustion from so much work, had buffered her somewhat from her thoughts, but there were still far too many moments when she wished she had never found out the truth about him, that the hurt and anger would all just go away. The distance between them the past two weeks had hurt, too, though she had tried to ignore it. Why had he shown up now, strolling into the middle of the overflowing mess with that indefinable grace of his?

Harmon groaned, straightening from his task. "Another strong back is just what we need! Take the other end of this table; it weighs a ton."

Max picked his way over the cluttered floor to help Harmon lift the table and put it where Claire had directed. Alma sailed out of the kitchen, and a glowing smile broke over her face when she saw Max. "Oh, hello! Did you volunteer, or were you kidnapped?" she asked, going over to hug him.

"I volunteered. You know what they say about mad dogs and Englishmen," he said, smiling as he returned Alma's hug.

Claire turned back to the box of books she'd been unpacking, a tiny frown darkening her eyes. She hadn't told Alma all the circumstances behind her move to Dallas, but neither had she thought that her family would be having any further contact with Max. Perhaps Martine had revealed some things, but Claire didn't know and didn't want to ask. Would Alma have been so friendly to Max if she had known the truth? This could be a little awkward; they knew Max as Max Benedict, but he was really Max Conroy. Should she let them continue thinking that was his name or reintroduce him? What could she say? "Conroy is Max's real last name; he just uses Benedict as an alias occasionally." She thought that Miss Manners probably hadn't ruled on this particular situation, so she decided to say nothing.

He fit in easily with her family, joking and conversing as effortlessly as he had before. They didn't know that this congeniality was a disguise for the driving power of his true personality. She watched him, but didn't talk to him except to answer direct questions and she sensed that he was watching her, too. She'd thought that he'd given up, but now she remembered telling Martine that he wasn't even familiar with the term. He hadn't given up; he'd simply been waiting. He calmly wrote down her unlisted telephone number, copying it off the telephone, and when he looked up to find her watching him, he lifted an eyebrow in silent invitation for her to make an issue of it. Claire simply turned away to continue her chores. Attacking him now over a telephone number would make her look like an ungrateful wretch after he'd worked tirelessly most of the day, helping her get settled.

It was late when everything was put in its place, and everyone was yawning widely. Rather than attempt the long drive back to Houston that night, her family had elected to stay in a motel and drive back the next morning. Somehow Claire found herself waving goodbye to them from her new porch, with Max standing beside her as if he belonged there.

"Why did you come here?" she asked quietly, watching the taillights disappear down the street. The warm night sounds of chirping insects and the rustle of leaves in the trees from a slight breeze surrounded them, where only a moment ago there had been laughter and noisy yawns and enthusiastic cries of "Bye! Take care now. I'll call you tomorrow!"

"To help you with your things," he said, holding the screen door open for her as she reentered the house. She didn't trust his bland tone for a minute. "And to make certain that you're comfortable. Nothing more sinister than that."

"Thank you for your help."

"You're welcome. Is there any coffee left in the pot?"

"I think so, but it is probably undrinkable by now. You drink too much coffee, anyway," she said without thinking, going into the kitchen to pour out the stale coffee. He stopped her as she was beginning to make a fresh pot.

"You're right; I don't need any more coffee," he said, taking the pot out of her hand and placing it in the sink. Grasping her elbow, he pulled her around to face him. "What I need is this."

His other arm went around her waist, bringing her up against him, and he bent his head. His mouth closed over hers, and the hot, heady taste of him filled her; he kissed her with deep, greedy hunger, until a painful hunger of her own began to coil in her body. Both angered and alarmed by the desire he could arouse so effortlessly, she jerked her mouth from his and pushed against his shoulders, feeling the heavy muscles beneath her palms.

To her surprise he let her go easily, releasing her and stepping back. Satisfaction was plain in his eyes, as if he'd just proved something to himself. He must have felt her response; for a brief moment she hadn't been able to prevent herself from melting against him, her body seeking his.

"I wish you hadn't come," she whispered, her dark eyes locked on him. "Why involve yourself with my family? How do I tell them that you aren't Max Benedict, after all?"

"You don't have to tell them anything; they already know. I've explained it to your mother."

Shocked, Claire stared at him. "What?" she stammered. "Why? When did you tell her? *What* did you tell her?"

He answered readily enough. "I told her that the takeover of Bronson Alloys by my company has complicated our relationship, but that I transferred you to Dallas so we would still be together and could work out the problems."

He made it all sound so simple, as if he hadn't abandoned her as soon as he'd gotten the information he wanted! It was true that he hadn't been expecting the phone call that had forced him to return to Dallas, but it was also true that he hadn't made any attempt to contact her after that until the actual mechanics of the takeover had put him back in Houston. Now, in his typical high-handed fashion, he believed that all he had to do was move her to Dallas and the "complications" would be settled.

Her expression was so troubled, for once so easily read, with all her doubts and hurt there for him to see, that he had to fight the urge to pull her against him and shelter her in his arms. Max had never known failure with a woman he wanted; they came easily into his arms and his bed, and they had always been so easy to read. It was ironic that Claire, the one woman he couldn't easily understand, should be the woman he wanted more intensely than he'd ever dreamed he would want a woman. He couldn't tell what she was thinking; her defenses were too strong, her personality too complex. Yet every glimpse he had of the inner woman only made him hungrier to find out more about her, to get deeper into her mind. Looking at her now, with her clothes grimy from the day's labors, her hair straggling down from its topknot, her face free of makeup and her velvety dark eyes full of pain and uncertainty, Max felt something jolt in his chest.

He was in love with her.

The realization stunned him, though now that he recognized it for what it was, he knew that the feeling had been there for some time. He had labeled it as attraction, desire, even challenge, and it was all of those, and more. Of all the women in the world, he hadn't loved any of the soft, willing beauties who had shared his bed and would have done anything for him. Instead it was a difficult, aloof, yet extraordinarily vulnerable woman who made him feel as if he would explode with joy if she smiled at him. He wanted to protect her; he wanted to discover all the hidden depths of her character; he wanted to lose himself in the unexpected and shattering passion she had to offer.

Claire moved away from him, rubbing the back of her neck tiredly and not seeing the arrested expression on his face. "How did you explain your change of name?"

It took a minute before he could gather himself and make sense of what she had asked. "I told her the truth, that I had been looking for certain information and didn't want Bronson to know my true identity."

Claire thought Alma was so charmed by Max that she would be prepared to believe anything he said. "What did she say?"

An appreciative smile quirked Max's mouth as he remembered exactly what Alma had said. That lady did have a way with words, though he could hardly tell Claire that her mother had said, "If you hurt my daughter, Max Benedict, or Conroy, or whoever you are, I'll have your guts for garters!" Claire didn't seem to realize how fiercely protective her entire family was of her.

"She understood," was all he said, watching Claire as she retreated even more, continually expanding the distance between them. She was so wary!

"I'm sure she did," Claire sighed.

Impatiently Max closed the gap between them, his quick strides carrying him to her side. Claire looked up, startled by his sudden movement, then gave a soft cry as he put his hands on her waist and lifted her up so her eyes were level with his. "Yes, your mother understood; it's a pity you don't!" he muttered, then put his mouth on hers.

There was a tiny, despairing cry deep inside her mind. How could she keep control of herself if he kept kissing her? Especially kisses like these, deep, hungry kisses, as if he couldn't get enough of her taste. His lips released hers and slid down to her throat, nipping at her skin as they went. He held her so tightly that his hands were hurting her, and she didn't care. Her eyes closed tightly, and tears welled beneath her lashes.

"Why do you keep doing this to me?" she cried rawly. "Do you just chase anything that runs? Did it hurt your pride that I told you to leave me alone?"

He raised his head; his eyes were burning green fire. He was breathing harshly. "Is that what you think? That my ego is so enormous I can't stand for a woman to turn me down?"

"Yes, that's what I think! I'm a challenge to you, nothing more!"

"We burned each other up in bed, woman, and you think it was nothing more than gratifying my ego?" He put her on her feet, infuriated that she continually put the worst interpretation on his actions.

"You tell me! I don't know you at all! I thought you were a gentleman, but you're really a savage in a tuxedo, aren't you? Your instincts are to win, regardless of how ruthless you have to be to get what you want!"

"You know me pretty well, after all," he snapped. "I go after what I want, and I want you."

Claire shivered, alarmed by the hard expression on his face. Swearing under his breath, he took her in his arms again, holding her head against his chest, his fingers threading into her soft hair. "Don't be afraid of me, love," he whispered. "I won't hurt you. I want to take care of you."

As what? As a mistress? She shook her head blindly, the motion limited by the way he held her to his chest.

"You'll trust me again, I promise." He murmured the words against her hair, and his hands slid down to stroke her back. Claire found that her hands were clenched on his shirt and that she was clinging instead of trying to push him away. "I'll make you trust me, love. We'll get to know each other; we have the time. There will be no more masks between us."

He bent his head and kissed her again, and this time Claire's self-control wasn't strong enough to keep her from responding. Blindly she rose on tiptoe, straining against him, her mouth opening under the probing of his tongue. She kept making foolish mistakes where Max was concerned, and the latest one was the idea that she would be able to keep him at a distance. Shaking with love and pain that mingled into a tangled knot, she let the pleasure sweep through her, because there was nothing she could do to stop it. His hand was on the buttons of her shirt, and there was nothing she could do to stop that, either; she trembled, waiting in an agony of anticipation for his touch, her body craving his heat and strength. Then his fingers were on her, sliding inside her opened shirt to cup her naked, swelling flesh, and electricity shot from her hardened nipples straight to her loins.

"I know you're tired, but I'm not a noble, self-sacrificing gentleman," he said harshly, lifting his head to look at her. "If you don't stop me now, I won't be leaving tonight at all."

She couldn't deny it, even to herself. He was giving her one last chance to reconsider. For a moment she almost pulled his head back down to her; then common sense asserted itself, and she pushed at his arms until they fell away from her. Her fingers trembled, and she couldn't look at him as she fumbled with the buttons of her shirt until at last she was covered again.

"Thank you," she said, meaning it. She felt exposed and vulnerable, because only his self-control had given her the chance to reconsider; she had had none at all, and he knew it.

He had offered, but that didn't help the frustration raging through his body. He glared down at her. "Don't thank me for being a bloody stupid fool," he said, his tone savage with temper. "I have to get out of here before I change my mind. Be ready at six-thirty tomorrow night; I'm taking you out to dinner."

"No, I don't think—"

"That's right," he interrupted, catching her chin in his hand. "Don't think, and above all, don't argue with me right now. I want you so much that I'm hurting. I'll be here at six-thirty; if you want to go out, be dressed. If not, we'll stay here. The choice is yours."

She shut her mouth. His mood was dangerous, his eyes glittering. He kissed her again, hard, then stalked out of the house.

When he was gone the house echoed strangely. She locked the doors and checked all the windows to make certain they were secure, then showered and got ready for bed. The furnishings were all familiar, and the bed was the one she had slept in for five years, yet she lay awake staring into the darkness. It wasn't the unfamiliarity of her surroundings, but her thoughts that prevented her from sleeping. Why had he given her the chance to stop? He'd said that he wasn't noble or self-sacrificing, but then he had made a self-sacrificing offer. He could have taken her to bed, and they both knew it. He had wanted her; there hadn't been any secret in the way he had pushed against her, letting her feel his arousal. So why had he given her that last opportunity to stop?

Pain squeezed her chest. Who was the biggest fool? Him for giving her the chance to stop, or herself for taking it? He had hurt her, and he had made her so angry that she had wanted to throw things at him, but none of that had stopped her from loving him. She wanted to cling to her anger, to use it as both a weapon and a defense against him, but she could feel it ebbing away from her and leaving her vulnerable to the truth. She loved him. No matter what happened, even if he wanted her only for a brief affair, she loved him. With that acknowledgment she felt her last defenses crumble inside her.

Nothing was working out the way she had planned. She hadn't intended to go out with Max again; she had intended to do her job and ignore him, but he hadn't given her a choice about that. He was taking over again, and with her defenses down she was helpless to do anything about it; all her intentions had gone down the drain with her anger. She could no longer make any plans or form any intentions; all she could do was face the fact that she loved him, and take each day as it came.

Claire was so nervous that she kept dropping the pins she was using to put up her hair. It was her first day on a new job, and Max was taking her out to dinner. She needed to concentrate on the job, but she kept thinking of Max. He simply wouldn't leave her head.

A pin flew from her trembling fingers again, and she muttered an impatient "damn!" as she leaned down to retrieve it. She had to calm down, or the day would be a disaster.

Finally she got her hair securely pinned, and with a frantic glance at the clock she put on the jacket that matched her gray skirt, grabbed her purse and left the house at a run. She wasn't certain how long it would take her to drive to the Spencer-Nyle building in the early morning traffic, so she had cautiously allowed an extra fifteen minutes, then used most of that picking up hair pins. What an impression it would make to be late on her first day!

But she made it with five minutes to spare, and a smiling receptionist directed her to Theo Caulfield's office on the fifth floor. A tall, dark man with a face like granite paused in passing, his dark eyes on Claire. She felt his gaze and glanced at him then quickly looked away. He was vaguely familiar, but she was certain she'd never met him. There was an almost visible force about him, and the receptionist became obviously nervous when she realized that the man was listening.

"Are you Claire Westbrook?" he asked abruptly, moving to Claire's side.

How had he guessed, unless he was Theo Caulfied? She looked up at him, feeling dwarfed by his powerful build despite the three-inch heels she wore, and hoped that he wasn't her new boss. He couldn't be a comfortable man to work with. Because he made her nervous, too, she reacted by hiding behind her usual mask of composure.

"Yes, I am."

"I'm Rome Matthews. I'll show you to your office and introduce you to Caulfield. Good morning, Angie," he said to the receptionist as he led Claire away.

"Good morning, Mr. Matthews," the receptionist said faintly to his back.

His name was familiar, too. Claire darted another look up at that hard, almost brutally carved face and remembrance shot through her. His picture had been beside Max's in that article she'd read, when she had discovered Max's true identity. He was executive vice president and Anson Edwards's right-hand man, his chosen successor. How did he know her name, and why was he personally escorting her to her office?

Whatever his reason, he wasn't inclined to make explanations. He asked polite questions, whether she liked Dallas, had she gotten settled yet, but she could feel him watching her. His hand was on her elbow, and she was surprised by the gentleness of his touch.

"Here it is," he said, drawing her to a halt and reaching out to open a door. "You'll have your hands full, you know. Your predecessor had to be on her new job today, so you'll be training yourself."

Claire thought of running while she still could, but a man came out of the inner office on hearing their voices, and she was trapped. To her relief Theo Caulfield was an ordinary man, middle-aged and thin, without the intimidating force of Rome Matthews. He, too, seemed nervous at the other man's presence and visibly relaxed when the short introductions were performed and the executive vice president took himself off to his own office.

To her relief her duties were fairly routine, and she settled in quickly. Theo Caulfield was quiet and meticulous, but not fussy. She missed Sam, but he was far happier in his laboratory than he had ever been in an office; perhaps the takeover had been best for him, as well as for the company.

Max called her just before the day was over—the only time she had heard from him—to tell her to dress casually for dinner. Claire hurried home to her little house, afraid that he would take it as a signal that she wanted to stay in if she weren't ready when he arrived. How casual was casual? She opted to play it safe with a plain skirt and blouse and flat heels, and was waiting to open the door before he could knock.

"Where are we going?" she asked, eyeing his slacks and open-neck silk shirt.

"We're having dinner with some friends of mine," he said, drawing her to him for a quick kiss. "How did it go today? Any trouble settling in?"

"No, it wasn't difficult. It's mostly routine secretarial work."

Max asked her several questions about her day, distracting her. She was still unfamiliar with the city, so she wasn't concerned with where they were going until she noticed they were in a residential section. "Where are we?" she asked.

"We're almost there."

"Almost *where*?"

"At Rome's house. We're having dinner with him and his wife, Sarah."

"What?" Claire asked faintly. "Max, you can't just take me to someone's house when they haven't invited me!" And Rome Matthews's house, of all people! She wasn't comfortable with him; he was the most overpowering man she'd ever seen.

He looked amused. "They *have* invited you. Sarah told me that if I didn't have you with me tonight, not to come myself." There was an unmistakable note of affection in his voice. He turned into the driveway of a sprawling, Spanish-style house, and Claire tensed.

He put his hand on her back as they walked up the brick walk to the front door, and if it hadn't been for that pressure at her back, Claire would have turned around and left. He rang the bell, and in a moment Rome Matthews opened the door himself.

Claire stared, almost not recognizing the high-powered executive in the man who stood there, clad in tight-fitting jeans that molded his powerful hips and legs, and a red polo shirt. His face was infinitely more relaxed, and there was amusement in his dark eyes. Even more amazingly, he held a chubby toddler in one strong arm and a tiny elfin girl in the other. Somehow Claire hadn't imagined him as a family man, especially one with young children. Then her eyes were drawn to the two children, and she gasped. "They're beautiful," she whispered, automatically reaching out her hands. The children both had their father's black hair and eyes and olive complexion, with the gorgeous rosy cheeks that only young children have. Two pairs of wide inquisitive dark eyes stared at her; then the baby gave a chuckle and launched himself out of his father's arms, straight into hers, his fat hands outstretched.

"Thank you," Rome said, his amusement deepening, and Claire flushed. She cuddled the little boy to her, loving the feel of his sturdy, wriggling little body. He smelled of baby powder, and she wanted to bury her face in his fat little neck.

"Here you go sweetheart," Max said, holding out his hands to the little girl, and with a giggle she, too, abandoned her father. She hugged Max around the neck and kissed his cheek; Max settled her comfortably on his arm and carried her into the house, keeping his other hand at Claire's back.

"The little tank you're holding is Jed," Rome said, reaching out to tickle his son. "The flirt around Max's neck is Missy. She's three, and Jed is almost one."

Claire was gently rubbing the baby's back, and he had nestled down against her as if he'd known her all his life. He was incredibly heavy, but his weight felt good in her arms. "You darling," she crooned to him, kissing his soft black hair.

Max looked up from the game he was playing with Missy, and his eyes flickered as he watched Claire playing with the baby.

A low laugh reached them, and Claire turned as a slim, delicate woman with white-blond hair came into the room. "I'm Sarah Matthews," the woman said warmly, and Claire looked into the most serene face she'd ever seen. Sarah Matthews was lovely and fragile, and when her husband looked at her it was with an expression in his dark eyes that made Claire want to turn away, as if she had witnessed something terribly intimate.

"Sarah, this is Claire Westbrook," Max said, his hand warm on Claire's arm.

"You have beautiful children," Claire said sincerely, and Sarah beamed with pride.

"Thank you. They're quite a handful. Your arrival has given Rome a rest," Sarah replied, slanting a teasing look at her husband. "They're always wild when he first gets home, especially Jed."

At that moment Jed was lying adoringly against Claire, and Rome laughed at his son. "He can't resist a pretty woman; he's the biggest flirt ever born, except for Missy."

Missy was perfectly content in Max's arms, and Claire noticed the tenderness with which he handled her, and the calm capability. She had noticed his skill with children before, soon after they had met. It had been while he was playing with Martine's children at the cookout that she had fallen in love with him. It had been that simple, that easy and that irrevocable.

"Enjoy the peace," Sarah advised, breaking into Claire's thoughts, and Jed chose that moment to lift his head from Claire's shoulder and look down at the scattered toys on the floor. With a grunt he pushed himself out of her arms. Claire gave a gasping cry and grabbed for him, and Rome did the same, leaping to snag his son out of the air. Sighing, he placed the baby on the floor. His attention completely on his toys, Jed toddled over to the red plastic truck he'd selected.

"He has no respect for gravity, and no fear of heights," Rome said wryly. "He's also as strong as a mule; there's no holding him when he decides he wants down."

"He scared me to death," Claire gasped.

"He's been scaring me since he learned to crawl," Sarah said with a chuckle. "Then he started walking when he was eight months old, and it's been even worse since. All you can do is chase after him."

It was impossible to believe that such a delicate woman had given birth to such a sturdy little boy who showed every sign of inheriting his father's size. The children resembled Sarah very little, except for Missy's delicate stature, and something in the shape of her soft mouth.

It was such a relaxed household, filled with the high-pitched giggles of happy children, that Claire forgot to be intimidated by Rome. Here he was a husband and a father, not an executive. It was evident that Max was a close friend who visited often, because the children climbed over him as enthusiastically as they did over their father, and he not only tolerated it, he seemed to enjoy it.

The children were fed and put to bed; then the adults sat down to dinner. Claire couldn't think when she had enjoyed an evening more; she didn't even shrink when Rome teased her. "I had to check you out this morning," he said, his hard mouth quirked in amusement. "Sarah was dying of curiosity."

"I was not! Max had already told me all about you," Sarah told Claire. "It was his own male curiosity Rome wanted to satisfy."

Rome shrugged lazily, smiling as he looked at his wife. Claire wondered what Max had said about her, and why he would talk about her, anyway. She glanced at him and blushed when she found him watching her intently.

It was late when Max drove her home, and Claire was sleepily curled in the corner of the seat. "I really liked them," she murmured. "I can't believe he's the same man who terrified me so this morning!"

"Sarah tames him; she's so incredibly serene."

"They're very happy together, aren't they?"

Max's voice roughened a little. "Yes. They've gone through some rough times; if they hadn't loved each other so much, they wouldn't have made it. Rome was married before and had two children, but his wife and sons were killed in an automobile accident. He was terribly scarred by it."

"I can imagine," Claire said, pain grabbing at her. She had never even held her child; it had been gone almost before she had been able to do more than dream of its existence. What would it have been like to have had two children taken from her in such a tragic way? She thought of the way Jed had nestled against her, and tears burned her eyes. "I miscarried. Right before my divorce," she whispered. "And losing the baby nearly killed me. I wanted it so badly!"

Max's head jerked around, and he stared at her in the dim, flickering glow of the streetlights they passed. An almost violent jealousy filled him because she had been pregnant, and it hadn't been with his child. He wanted her to have his baby; he wanted his children to be *her* children. She was a natural mother, so loving with children that they instinctively clung to her.

When they reached her house, he went inside with her and quietly locked the door behind him. Claire watched him, her dark eyes becoming enormous as he came to her and caught her hands in his.

"Max?" she whispered, her voice shaking.

His face was both tender and wild, and his eyes glittered. He put her hands around his neck, then drew her close to lie full against him.

"I'm going to take you to bed, love," he said gently, and a hot tide of pleasure surged through her body at his words. She drew a deep breath and closed her eyes, the time for protests gone. She loved him, and now she realized exactly what that meant; she loved him too much to preserve any distance between them.

He carried her to her bed, and this time he was slow, gentle, taking his time to kiss her and caress her, arousing her to fever pitch while he kept tight control over his own body. Then he eased inside her, and Claire cried out as he filled her. Her nails dug into his back; her hips arched wildly toward him. Max's control broke, and he gave a hoarse cry as he grasped her hips and began driving into her. That same wild, ungovernable need exploded between them, just as it had the first time. They couldn't get enough of each other, couldn't get close enough; their joining was as elemental as a storm, and as violent.

In the silent aftermath Max held her close, his hand on her stomach. It had happened again, and he couldn't regret it. This woman was his; he could never let her go. She was tender and loving, sensitive and vulnerable and easily hurt. He would gladly spend the rest of his life protecting her from those hurts, if she would only stay with him.

Claire watched with wide, unfathomable eyes as he rose on his elbow and leaned over her. He was very male, and never more so than when he was nude, the power of his body exposed. She put her hand on the brown tangle of hair that covered his chest, stroking gently. What was he thinking? He was serious, almost stern, his sea-colored eyes narrowed to brilliant slits, and he was so beautiful that he took her breath away.

"I may have made you pregnant tonight," he said, his fingers sliding over her stomach. Claire inhaled slightly, her eyes widening. His hand slid down even farther to touch her intimately and explore her in a way that shot rockets along her nerves, making her arch and twist against his fingers. He leaned even closer, his mouth finding hers. "I want to make you pregnant," he groaned, the thought so erotic that his body was hardening again. "Claire, will you have my baby?"

Tears streaked silvery trails down her cheeks. "Yes," she whispered, reaching up to hold him with both hands as he rolled onto her. He thrust deeply into her, and they stared into each other's eyes as they made love, moving together and finding incredible magic. If she could have his child, she would never ask anything more of life. She moved under him. She felt; she loved; she experienced; and she cried.

He lay on her, still deep within her, and kissed away her tears. Incredible contentment filled him. "Claire," he said, holding her face still in his hands, "I don't think anything but marriage will do."

Chapter Eleven

Claire felt as if her heart had simply stopped beating; everything inside her went still, waiting for that moment when time would begin again. She couldn't breathe, couldn't speak, couldn't move. Then, with a little jolt, her heart resumed its function, freeing her from the temporary paralysis. "Marry?" she asked faintly.

"My mother will be in ecstasy if you make an honest man of me," he said, tracing her lower lip with his finger. "She's quite given up on me, you know. Marry me, and have my children. I find that I want that very much. When I saw you holding Jed tonight, I thought how perfect you look with a baby in your arms, and I want it to be my baby."

There was nothing about love in his proposal, but Claire found that there didn't have to be. She could accept the fact that he didn't love her; she would take whatever he offered her and do anything she could to make him happy with his decision. Perhaps she should have more pride than to settle for anything less than love, but pride wouldn't gain her anything except an empty bed and an empty life. Happily ever after was a fairy tale, after all.

"All right," she whispered.

His shoulders relaxed almost imperceptibly, and he eased away from her to lie beside her, hugging her against him. His free hand absently stroked her satiny shoulder, and his handsome face was thoughtful. "Does this mean you've forgiven me?"

She wished he hadn't asked that; it touched on a wound that hadn't healed, reminded her of pain that still lingered. She didn't want to think of the past, not now, when she had just agreed to take a step into the future, a step that terrified her with its enormity. If Max were just an ordinary man perhaps she wouldn't feel so uncertain, but Max was extraordinary in every way, and she was filled with doubts that she would ever be able to satisfy him.

"It seems I have to, doesn't it?"

"I never intended to hurt you; I wanted only to get the business part of things over with, so I could concentrate on you. I've wanted you pretty desperately from the first," he admitted wryly. "You wreck my self-control, but that's obvious, isn't it?"

Her head found the hollow of his shoulder, nestling there comfortably. "Why is it obvious?"

He gave a short laugh. "Bloody hell, you can't believe I normally go about attacking women on a table in the foyer? You kissed me back, and I went mad. I couldn't think of anything but being inside you. It was like being picked up by a storm, unable to do anything but go along for the ride."

It had been like that for her, too, an explosion of the senses that obliterated everything else in the world except that moment, this man. The memory of that first lovemaking would make her blush for the rest of her life, because she hadn't known she was capable of such passion. Since then she had come to expect that inner burning whenever he touched her.

She sighed, suddenly so tired that she could barely keep her eyes open. Max kissed her then untangled himself from the bed and got up. Claire opened her eyes, watching him in bewilderment as he sorted out his clothing and got dressed.

"If you weren't half-asleep already, we'd make wedding plans," he said, bending over to tuck the sheet around her naked body. "But you're tired, we have to work tomorrow, and all my clothes are at my apartment, so it's best that I leave."

There would be a thousand-and-one problems to work out, some small and some not so small, but she couldn't think of them now. She was drowsy, her body satisfied, and though she was disappointed that he wouldn't be spending the night with her, she realized that it wasn't practical. He kissed her, his hand stroking over her body in blatant possessiveness.

"I hope you like big weddings," he murmured.

Her lashes fluttered. "Why?"

"Because I have hundreds of relatives who would die of terminal dudgeon if they weren't invited to my wedding."

She chuckled, snuggling deeper into the bed. Max kissed her again, so reluctant to leave her that he considered saying to hell with work and climbing back into bed with her. She was so warm and rosy and relaxed, and he knew it was from his lovemaking. There was nothing quite like the feeling of certainty that he had left her satisfied, and his emotions ran the gamut from pride to possessiveness to wonder. Under all that lay his own bone-deep satisfaction. Beneath her cool, self-possessed mask was a passionate nature; other people saw only the mask, but she burned for him with a sweet fire that left its scorch marks on his heart and branded him as hers.

She was asleep, her breathing soft and even. With one last look at her, Max quietly turned out the light and left the bedroom. Soon they would be sharing a bedroom and a name, and his ring would be on her hand.

When she woke the next morning, Claire had the confused feeling that it had all been a dream, a wonderful, impossible dream. Had Max actually asked her to marry him, or had her imagination conjured up the fantasy? Then she moved, and the startled realization that she was naked brought back clear memories of the night before. He had made love to her; then he'd asked her to marry him, and she had agreed. Panic twisted her stomach. What if it didn't work out? What if they got married and he decided that she didn't suit him, after all? What if she failed to satisfy him, just as she had failed with Jeff? What if he already regretted asking her? Men sometimes said things in the heat of passion that they later wished had never been said.

The phone rang beside her, startling her, and she almost dropped the receiver as she grabbed it. "Yes? Hello?"

"Good morning, love," Max said, his voice warm and intimate. "I wanted to make certain you didn't oversleep. I forgot to turn on your alarm when I left last night."

Even though he couldn't see her, a deep blush covered her body, and she pulled the sheet up high under her chin. "Thank you," she said, not hearing the uncertainty in her voice.

Max paused. "We'll go tonight to pick out the rings, shall we? Are you going to call your parents today, or wait until the weekend when you visit them?"

Claire closed her eyes on an almost painful surge of relief; he hadn't changed his mind. "I'll call them. Mother wouldn't forgive me if I kept it a secret until the weekend."

He chuckled. "It's the same with my mother. I'll call her in a moment, and she'll be on the phone for the rest of the day calling everyone in the far-flung family. How soon do you think we can manage the deed? Poor Theo. He's just gotten you, and now he'll have to find another secretary."

"Another secretary?" Claire echoed in surprise.

"Of course. You can't continue to be his secretary after we're married. We'll decide tonight on a date for the wedding, and you'll know when to turn in your notice. I'll see you at work, love; take care."

"Yes, of course," she said, still holding the receiver after he'd hung up and the dial tone was buzzing in her ear. Slowly she hung up, a frown pulling at her brow. She was expected to give up her job when they were married?

She fretted about it while she showered; on the one hand, she could see that it wouldn't work for both of them to be employed by Spencer-Nyle, and as his salary was far more than hers, it was logical that she should be the one to quit. On the other hand, she had struggled for years to establish her own independence, and it was important to her own sense of self-worth that she continue to support herself, or at least feel as if she were making a contribution to their lives. It wasn't just that Max expected her to quit Spencer-Nyle; Claire had the feeling that he expected her to quit working completely, and the thought made shivers of alarm race down her spine.

What sort of life would they have together? She didn't even know if she could expect him to be faithful. Women melted around him; how could a man not be tempted when he was surrounded by constant opportunities to wander? Given that, she would be incredibly foolish to stop being self-supporting. She only hoped he would be sensible about it.

She didn't have time to call Alma that morning, but found a pay phone at lunch and sat chewing her lip, listening to the ringing on the other end of the line. At last she hung up, both relieved and disappointed that Alma wasn't at home. She didn't know how she felt about marrying Max, either; part of her was ecstatic because she loved him so much. Another part was plain terrified. What if she couldn't make him happy? He was so intelligent and sophisticated and supremely self-confident; he made Jeff look like a lightweight, and Jeff had turned from her to someone more poised and polished.

Max was waiting in the office for her when she returned from lunch, and a warm, intimate smile touched his chiseled mouth when he saw her. "There you are, darling. I'd hoped to take you to lunch, but I couldn't get clear in time. Was your mother pleased?"

Claire glanced at Theo's office, relieved to see that he hadn't returned from lunch. "I just tried to call her, but she wasn't at home. I'll call her tonight."

He put his hands on her waist and drew her to him for a quick kiss. "*My* mother was all but dancing on the table," he said in amusement. "By now half of England knows."

He was in a good mood, his eyes sparkling like sunlight on the ocean, and she felt her heart give that little jolt again. Uneasily she watched the door, trying to draw back from him. "Should you be in here?" she asked, worried. "What if someone saw you kiss me?"

He actually laughed. "Is it supposed to be a secret that we're getting married? I told Rome this morning, and he's already called Sarah to let her know. Then I told Anson, who asked if I couldn't have proposed to you in Houston, rather than rearranging the entire office to empty a position for you. So you see, it's already common knowledge. The news will have gone around the office at the speed of sound."

Claire flushed, staring at him in mortification. "You *made* this job me?" And did the entire office know that he'd brought her to Dallas for himself?

"No, love, the job is a legitimate one. I simply made it available by promoting and shifting some people who, incidentally, are all thrilled with their new positions." Gently he touched her pink cheek. "You don't have any reason to feel embarrassed."

He kissed her again then reluctantly let her go. "Have you been thinking about the type of ring you would like?"

She hadn't, and surprise was plain on her face. "No, not really. I think I'd like a plain wedding band, though." The rings Jeff had given her had been encrusted with yellow diamonds, and she had never really cared for them. The stones had been so large, almost ostentatious, as if they were only what was expected of the Halseys. She had returned them to him after the divorce and never missed them.

He watched her, wondering what memories had caused the brief sadness that darkened the soft brown of her eyes. "Whatever you want," he promised, wishing that he would never see sadness on her face again. For a brief moment she had drifted away in her thoughts, leaving him behind, and he resented even a minute when she wasn't with him.

Max was at her house that night when she finally got Alma on the phone, and he lounged across from her, smiling as he listened to the conversation. Alma laughed, then she cried. Then she had to speak to Max, who assured her with quiet sincerity that he would take care of Claire. When he gave the phone back to Claire, she gave him a look of gratitude for being so understanding with Alma.

"Have you set a date?" Alma asked excitedly.

"No, we haven't had time to talk about it. How long will it take to arrange a church wedding?" Claire listened then turned to Max. "How many of your family do you think will attend?"

He shrugged. "At an offhand guess—seven hundred, give or take a hundred."

"Seven hundred?" Claire gasped, and on the other end of the line Alma gave a small shriek.

"I've mentioned that I have a large family. That also includes friends; Mother will be able to give us a list in a week or so." He motioned for the telephone, and Claire gave it to him again. "Don't panic," he said soothingly to Alma. "Perhaps it would be easier if we were married in England. How many people would we have to transport?"

Claire tried to think of how many people would be invited to her wedding; her family was small, but there were friends of the family who would have to be included. But if they were married in England, how many of them would be able to attend? And if they were married in Texas, how many of his family and friends wouldn't be able to make a transatlantic trip? Suddenly the wedding was assuming horrendous proportions.

"Accommodations aren't a problem," Max was saying soothingly, so Claire guessed that Alma was having hysterics at the thought of moving the family, lock, stock and barrel, to England. "There are plenty of spare bedrooms scattered around the family. The church? Yes, the church is large enough to handle a wedding of that size. It's an enormous old rock pile." He listened a moment, then laughed. "No, I don't care where we're married. England or Texas doesn't matter to me, so long as I get Claire and it doesn't take an eternity to do it. How long? Six weeks is my limit."

Even sitting across from him, Claire heard the loud protest that Alma was making. Max merely said patiently, "Six weeks. I'm not waiting any longer than that. Claire and I will visit this weekend, and we'll make our plans."

Claire stared at him in horror as he hung up with an air of patent satisfaction. "Six weeks?" she echoed. "It's impossible to put on a wedding for more than seven hundred people in six weeks! That takes months of planning!"

"Six weeks, or I'll carry you before a judge and do the deed. I'm being generous, at that. My inclination is to marry you this weekend, and it's damned tempting. The only thing is, a lot of people would never forgive us."

He flashed her a brilliant smile, standing and holding his hand out to her. Claire put her hand in his, and he pulled her to her feet and into his arms, kissing her long and hard. "Don't worry. Between your mother and mine, this wedding will be perfect. Nothing would dare go wrong."

To Claire's consternation, he didn't take her to one of the small jewelry stores she'd anticipated. Instead she found herself seated in a luxurious salon while the manager brought trays of glittering jewels for her inspection. What on earth was Max thinking about? Surely he didn't think he had to compete with Jeff Halsey in the material things he could give her? Claire knew that Max was certainly not poor; his salary was far more than comfortable, but it didn't make him a millionaire. He didn't have to compete with Jeff in anything, because he had Jeff outclassed in everything.

But there the rings were, waiting for her to make a selection. "What I really want is a plain simple old-fashioned wedding band," she said, frowning slightly.

"Certainly," the manager said politely, starting to take away the tray of diamonds and emeralds and rubies.

"No, leave that," Max instructed. "We'll look these over again while you're bringing the tray of wedding bands."

Claire waited until the manager was out of hearing then turned to Max. "I prefer a wedding band, truly."

He looked amused. "Darling, we'll have our wedding bands, and don't look so surprised. Of course I intend to wear a ring. I've waited long enough to be married; I'm not going to waffle about it. But this is for your engagement ring."

"But I don't need an engagement ring."

"Strictly speaking, no one *needs* any sort of jewelry. An engagement ring is just as old-fashioned and traditional as a wedding band, a symbolic warning to other primitive and marauding males that you aren't available."

Despite her misgivings Claire couldn't keep herself from smiling in answer to the twinkle in his eyes. "Oh, is that what you're doing, warning off other primitives?"

"One never knows what caveman instincts lurk beneath a silk shirt."

Claire knew. She looked at him, and her breath caught as she remembered the wild sensuality behind his calm mask. Most people would never realize just how primitive he really was, because he disguised it so well with his lazy, good-humored manner. He was tolerant, so long as he could get his way with charm and reason, but she sensed the danger in him.

"That was supposed to be a joke," he said lightly, touching her cheek to dispel the look she was giving him. "Take another look at these rings, won't you, before the poor man gets back with that other tray."

She did look at them then shook her head. "They're too expensive."

He laughed; he actually laughed. "Love, I'm not a pauper. Far from it. I promise you that I won't have to go in debt for any of these rings. If you won't choose, I'll do it for you."

He bent over the tray, eyeing each ring carefully. "I really don't care for diamonds," Claire tried, seeing that he was determined.

"Of course not," he agreed. "They wouldn't suit you, not even with that sexy black velvet gown of yours. Pearls are for you. Try this ring." He plucked a ring from its velvet bed and slipped it on her finger.

Claire looked down at it, and a feeling of helplessness came over her. Why couldn't it have been a truly hideous ring that she would have hated on sight? Instead it was a creamy pearl, surrounded by glittering baguettes, and it looked just right on her slender hand.

"I thought so," he said in satisfaction as the manager returned with a tray of wedding bands.

Claire was silent as they left, still trying to come to terms with the changes this wedding would bring in her life, had already brought even though they weren't married yet. Max put his arm around her and held her close, as if trying to shield her from the worries that darkened her eyes.

"What is it, love?" he asked, following her into the tiny house that she liked so much, but which had turned out to be only a temporary stopping place in her life.

"There are so many problems, and I'm not certain how to deal with them."

"What sort of problems?"

"The wedding for one thing. It seems impossible, with so much to be done and the distance involved, the problems of transportation and housing and getting everything coordinated. The cake; the dresses; the tuxedos; the flowers; the receptions. Not only that, I've been divorced, and a white wedding is out of the question, if we can even have a church wedding at all."

He held up his hand, halting her tense litany. "What did you just say?" he asked politely.

She sighed, rubbing her forehead. "You know very well what I said."

"Then let me reassure you on two points, at least. One, we will be married in my family church, and no one will think anything of the fact that you've been married before. Two, you will definitely wear white."

"That's totally unsuitable."

"Let's talk it over with your mother, shall we? I think she'll agree with me."

"Of course you think that! Has any female ever *not* agreed with you?" she said with a groan.

"You, love," he teased. "Is there anything else bothering you?"

It was obvious that she wasn't getting anywhere with him. She sat down and twined her fingers together, watching him with somber dark eyes. "I've been thinking about my job. I realize that it's only reasonable that I leave the company after we're married, and I certainly haven't been there long enough to get attached to the job, but I do want to continue working somewhere."

He watched her in silence for a moment, as if trying to read her thoughts. "If that will make you happy," he finally said in a gentle tone. "I want you to be happy with our marriage, not trapped in a gilded cage."

She was wordless; he'd never suffered from self-doubt, so how could she tell him that she wasn't worried about herself being happy but rather that he wouldn't be happy with her? He sat down beside her and eased her into his arms, cradling her head against his shoulder. "Don't worry about any of that, love. Let our mothers worry about the wedding, and we'll just enjoy watching them run about. I expect we'll have our share of problems after we're married, but let's not anticipate them, hmmm? They may never materialize."

Whenever he had her in his arms, Claire felt reassured. Her hand drifted across his chest, absently stroking the hard muscles she found there. Beneath her ear his heartbeat picked up a beat in speed.

"I believe we've found another subject that needs discussing," he muttered as he tightened his arms around her. "How likely is it that you're pregnant after last night?"

She caught her breath then concentrated and counted in her mind. "It isn't likely, not right now."

His mouth nuzzled under her ear, finding the soft little hollow there and filling it with kisses. Claire caught her breath again, her eyes closing as pleasure began heating her blood. Her breasts tautened, aching for his touch, and his uncanny sense of timing told him exactly when to cup his palm over her.

"I'll be more cautious until after we're married, then, but I damned well refuse to do without you for six weeks." His mouth was at the corner of hers, his breathing mingling with hers. Blindly Claire turned her head until the contact was complete, her arms sliding around his neck.

Much later he swore softly as he got out of bed. "I'm not fond of this business of leaving you in the middle of the night," he said in sharp displeasure. "Why don't you move in with me?"

Claire drew the sheet up to cover her, a little alarmed by the thought of living with him. Of course they would live together after they were married, but she would have six weeks to get used to the idea. She had lived alone and liked it for quite some time now. The loss of privacy wouldn't be an easy thing to handle. "Where would I put my furniture?"

"Don't be logical," he said in frustration, buttoning his shirt. "Bloody hell, we do have some details to work out, don't we? Would you prefer to live in my apartment, or should we go house hunting?"

"I've never seen your apartment," she pointed out.

He shrugged. "I suppose we should begin looking for a house, as we'll need one eventually."

For the children he planned, she thought. She lay on the bed watching him dress, her body nude and still throbbing from the power of his lovemaking, and she thought of being pregnant with his children, of nursing them and watching them grow. "How many children do you want?" she whispered.

He looked down at her, seeing her soft, slim body outlined by the sheet, and the dark wells of her eyes. His hands stilled on the buttons. "Two, I think. Perhaps three. How many do you want?"

"That doesn't matter. I would be content with one, or half a dozen." No, the number wasn't important at all.

Slowly he began undoing his buttons and stripped off his shirt again. Tossing it aside, he unzipped his pants and stepped out of them. "You make me react like a teenager," he said, his eyes narrow and bright. Lowering himself onto the bed with her again, he forgot the irritation of living apart, and Claire forgot to worry. When he was making love to her, nothing else was real.

Instead of making the long drive to Houston, they flew down that Friday afternoon, and Max rented a car at the airport. It was already night, but the humid heat enveloped them like a wet blanket, and Claire sighed tiredly. It had been a hectic week, though they hadn't really done anything. But, rather than wait for the weekend, Alma had called every night about some detail that had to be discussed immediately.

She closed her eyes, wanting to rest on the drive to her parents' house. As excited as Alma was, Claire had no hope of getting to bed before midnight; there would be endless discussions about subjects they had already discussed endlessly.

"We're here, love," Max said, touching her arm to wake her.

Claire sat up, startled that she had dozed so quickly. She started to get out of the car, then sank back against the seat. "We aren't at Mother's."

"No, we aren't," he agreed, taking her hand and urging her from the car.

"You kept the apartment?"

"It seemed reasonable. I knew I would have to be coming here on business several times a year, and we'll be visiting your parents. Until the original tenant returns, I see no reason to give it up."

Claire was oddly reluctant as they went up in the elevator; she hadn't been in his apartment since the night they had first made love. Her face was burning as he opened the door and she stepped into the elegant black-tiled foyer, with the gilt-framed mirror over the lovely Queen Anne table. She had a vivid memory of her underwear lying discarded on the black tile.

Max dropped their overnighters where he stood and locked the door. His eyes were hot. "We'll go to your parents' house tomorrow."

By now Claire was intimately familiar with that look. She retreated, her heart pounding, and stopped abruptly when she came up against the table.

"Perfect," he crooned, his strong hands closing on her waist and lifting her up.

She buried her hot face against his shoulder. "Here?"

"It's my favorite memory, darling. You were so beautiful...so wild...so ready for me. I've never wanted any woman the way I want you."

"I hated myself for being so shameless," she confessed softly.

"Shameless? You were so beautiful, you took my breath."

Beautiful wasn't a word that Claire was accustomed to hearing in connection with herself, but that night, in Max's arms, she felt beautiful. She would always blush when she remembered that foyer, but thereafter it was with excitement and remembered pleasure, never again with embarrassment.

"I don't see why you shouldn't wear white," Alma said, making a note in a thick notebook she'd already half-filled with reminders. "This isn't the fifties, after all. Not white-white, of course, that's not your color, but you've always looked beautiful in a creamy golden-white."

Alma and Martine had a full head of steam going, making plans enthusiastically. It was her wedding, but Claire was the only calm one. Since she'd arrived that morning, she had listened to the constant chatter, letting them discuss every detail to death before they remembered to ask either her or Max's opinion. Occasionally she looked at Max, and the amusement in his eyes helped her to remain rational.

"The wedding will have to be in England," Alma pronounced, pursing her lips thoughtfully. "I checked, and it's impossible to reserve a church here that's large enough to hold that many people on such short notice. Max, are you certain there won't be any problem in getting your church?"

"I'm positive."

"Then it's England, and let your mother know. Better yet, give me her number and I'll call her. This schedule is going to be murder. Claire, you have to have your dress made here; there won't be time after we get to England. And we'll have to find one of those big garment boxes for shipping the dress over, but I suppose the dressmaker can help with that."

"I could buy a ready-made dress in England," Claire suggested.

"And take the chance of not being able to find what you want? No, that would be awful. Let's see, we'll need to be there at least three days early. Make that a week. Will that inconvenience your family, Max?"

"Not at all. There are so many of us, a few dozen more won't even be noticed. If you don't mind, I'll handle the plane reservations for the group. Do you have a list of everyone?"

Alma scurried around for her list of guests and wrote out another copy of it for Max. He glanced at it, then folded it and put it away in his pocket, not at all dismayed by the prospect of organizing the transportation of so many people to another country. Knowing what she did about executives, Claire thought that his secretary would probably inherit the burden.

"I have a few names to add to the list, but they'll be flying out from Dallas. I'll arrange for everyone to connect in New York."

Rome and Sarah would probably be attending, Claire realized. She had seen the length of the list and was surprised that so many people would travel so far to see a wedding. Even Michael and Celia were going, and she would have thought they would never want to travel again after moving from Michigan to Arizona in a station wagon.

She scarcely had time to wave at Max before she was whisked away to the fabric store to pore over pattern catalogs and bolts of cloth. From there they went to the dressmaker's, and Claire was measured for what seemed like hours. Then Alma insisted that they find the shoes to go with the gown, since it was almost June and that led to a tooth-and-nail battle over anything connected with weddings.

By the time they returned home, Claire was exhausted. Alma and Martine were still going strong, high on adrenaline, and she wondered what kept them from collapsing. Max was waiting for her, and he looped a sheltering arm over her shoulders to hug her to him.

"Shall we leave?" he asked quietly.

She closed her eyes. "Please. I'm so tired I can't think."

Alma started to protest that Claire could spend the night with them then glanced at Max and swallowed the comment. Claire belonged with him now; he had made that plain, though there were still five weeks until the wedding. For all his golden beauty there was a strength in Max that wouldn't permit any interference between him and the woman he'd chosen.

"This is so exhausting," Claire sighed as he drove them back to the apartment. She slipped off her shoes and wiggled her toes, wondering if they would ever feel normal again. "I think digging ditches wouldn't be as tiring as shopping. I can work all day and do chores at night without feeling half as wiped out as I am now. The terrible thing is, I'll have to come back every weekend for fittings!"

"But I'll be with you," Max said. "If it gets to be too much for you, we'll leave it and go back to Dallas."

"Then everything won't get done."

"I would rather have something left undone than to have my wife collapsing of exhaustion."

His wife. More and more Claire was coming to believe that it was really so, that it was really going to happen. She looked at the pearl-and-diamond ring on her left hand then at Max. She loved him so much that it swelled within her like a tide, relentless and eternal.

When they were in bed, she curled her arm around his neck and pressed against him, sighing as her tired muscles relaxed.

Max cuddled her, loving the feel of her body in his arms, right where she belonged. As usual when he was near her or thought about her, he wanted to make love, but she was too tired. He kissed her forehead and held her until she was asleep.

"Just five more weeks, love," he whispered into the darkness. She would be his wife, and he would no longer have this unreasoning fear that she was going to slip through his fingers like mist melting away before the sun.

Chapter Twelve

Claire managed a tight smile for the airline attendant as she refused a refill of her tea. They would be landing at Heathrow within the hour; she was relieved that the long, monotonous flight was nearly at an end but she tensed inside whenever she thought of meeting Max's family. She had spoken to his mother on the telephone and felt the warmth of the older woman's greetings, but she wondered how she would get through the ordeal of actually meeting all of them. She had memorized the names of his brother and sisters, as well as that of their spouses and the swarms of children, but that was only scratching the top of the list. There were aunts, uncles, cousins, in-laws, grandparents, great-aunts and uncles, as well as their children and spouses. Such a large family was beyond her experience.

Alma and Harmon were sitting directly ahead of them. It was exactly a week before the wedding, and Alma had been working on her ever-present list most of the flight. Martine and Steve and the children would be flying over in three days, followed the next day by the remainder of the guests. Rome and Sarah were attending, with Missy and Jed. Sarah had suggested leaving the children with a sitter, but Claire had become inordinately fond of the two little imps and wanted them present. After all, her wedding would be swarming with children; what difference would two more make? Rome and Sarah would be bringing a young friend, Derek Taliferro, who was home from college for the summer and who spent a lot of time with the Matthews. Claire had met Derek only twice, but had liked him on sight, and that was unusual for her. She was usually far more cautious with strangers, but there was something about Derek that relaxed her. He was inordinately handsome, with curly black hair and calm golden-brown eyes that reached deep into her mind, yet his handsomeness would normally have made Claire distrust him. But the tall, muscular youth had such enormous self-possession and purpose about him, and he was so tender with the children, who adored him, that instinctively she trusted him, too. For all his lack of years Derek was more of a man than most males who were twice his age. Max and Rome treated him as an equal, and they weren't ordinary men themselves.

Claire glanced quickly at Max, wondering if he had any doubts surfacing about the wedding as it drew closer, but she could read nothing in his expression. For all the passionate hours she had spent in his arms, she still sometimes felt as if he were a stranger to her, a handsome, aloof stranger who gave her his lust but not his thoughts. He was affable, charming, attentive, but she always felt as if he were holding something back from her. She loved deeply but had to keep her love hidden, because he didn't seem to want that sort of devotion from her. He wanted her companionship, her body beneath his in the night, but he didn't seem to want her emotions. He asked for none, and he gave none.

That was the real basis for her unease, she realized. She could have faced an army of relatives with poise if only she were certain of Max's love. All those people would be watching her, measuring her, just as she had been watched when she had married Jeff. How would she fit in with such a family, who were so far-flung and numerous, but oddly close for all that? It had never been easy for her to make friends, and his entire family all seemed to be so warm and outgoing. How could they understand her difficulty in warming up to people? Would they think her cold and unfriendly? Her hands were icy, and she clenched them together in an effort to warm them.

The No Smoking sign flashed on over their heads, and a huge knot formed in Claire's chest, making it necessary for her to breathe in swift, shallow gulps. Max didn't notice her anxiety; he was looking forward to seeing his family again, anticipation making his eyes gleam like jewels set in a golden idol's head.

Heathrow was sheer pandemonium, with the summer crowds thronging the airport. Max didn't turn a well-groomed hair at the hurly-burly; he secured a porter with a lifted finger, and just as the last of their luggage came around on the carousel, a joyous, lilting cry of "Max! *Max!*" soared above the noise.

He turned and a grin split his face. "Vicky!" He held out his arms and a tall, blond woman hurled herself into them. He hugged and kissed her enthusiastically, rocking her in his arms. Then he freed one arm to reach out and pull Claire to him. "Claire, this hoyden is my youngest sister, Victoria. Vicky to those of us familiar with her unruly behavior. Vicky, Claire Westbrook."

"Who became instantly famous when she snared the *in*famous Maxwell Conroy," Vicky teased, then enveloped Claire in a warm hug. Claire smiled quietly, thinking that she liked this unpretentious young woman. The family resemblance was strong; Vicky was tall, with the same golden hair, but her eyes were cerulean blue, and her face wasn't as sculptured. Still, she was a striking woman.

Introductions were made to Alma and Harmon; then Victoria led the way out of the air terminal. "How did you end up with the welcoming duties?" Max asked. His left arm was around Claire, and Victoria clung happily to his right.

"Oh, I'm not the lone delegate," Victoria said lightly. "Mother is waiting in the car; she didn't want to brave the hordes, but she couldn't wait for us to get home before she met Claire."

The knot in Claire's chest, which had subsided a bit on meeting Victoria, now rose to lodge in her throat. Max's mother! From the way he talked about her, Claire knew that he adored his mother, and it went without saying that she adored him. What woman wouldn't?

"We brought two cars, because of all the luggage," Victoria explained, smiling at Claire and her parents. "Mother will insist on Claire and Max going with her, if you don't mind. I'm really a safe driver."

"Really?" Max inquired, looking astonished.

"Of course we don't mind," Alma said.

As they approached the parking area, a man in a dark suit opened the door of a black four-door Jaguar, and a tall slender elegantly-dressed woman got out. "Max!" she called, waving her hand; then dignity was forgotten as she raced to meet him. Max laughed and left Claire and Victoria to sprint across the tarmac. He scooped the woman up in his arms and hugged her tightly.

"So much for our famous British reserve," Victoria observed humorously. "Everyone is always so happy to see Max again that we make absolute fools of ourselves, but there's no resisting him, is there?''

"None at all," Claire replied, watching him. Was that his *mother*? That lovely, too-young woman, with a sleek knot of blond hair just beginning to fade in color?

Before she could get herself under control and readjust her expectations from a gray-haired proper matron to the sleek reality, Max was walking toward her with his mother on his arm. "Mother, my future wife, Claire Westbrook. Darling, this is my mother, Lady Alicia Conroy, dowager countess of Hayden-Prescott."

Lady? *Countess?*

Claire was numb. Somehow she managed to smile and murmur something appropriate. The general enthusiasm of the all-around greetings continued as Alma greeted Lady Alicia, with whom she had had several long telephone conversations. Max's mother was smiling and gracious and seemed genuinely delighted by the occasion. It was several minutes before all the luggage had been packed into the cars and everyone sorted out, Alma and Harmon into Victoria's blue Mercedes, and Max and Claire, with Lady Alicia, into the Jaguar, which was driven by the chauffeur, Sutton.

"Has the mob begun arriving yet?" Max asked, smiling at Lady Alicia and an answering twinkle lit her green eyes.

"Not yet. We expect another few days of relative quiet, though of course those within easy traveling time will have to come over for tea. Did you expect it to be otherwise?"

"I hoped, but no, I didn't *expect* it. Would it be possible for me to reserve any of Claire's time during the next week?"

"Highly doubtful," Lady Alicia said briskly, though the twinkle remained. "There's entirely too much to be done. There hasn't been such excitement in the family since the war ended; even Great-Aunt Eleanor will be attending, and you know she seldom gets out."

"I would be honored, but I know she isn't venturing out on my account."

"Of course not; everyone knows *you*. It's Claire they're interested in."

Claire didn't want everyone to be interested in her; she hated being an object of curiosity. She would become awkward and silent, afraid of doing anything for fear of making a mistake. What had Max done to her? It had been difficult enough to imagine facing an enormous family; why hadn't he told her that he was a member of the British aristocracy? She should have guessed; would the average Englishman have quite that degree of mixed elegance and arrogance? His accent, his insouciant sophistication, his rather formal manners, all indicated a circumstance of birth and breeding that was far from the ordinary.

"You're very quiet, love," Max said, reaching out to take one of her hands and frowning when he felt its chill. It was, after all, the middle of summer, and was an unusually warm day for London. "Suffering from jet lag?"

"I do feel . . . disoriented," she replied quietly.

"There's no wonder at that," Lady Alicia said. "I always need a long nap after a trip, and I've never been quite so far as the States. Don't worry, dear, there's no one descending on us today to meet you, and even if there were, I would send them away."

Lady Alicia was warm and friendly, and it was soon plain that Max had inherited his wry humor from her.

On closer inspection it was possible to place her age at perhaps sixty, but it was a very young sixty. Her skin was smooth and virtually unwrinkled, except for the laugh lines at the corners of her eyes, and her hair was still thick, though fading in color. She enjoyed life and enjoyed her family; love was plain in her eyes when she looked at Max.

Claire listened to them talk, answering whenever she was asked a direct question, but for the most part she was quiet, wondering what else she should expect.

The estate was almost two hours' drive from London, but finally the Jaguar slowed, then turned left through a set of gates guarded by a thatch-roofed gatehouse. Victoria and Claire's parents followed closely behind in the Mercedes. "We're almost there," Max said. "You can just see the chimneys now. By the way, Mother, where have you put us?"

"Claire and her parents are to be with me at Prescott House," Lady Alicia said serenely. "You'll have your old room at Hayden Hill."

He didn't like that; his eyes narrowed and darkened to green, but he held his tongue. Claire was grateful that he hadn't demanded that they be given a room together; he was possessive enough and arrogant enough to do exactly that. His fingers tightened momentarily on hers, and she realized that he had sensed her feelings.

Then they rounded a curve, and Hayden Hill came into view. It wasn't a castle, but it was one of the old, enormous manor houses, with chimneys sticking into the sky like sentinels, the yellow brick mellowed with age to a dull gold color. The lawn was immaculately manicured, the hedges sculptured, the rose beds perfectly tended. This was where Max had grown to manhood, and Claire felt the gulf widening between them.

They drove past Hayden Hill down a narrow, paved lane. "My house is just down here," Lady Alicia explained. "It's the traditional dowager house, and I decided to honor tradition by moving into it when Clayton married."

"Not to mention escaping the bloody rows Clayton and Edie used to have when they were first married," Max added, his eyelids drooping.

Lady Alicia smiled at Claire. "My eldest son was very much the earl when he and Edie married," she explained placidly. "It took her the better part of a year to instruct him on the finer points of marriage."

Prescott House was less than half the size of Hayden Hill, though built in a similar style and with the same mellowed brick, but Claire soon found that it possessed eighteen rooms. Both Hayden Hill and the dowager house had been built in the late 1700s, after the original manor house had been destroyed by fire but both had been extensively modernized as time passed. Therefore, unlike many of the old manor houses, Hayden Hill and Prescott House both had efficient wiring and plumbing, while modern insulation and heating made it possible for the enormous fireplaces to be used for pleasure rather than for actual heating purposes. There was even a fireplace in Claire's bedroom, and when she was finally alone, she ran her hand lightly, dreamily, over the polished wood of the mantel. It was a beautiful room, with white lace curtains and a matching bedspread. A rose-colored carpet covered the wooden floor. The furniture was rosewood, and the bed was an enormous four-poster, so high off the floor that she had to mount steps to crawl onto it. A private bath and wardrobe adjoined.

How could Max not have mentioned all of this? It wasn't as if it were an insignificant detail. She had worried about living up to the Halseys, and now she had fallen in love with a man who made the Halseys look like Johnny-come-latelies.

She took a quick shower, unable to stand the grime of travel a moment longer. A thick, fleecy toweling robe hung on a hook behind the door, and Claire wrapped herself in it rather than try to hunt hers out of the pile of luggage. Leaving the bathroom, she stopped short when she saw Max lounging in the reading chair. He looked up, that intent look coming into his eyes when he saw her shiny face and warm, damp body wrapped in the robe.

"My mother can have the most perverse sense of humor at times," he said, holding out his hand to her. "Come here, love, and let me hold you for a little while before I'm banished to Hayden Hill."

She put her hand in his and found herself gathered close, then perched on his lap. Sighing, Claire put her head on his shoulder and felt his arms close around her with steely strength.

"You've been quiet since we left New York," he murmured. "Is something wrong, or is it just jet lag?"

While he held her, nothing was wrong, but she couldn't spend the rest of her life in his arms. "No, there's nothing wrong."

He slipped his hand inside the robe and cupped her breast, stroking her flesh with gentle fingers. "Shall I leave you to your nap, then? Your mother and father have already gone to their room; the telephone is ringing constantly, but Mother is fending everyone off."

She clutched at his shoulders. "Don't go, Max, please. Hold me for a little while longer."

"All right, love." His voice was low. He tipped her face up and kissed her slowly, his tongue probing into her mouth, and his hand was no longer quite so gentle. "This is going to be an endlessly long week," he said, moving his lips down her throat. "I may kidnap you one afternoon and take you to a place where we can be alone."

If only he could kidnap her and take her away now. If only the wedding were behind them and they could return to Dallas.

It only got worse. Sometimes it seemed as if she never had a moment to herself, and every day there were more and more people to meet. Max's wedding was an excuse for a party every night as the celebration escalated. Alma was in her element, and Harmon was perfectly comfortable with the life of an English country gentleman. Then Martine and Steve arrived with the children, and they were exuberantly welcomed. Martine got on like wildfire with Max's outgoing sisters, Emma and Patricia and Victoria, and Prescott House rang with their chatter and laughter.

There were lunches, afternoon teas and endless visits sandwiched between appointments with the photographer, the caterer and the florist. The gowns were pressed and ready, and the tuxedos had arrived from the dry-cleaners. The most amazing thing to Claire was that no one had had to rent one. It was a gracious, cushioned life, marching to a well-ordered beat, with privileges taken for granted.

There was no time to see Max alone, but becoming acquainted with his background told her more about him than what she had learned before. He had been born superior and saw nothing unusual about his life,

even though he was the family maverick. He was a
Conroy of Hayden-Prescott. The earldom was a rich
one, and his family estate had not been opened to tour-
ists in an effort at survival. Max's inheritance made him
independently wealthy; it was only his own restless
genius and drive that sent him first to Canada then to
the States to take on the challenge of high-level corporate dealings. Centuries of aristocratic breeding ran in
his veins.

She couldn't fit into his world. A man in his position
needed a wife who was comfortable in society, and
Claire knew that she would always prefer a far more
private life. She had driven herself into the ground trying to be suitable for the Halseys and had failed. How
could she possibly measure up to the standards of the
Conroys of Hayden-Prescott? They were the elite, and
she was a secretary from Houston, Texas.

The celebrations going on around her took on an un-
real, circus quality, and she went through the motions,
doing as she was told, going where she was guided,
while the certainty grew inside her that it was all a mistake. Max would soon come to see how unsuitable she
was, and he would be impatient. She knew all the stages
well, having suffered through them before. First he
would be impatient because she wasn't living up to expectations; then would come indifference, when it no
longer mattered. And, finally, he would pity her. She
didn't think she could bear that, to have him pity her.
Isolated from him, without even the reassurance of his
passion, Claire withdrew as she had always done in an
effort to protect herself. Their marriage wouldn't have
a firm base even under the best of circumstances, with
only a lopsided love holding it together. Max's reasons
for proposing to her weren't clear. Perhaps he thought

she would be suitable; perhaps he was ready to begin his own family. But he hadn't proposed out of love. Even during all the times when they had made love, with passion burning so high between them that sometimes she felt she would shatter in his arms, he'd never said anything about love.

She had to call it off before it went any further. When she thought of what she was about to do, of the scandal it would cause, Claire went cold, but she couldn't see any other alternative. The marriage simply wouldn't work, and it would destroy her if one day Max despised her for her inability to be what he wanted, what he expected, what he *deserved*.

She reached that conclusion the day before the wedding, but she had no opportunity to talk to him. They were always surrounded by family, both his and hers, and Rome and Sarah had arrived to add to the crowd. The wedding rehearsal went off without a hitch. Everyone was in high spirits, laughing and joking, and the ancient enormous stone church echoed with their joy. Claire watched it all with dark, stricken eyes, wondering what they would all think of her when they knew the wedding had been called off.

Dear God, she couldn't just leave him standing at the altar. His fierce pride would never forgive her for that, and she couldn't live if he hated her. Determined to talk to him, Claire threaded her way through the crowd and caught his sleeve. "Max?"

He smiled down at her. "Yes, love?" Then one of his cousins hailed him, and she lost his attention. Her nails bit into her palms as she stood beside him, trying to smile and act normally when she felt brittle inside, as if she would shatter at the slightest touch.

"Max, it's important!" she said desperately. "I have to talk to you!"

Max looked down at her again, and this time he saw her pale, taut face, the tension in every line of her body. He covered her hand with his, holding her fingers to his arm. "What is it? Is something wrong?"

"It's private. Can we go somewhere we can talk?" Her eyes begged him, and automatically he put his arm around her as if he could shield her from whatever was bothering her. "Yes, of course," he said, turning to walk with her to the door.

"Oh, no, you two lovebirds!" someone called. "You can't sneak out on the night before your wedding!"

Max looked over his shoulder. "Don't be ridiculous," he said, ushering Claire out the door. "Of course I can."

He led her outside into the cool English night, and the darkness folded around them as they walked down the lane toward Prescott House, leaving behind the brilliantly lit church. Their steps crunched on the loose gravel, and Max pulled her closer in an effort to keep the chill from her bare arms. "What is it?" he asked quietly.

She stopped and closed her eyes, praying for strength to get through this. "It's all a mistake," she said in a muffled tone.

"What is?"

If only he didn't sound so patient! Tears blurred her eyes as she looked up at him in the darkness. "This is," she said, waving her hand at the church behind them. "All of it. You, me, the wedding. I can't go through with it."

He drew in a sharp breath, and tension invaded his muscles. "Why is it a mistake? I thought everything was going along well. My family likes you, and you've given the impression that you like them.''

"I do." Tears were making her voice ragged, and she wondered how long she could hold out before dissolving into sobs. "But can't you see what a mismatch we are? I told you the first time we went out together that I'm not in the same league with you, but I didn't know how right I was! I don't fit in here! I can't be more than what I am, and I'll never be the aristocratic wife you need. Your... expectations are too high." She choked and couldn't say anything else, but perhaps it was just as well. Wordlessly she pulled off the pearl-and-diamond ring and extended it to him. He didn't take it, only stared down at it as she held it out in her shaking hand.

Claire couldn't hold back the sobs any longer. Grabbing his hand, she put the ring in it and folded his fingers over it. "It's for the best," she wept, backing away from him. "I love you too much to disappoint you the way I would."

She fled down the dark lane, too blinded by tears to be able to see where she was going, but she knew that Prescott House was down the lane, and she would eventually get there. Misery choked her; she didn't hear the running footsteps behind her. A hard hand grabbed her, swinging her around, and a small scream broke from her throat. She had a glimpse of his face, hard and furious, before he tossed her over his shoulder and started back up the lane.

"Max—wait!" she gasped, startled out of her tears. "You can't—what are you doing?"

"Taking my woman away," he snapped, his long legs eating up the distance as he strode toward the church.

People were milling around in front of the church, chatting before going on to Hayden Hill for the after-rehearsal party. When Max strode into view, there was a moment of dead silence, and Claire buried her face against his back.

"I say," his brother Clayton drawled. "Isn't there time enough for that tomorrow?"

"No, there's not," Max snapped, not even looking around. "I'm taking your car."

"So I see," Clayton said, watching as Max opened the door of a Mercedes and put Claire inside. Claire dropped her face into her hands, so miserable that embarrassment was only a small part of her woes.

Rome Matthews grinned, thinking of a time when he had carried his woman away from a party.

Standing on the steps, elegant in an oyster-white linen suit and pearls, Lady Alicia watched her son drive way with his intended bride. "Do you suppose," she mused, "there's any point in waiting for them? No, of course not. We'll have the party without them," she decided.

Max drove for a long time, his temper crackling around him like a visible flame. Claire sat silently, her eyes burning, wondering if he were taking her anywhere in particular, or if he were simply driving aimlessly, but she didn't dare ask him. She had the answer to her question when he pulled into the courtyard of a small inn.

"What are we doing here?" She gasped as he got out of the car and reached in to pull her out. Roughly he put the pearl ring back on her finger.

He didn't reply but pulled her into the inn. It was small and rustic, just the sort of inn that had lined England's roads for centuries. It was a pub on the bottom, with rooms on top. Max signed the register, paid the landlord and towed Claire after him up a narrow flight of stairs, while the landlord watched them with mild curiosity. Stopping before a door, Max unlocked it and pulled Claire inside, then turned to lock the door again.

"Now," he said, his voice almost guttural with rage. "Let's talk about this. To begin, the only standards and expectations you are measuring yourself against are your own. No one else expects or wants you to be anything other than yourself. I don't want you to be perfect; that would be bloody hell for me to try to live up to, because I'm not perfect. I don't want a china doll who never makes mistakes; I want *you*. As for that garbage about the aristocratic wife I deserve—" He broke off, his fists clenching with rage. Claire found that she had backed across the room, her eyes enormous as she stared at him. She couldn't believe the fury that burned in him; his eyes were like lasers, searing her.

He began unbuttoning his shirt with rough movements. "I'm a man, not a title, and the bloody damned title isn't mine anyway. My brother is the earl, and thank God he's healthy, with two sons to inherit before it would come to me. I don't want the title. I have American citizenship now; I have a job with a lot of damned responsibility that keeps me interested the way an earldom never would, and I have a family I love. I also have the woman I love, and I'll be bloody damned to hell and back before I let you walk out on me now." He pulled his shirt off and tossed it aside then unbuckled his belt and unzipped his pants.

"If you don't want to get married, all right," he bit out, stripping naked. Claire stared at him, her mouth going dry. "We'll just live together, but don't ever think that we *won't* live together, married or not. You're the only woman I've ever met who can drive me so wild that I lose control, and you're the only woman I've ever met whom I love so much I ache with it. I nearly ruined it in the beginning by not being completely honest with you, and you stopped trusting me. You've never trusted me again, have you? Too bloody damned bad, because I'm not letting you go. Is that clear?''

Claire swallowed, looking at him. He was so beautiful that she hurt. "Do you know how many 'bloody damns' and 'bloody hells' you've just said?'' she whispered.

"What the bloody hell difference does it make?'' he asked, stalking across the floor to grab her and toss her onto the bed.

She bounced and grabbed at the covers to keep from flying off. "You never told me before that you loved me.'' Her voice sounded strange, too high and tight.

He glared at her, reaching behind her for the zipper on her dress. "Is that an unforgivable sin? You never told me that you love me, either, until you blurted it out at the same time you said you couldn't marry me. What do you think that did to me? I've been trying for weeks to make you trust me again, wondering if you'd ever love me, and you throw it at me like that.''

He pulled her dress off, and Claire put her hands on his chest, her heart pounding so hard that she could barely think. "Max, wait. Why are we here?''

"It's obvious, isn't it? I'm having my wedding night, even if you're determined not to have a wedding. I love you, and, I repeat, I'm not letting you go.''

"What will everyone think?''

"I don't care.'' He stopped, looking down at her with burning eyes. "I love you. You're more important to me han anyone else on this earth, and I'd walk on live coals to get to you."

He had managed to strip her completely, and his gaze wandered down her slim body. He had been rough before, but his touch now was so gentle that it was almost like a whisper of wind as he parted her legs and eased into her. Claire accepted him, her body arching in pleasure, her hands clinging to him. She loved him so much that she thought she would burst with it, and it was in her eyes as he propped himself on his elbows over her.

"Let's try this again," he whispered. "I love you, Claire Westbrook, for all the things you are. You're gentle and loving, and you have dreams in your eyes that I want to share. Will you marry me?"

She would never have believed that she could soar so high. With her arms locked around his neck, straining up to put her mouth to his, Claire looked up into those brilliant sea-colored eyes and said, "Yes."

She walked down the aisle of the huge, drafty old church with her cream-colored satin gown rustling and the veil trailing behind her. Her father's arm was steady under her hand. Familiar and beloved faces turned toward her as she walked: the faces of the many people she had met this past week, all beaming at her; Sarah Matthews, pale and serene, with her children beside her; Derek Taliferro, his golden eyes wise beyond his years, smiling as he watched her. Alma, smiling and crying at the same time and still looking lovely while she did it. Lady Alicia, her eyes brimming with pride. At the altar, waiting for her, were Martine, and Max's sisters, four heads in varying shades of blond. Rome Matthews stood beside Max, his dark eyes seeking out his wife where she sat in the pews, and a silent message passed between them. Clayton also stood there, and two of Max's cousins.

And Max. Tall, impossibly handsome, and so beloved that it hurt her to look at him. His image was blurred by the veil she wore, but he watched her, and there was a moist glitter in his eyes, like that of the sea.

Her father gave her hand to Max, who moved to stand by her side. The pearl on her hand gleamed in the golden candlelight of the many tapers that flickered throughout the church.

Max pressed her hand warmly, and she looked up at him. His eyes were steady. Hers were dark, secretive pools, but there were no more secrets between them. Turning toward the altar, they began speaking their vows.

Available mid-September from
New York Times bestselling author

LINDA HOWARD

Had he given his heart to the enemy?

Robert Cannon feels there is little doubt that
Evangeline Shaw is the key to the conspiracy that
threatens his company. Classified software developed
by Cannon's group is being sold to a foreign
government, and it isn't just theft or a case of
corporate espionage—it's treason. And the
trail leads to Shaw—a woman who by all
accounts has the means and motives.

Even though the facts still seem pretty black-and-
white, Robert's heart tells him she's no Mata Hari—
her small-town innocence is the real thing.

LOVING EVANGELINE

Would Rhy Baines recognize his wife?

New York Times Bestselling Author

LINDA HOWARD

Sallie Jerome, a.k.a. Mrs. Baines, had picked up the pieces of shattered dreams after Rhy walked out seven years ago. A news reporter for one of the nation's leading magazines, she'd become the independent, self-possessed woman Rhy had always wanted. Only, now *she* didn't want him. Or did she?

An Independent Wife

"Howard's writing is compelling."
—*Publishers Weekly*

On sale mid-April 1999
wherever paperbacks are sold!

One of America's best-loved authors

DIANA PALMER

Introduces her most mesmerizing hero yet, in her new novel

ONCE IN PARIS

It was in Paris that she first saw him—tall, handsome and utterly dangerous. Brianne Martin saved a grief-stricken Pierce Hutton but the older man was strictly off-limits for a romance.

It was in Paris that she fell in love—with a man she couldn't have. She was being relentlessly pursued by a corrupt business associate of her stepfather's who wanted to merge their powerful families. And now it was Pierce's turn to save Brianne....

MIRA

On sale mid-November 1998 wherever paperbacks are sold!

MDP470